S E MORC

THE
KING
OVER THE SEA

PASSION, TREACHERY, SURVIVAL

Cover design by 100Covers.com
Formatted by FormattedBooks.com

Acknowledgements

I must thank the generosity of a number of friends in lending their time and energy to my endeavours notably:

Richard Hibbs for his helpful comments and suggestions on the earliest draft.

Sian Stewart for her enthusiasm, advice and support, as well as fact checking from a historical perspective.

Cardiff Writers Circle, as always, provided thoughtful and constructive criticism, as well as moral support, enthusiasm and general fun.

Pamela Cartlidge, for her beta-read skills and saving me the embarrassment of excessive typos.

Rebecca John, editor at Cadogan and Quill was once again, insightful as to what needed changing to improve my story.

Fortune smiled when I found an Irish copy editor and ancient Ireland enthusiast in Fionn Ó Cahthláin.

CONTENTS

Chapter 1 1

Chapter 2 10

Chapter 3 21

Chapter 4 28

Chapter 5 44

Chapter 6 56

Chapter 7 71

Chapter 8 84

Chapter 9 94

Chapter 10 116

Chapter 11 123

Chapter 12 128

Chapter 13 139

Chapter 14 155

Chapter 15 179

Chapter 16 194

Chapter 17 204

Chapter 18 221

Chapter 19 232

Chapter 20 246

Chapter 21 257

Chapter 22 261

Chapter 23 272

Epilogue 291

Key References 299

List of main characters 301

CHAPTER
1

Autumn 443 AC

Our royal dún had been preparing for days. At last, we heard them, felt their approach deep in our bones. Thud, thud, thud, beat of sword on shield, iron on yew and leather. The first of the fianna were coming. My father's men roared derision and challenge behind the timber palisade; "Niall, Niall," they chanted, as our hounds bayed death.

I was hopping with excitement, a puppy scuttling between warrior's legs, in the way, but tolerated with affection.

Breathless, I poured out questions. 'Conall they're here at last. Who will arrive first? Math, will you win great prizes? I think you must, you are the biggest man I know, except for Father and he's old and fat.'

I gazed up at Math, muscular, wide-necked and handsome, black beard neatly groomed, battle gear oiled and gleaming.

The two laughed. Math pushed me aside gently saying, 'Little Lord be gone to your mother; we must greet our brothers in arms.'

My uncle's fiann was at the gate; the men of the swan. At their head, astride a bronze and bone-decorated war chariot balanced Father's oldest brother, Fiachrae. Battle-hardened Nathi, Fiachrae's only son stood beside him, tugging hard at the horses' reins. Flecks of spume at their mouths. On each warrior's shield was painted a white swan neck, red-eyed and sharp-beaked. In the distance, other bands of men marched towards us.

Autumn had returned; the kings and chieftains of Ireland were coming to Tara. They came to pay respect to the High King: my father, Niall Noígíallach, bringing plunder from over the sea as tribute. They had raided the coasts of Britannia and Armorica over the long summer.

Come to feast and fight, to see champions named when Father would gift the victors rich prizes. It was nearly Samhain; the harvest gathered in; as nights lengthened the spirits of the dead walked our land. Slaves carried up frothing horns of mead in welcome, as my father greeted his brother with a bear hug. I admired their splendid garments; rich woollen cloaks held in place by ornate pins; heavy gold torcs glinted at their necks and battle rings aligned along hairy, scarred arms. Fiachrae, sinewy and short, tattoos on each cheek framing his luxuriant moustache, laughed as I ran to him.

'Growing still, Maelon. You will soon be strong enough to join the fiann, like your half-brothers.'

I smiled up at him in awe. Yes, that was my plan. I would be the strongest and bravest of warriors, tales of my high deeds toasted in halls across Ireland. Every day I pestered my older brothers to train me with sword and shield. I spent hours practising my slingshot and short bow; as long as Sylvester, our priest didn't find me for lessons.

I tasted bitter gall as my father rumbled a reply.

'No, the boy's path lies elsewhere.' He gestured to my half-brothers. 'Too many,' then at me, 'too young, I am sending him to Wales, his mother's home. He will become a priest, so my name is remembered and blessed.'

My father was an enthusiastic convert to Christ. I hated him at that moment, as he confirmed his plans for me.

Over two days, war bands arrived from across Ireland. Each kingdom and clan sent warriors to present him with a portion of their reaving from the lands over the sea. He would give much away, binding men to him with his generosity. Fine cattle, iron daggers, silver encrusted mead horns and other treasures presented to those he favoured.

Finally, the contests between champions could begin. Each man carried his clan buckler shield, freshly painted bright white, red or black, along with a sword, axe or spear. The kings clustered on the grassy mound of the tournament field to watch, dressed in their finest, heavily adorned with ornament. Gold arm-rings, garnet encrusted necklaces, bronze shields and hilts glistened in the afternoon sunlight.

At the centre of the rise, beside my father, stood his three wives. To his left Rignach, the Irish Queen, older, grey, sharp-faced, watching for any insult to her pride. Her keen eyes searched out her sons, hoping they would fight fiercely.

Standing nearby was my mother Inne, the Welsh Queen, lovely, twenty-six years old. She'd been sent to Ireland at fifteen for Niall to marry. Mother wore a cloak dyed a soft woad-blue, held by an ornate circular gold brooch above a simple shift. Around her neck was an ancient band of twisted gold, her long dark hair dressed with beads.

To my father's right was Ness, white skin, flame-red hair. She wore no jewels; a gown of fine green fabric outlined her firm body. Youth gave her a glow that made trinkets redundant; the Red Queen.

I ran to my mother's side and she rested her hand on my shoulder. Each warrior came to bend his knee, to offer his sword to his king. Math, my friend, Father's champion and captain of his household guard approached. Mother's eyes met his; I felt her grip tighten.

My father nodded. 'Fight well my Champion.'

Mother added under her breath, 'and safely.'

Rignach's sons approached, offering fealty. I beamed at them, proud of my tall half-brothers, my heart felt fit to burst.

I whispered to Rignach as they left, 'I have the bravest brothers in Ireland.'

'I hope so little one, but the tournaments will test them.'

That night the Samhain bonfires flickered red, sparks lighting the night. Cattle were driven between them, young men leapt across the flames to impress giggling girls, as feasting began. In the peat scented great hall our bard, Laidcenn, took up his harp, singing a favourite tale; the Cattle Raid of Cooley. Servants brought in a roast boar for my father to divide as he willed. Math had beaten all rivals and remained champion; he would receive the choicest portion and richest prizes.

A shout rang out; it was Nathi, my cousin. 'I call for my right to challenge the High King's champion in combat.'

His father, Fiachrae's face showed dismay, as did Mother's; my father seemed detached, unconcerned. I turned to see how my hero Math would react.

Math looked nonplussed and drowsy. Along with every man in the hall he had started drinking hours ago, once the tournaments finished. Nathi was a fine warrior but no match for Champion Math, captain of the High King's household warriors; however, Math was in his cups. Nathi looked fresh, he had not fought. There was no mead cup near his place at the high table. This challenge had been planned.

Around the room men banged cups and fists on the table, stamped on the mud floor.

'Fight, fight.'

The noise swelled around us deafening, rhythmic. It was not a challenge Math could refuse, nor Nathi withdraw. Math had the right to choose weapons. He stood and gestured his agreement, but swayed drunkenly as men cheered. Math called for his long sword and the crowd stilled.

Nathi smirked and sent a slave to the guardhouse to collect his heavy weapon. Everyone waited, murmurs of excitement growing louder. My cousin's pox scars above his pointed chin and neat beard were accentuated by the shadows in the torch-lit, timbered hall. A light short-sword was balanced on a bundle near his seat. He was up to something. I slipped across to Finn our master of hounds.

'Finn, Nathi has a second weapon ready. He is sly, something is going to happen. I can feel it. Math needs a lighter blade. What can we do?'

Finn pursed his lips. Every visitor was expected to surrender their weapons at the gate of the dún[1]. There should not have been a second blade. Finn glanced pointedly at the pile of plunder in the corner. At the mound's edge was a sharp, slim sword. I grinned and crept towards it.

---

1   dún -ancient fort

No one saw me. Every eye watched the warriors, as they warily circled the central hearth and steaming bronze cauldron. I slipped the weapon inside my tunic. Then slid through the legs of the watchers gathered around the two men and placed it on a bench at the edge of the space.

Math shook his head, trying to clear it, flexed his back and raised his weapon ready. Without warning Nathi lunged at him, forcing Math to step back. Their weapons crashed together, metal ringing out as the room gasped. The heavy sword shook with the blow. Math swung back viciously, muscles hard and rippling beneath his leather shirt. Nathi deflected the stroke with ease, but his sword shattered at the blade's impact.

Nathi did not look alarmed, he threw down the bronze hilt and grabbed for his lighter weapon. He stood firm, facing a drunk and befuddled Math. Snake-like he twisted, agile and flexible; the sword above his head hissed as it travelled down through the air. Math, slowed by his massive sword, fielded lightning blow after blow from his clear-headed opponent. Math was forced to retreat backwards again. His face a mask of determination, beads of sweat trickling down his brow. How could he possibly keep up with the flurry of strokes? A scythe like swipe grazed Math's bare forearm. Droplets of deep red blood appeared as pinpricks along the cut, glistening in the flickering lamplight. The watchers groaned as I gritted my teeth in horror. The thought that my friend and Tara's champion could be beaten, unbearable.

I didn't like or trust Nathi. He was older than my brothers and I'd heard talk about his cruel tricks toward fellows when fostered by my father. I'd seen him beat slaves for no good reason.

Finn leant forward and whistled sharply, carefully holding up the replacement weapon by its shank, handle reaching toward Math; who, dropping his heavy sword grabbed for it, attacking back in an instant.

It was Nathi's turn to look anxious. He had not anticipated Math being able to match him weapon for weapon. The crowd roared approval as Math, the more skilled warrior, moved in. Nathi deflected a blizzard of sharp strikes, dodging and ducking desperately. Although sober to Math's drunkenness, he was unequal to the stronger, younger man.

In seconds' Nathi overreached himself under the speed and weight of the onslaught. He swung wildly, a slicing cut that missed his opponent and lost his footing. He lay sprawled in the straw and mud and froze as Math held a wicked point to his throat.

Challenges were to the death. Math should let blood flow to appease the gods. He hesitated to kill the son of a king; held back from the final thrust. He looked uncertain; the mead made him indecisive. King Fiachrae would surely kill him if his son died. Math stood breathless and bewildered, his sword pointing at my trembling cousin, ready to end a life. I had to do something.

I launched myself at them. 'Stop. Please don't kill my cousin, Champion Math. Father, allow mercy in the name of the new Lord Jesus. Please, Father.'

The room was silent; every man and woman waited agog for the outcome.

My father stood slowly, pushing up his massive weight using the arms of his tall-backed throne, his great belly pressed into the tabletop. Twisting the end of his thick moustache, he rasped out his decision.

'My son has asked for a boon in the name of Jesus, on the very day I told him he is to become a priest. He is to go to a monastic school in Wales to learn the Lord's way. I will give him this gift, for his and my brother's sake. I give him his cousin's life.'

There was a murmur of approval around the room. Tension drained from the two bodies. Math clapped me on the back in gratitude. Nathi scrambled away, humiliated at the failure of the challenge and that a child had intervened to save his life. Rescued by a ten-year-old, he had cause for gratitude, but somehow, I doubted he was.

Tara had been told of my departure directly, no rumours of machinations and deceit would spread when I left. Always clever my father, Niall, but today I matched him. I stared at him defiantly. He'd rejected me again, demonstrated he placed my older brothers before me. I wouldn't show him that I cared.

Niall looked first at Finn and then me. He missed nothing, judging all who stood before him, always. He knew who'd filched Math's replacement sword.

'I will distribute tribute now. First to receive a prize is my son, who has saved this night from tragedy.

'Approach Maelon, what will you take? I think you have already examined the treasure?'

I blushed at the truth of his words. That afternoon Conall, Loegaire and I crept in behind the guards' backs to marvel at the piles of plunder. I had noticed three sets of wonderfully worked gold arm-rings; one pair was decorated with finely worked hound heads at each end, deep red garnets glimmered as eyes. I had longed to own those rings but realised they could never be mine. Why would a child be given such precious objects?

'I would like the pair of hound arm-rings Father,' then chancing my luck I continued, 'and for Conall and Loegaire: could Conall have the raven, and Loegaire the boar rings? We would be the same, that would be wonderful. My arms are too small to wear them, but in years to come they will remind me of home.'

Clicking his fingers for a servant to fetch them, he presented them to me with resigned amusement; he could not refuse. He glanced at my mother who'd sat beside him, still as stone throughout the fight, and his smile faded.

CHAPTER
2

To begin at the beginning is best, and my beginning was in Ireland. I was third youngest of ten sons of the High King, Niall Noígíallach, he of the Nine Hostages. The second of Niall's three wives, Mother, had given him a son and his only legitimate daughter. At the time of their marriage my father worshipped the old gods, such kings took many wives, concubines and mistresses.

All was well until my father became Christian; when the priests made him choose one wife. My father picked the youngest, Ness, who'd born him twin boys when I was nine. We'd thought him a fool.

If he'd confirmed his first wife, Rignach, mother of seven sons, five already trained warriors, it would have been accepted by his people. If he'd chosen my mother, Inne, who had powerful relatives across Ireland and Wales and an ancient lineage, that would have been respected. Instead, Niall took the seventeen-year-old red-head as his Christian wife.

Daughter of a freed slave woman, Ness had no kin or connections. No adult sons to carry on the line, just a winsome smile and an ability to bend him to her whims. Resentment festered between the three wives and their children. Rignach and my mother did all they could to undermine this worthless woman, a chit, younger than his oldest sons.

My father appeared to have little interest in his many offspring, but attended to every detail; saw everything. Niall paid no more heed to any of his brood of eleven acknowledged children than he did me, even-handed in that singular way. He showed no favouritism; gave no indication who was to succeed him as High King.

The tournament was not, in fact, the first time I'd heard of my father's plans. Days earlier he called me to Mother's hut and she cried bitterly at the news. Father started to walk out but then turned.

He explained gruffly, 'Maelon has to leave for his own safety, Inne. I have seven sons by Rignach. They are waiting for me to die so they can divide the kingdom. My brothers and I did the same. I know the dangers well. I needed to be the strongest and yes, the most cunning to become High King. I had to be careful of my step-mother, Mongfind. She was more dangerous than my four half-brothers put together.'

'But surely you don't need to send him yet? He is only ten. Why must he go so soon?' she pleaded, her lilting accent soft, musical and sad.

'We can delay a year, maybe two but then he must leave. If Maelon is in Tara after I am gone, his brothers might kill him; he would be a threat to their rule. It would be disastrous for my line.'

'I don't understand. Why is he so much more of a risk than any of his half-brothers?' Her dark brown eyes gazed at him bereft.

'I married you because of your lineage, Inne, not for your beauty nor your meagre dowry. Maelon's ancestry means he could be used as a pawn by many. Some might believe him the rightful heir to my kingship. It is not only your bloodline that makes him dangerous; I was the youngest of my father's sons remember, and I inherited.

'If we give him to the church, he will be safe. Neither his brothers nor uncles would have reason to fear him if he is a priest. He could become a bishop, or a saint like his great-grandmothers, who knows. He could marry and live a good life. If he wishes to throw his hand for the throne after I'm dead I can't stop him. However, if Maelon stays in Ireland he may not reach adulthood.'

Mother had looked angry when he mentioned her bride price; clenched her fist behind her back and bitten back a retort. For a High King, it may have been meagre, but for most chieftains it was a fortune and my grandfather, Anlach, had dug deep to find the gold.

He rumbled on, 'I know Rignach befriends you and sets you against Ness. Be careful; she puts her sons' interests before all else. When I die you should return to Wales. Had I married you, not Ness, I doubt Maelon would still be alive. It would have given him precedence over his brothers. Rignach would never have tolerated that.'

Mother gasped, wanting to deny the truth of all he said, but her eyes showed she believed him. As usual Niall had plotted and planned his marriage. Even as a ten-year-old I realised that my father had implied Ness and her baby sons were of no account; as disposable as the many other children he had fathered by slaves and concubines.

My mother, brothers and our hounds were my whole world. Mother had brought three wolfhounds as a portion of her bride price. Those dogs, *Cú Faoil*[2] were valuable, worth many slaves.

---

2   Cú Faoil- Wolfhound

In recognition that the hounds came from my Welsh grandfather, years earlier, Finn encouraged me to work with the huge animals. They were trained to attack strangers, wolves or other dogs, but were quiet and obedient if you understood them. He taught me to train and control them as if I was his successor, not a princeling. By the age of ten, I could manage the pack with an ease my brothers envied. When I took them out hunting, I imagined myself a figure to be feared; any man or animal could be killed in moments on my orders. That Finn followed closely, watching over me, I didn't notice. I loved the hounds for what they were, beautiful, intelligent friends. When I was nearly eleven, Finn set me to train one, Kira, from a puppy. She was beautiful, my Kira, the colour of ripe wheat, standing half the height of a tall man. She had a slim body, legs that rippled with muscle and teeth like blades. Mother didn't complain that Kira slept on my bed; it would be a foolish man to attempt to harm me with her there.

Early one spring morning I heard the hounds howl as they raced past the boys' hut. I was up, dressed and out in a trice, whistling for Kira to follow. At the palisade gate a meaty arm grabbed my tunic, jolting me to a stop. I wriggled and squirmed, annoyed to be thwarted and was about to kick back at the shin of the man holding me when I realised who it was. I froze motionless. I'd nearly kicked my bear of a father.

Breathless already, his purple lips wheezed out, 'Not today Maelon, you can't follow the pack. It's not game the dogs are after, it's a hostage.'

He reached down to fondle Kira's ears. All the while, he gazed around suspiciously. Was it one boy or had other hostages joined his attempt at flight? Father was, 'The Noígíallach,' that title, "Of

Nine Hostages" was entirely justified; he held more than nine hostage and fostered other princelings.

Aed, one of Father's hearth warriors ran up. 'Only one boy is missing,' he hesitated, 'your nephew, Fergus. He's been gone an hour, no more.'

I gasped, at fourteen Fergus was the same age as Conall's and his close friend...

'Damnation, why would he try something so stupid?' asked my father.

I'd had exactly the same thought. Why would Fergus run when Father taught him how to fight and lead? He sent foster sons and hostages alike out to raid foreign shores with the protection of the strongest fiann in Ireland. Few needed to be fettered. It was an honour as well as a trial to be held hostage by Niall.

In the distance I watched Finn's sturdy pony chasing after the hounds. Would he reach them in time? We waited silent and alert. Father had kept hold of my puppy; I didn't dare leave.

More and more men came to stare outside the palisade. All my brothers were there, hearth warriors, everyone that could, came to watch. Half an hour later we heard distant barking, as a horn sounded, the pack was returning. At their head rode Finn, a small figure was held in front of him.

Fergus had stood no chance. The dogs had been given his clothing and tracked him relentlessly. Once they caught him, the loss of his arm, or if seized by his throat, his life, likely.

Conall came to stand beside Father and me, face drawn, worried for his friend. Diffidently he cleared his throat. Father's sharp eyes peered at him.

'Well?'

'Fergus's mother is ill, he's been worrying for weeks. He was too afraid to ask if he might go to see her. He thought you'd refuse.'

Father sucked at his teeth, thinking.

Finn's pony trotted through the gate. I couldn't see any blood, that was good. Finn jumped down and dragged a trembling Fergus to my father's feet.

'He had the sense to climb a tree,' said Finn.

Fergus didn't move, he lay huddled into a ball, terrified, whimpering. We knew why. Three months ago an older hostage had tried the same thing; he'd been captured as quickly. Father ordered the boy's head cut off; then sent it to his home in a bloodied linen sack, demanding a replacement child. The family had dared not refuse, that boy's brother was kept in chains to remind and deter others.

Father stroked his cheeks, pulling at his beard. Leaning down, he picked Fergus up by his throat in one hand. His biceps bulged, thick fingers biting into the boy's jaw. Holding him up level with his face, Father glared at him.

'So, Nephew, you have rejected my hospitality. I am disappointed. I'm told your mother is unwell. Is that why you snivel like a baby before me?

Fergus nodded, too afraid to speak.

Father rumbled a laugh. 'You should have asked. I can see you are still attached to her skirts, you are too weak for my court. I will send you home to your mama. You may leave Tara. I give you one month, then return. If you ever,' he tightened his grip on the boys throat, 'attempt to run again, I will feed you to my hounds and your mother with you. You understand?'

Fergus had turned red, was barely able to breathe from the throttling, but he managed to signal agreement. Niall dropped him to the ground and stalked away, leaving the boy gasping and coughing in his wake.

'I smell fresh bread. Sons follow me.'

All eight of us obeyed, instantly. My oldest five brothers were brawny young men; rumbustious, ready to fight and take offence, good with weapons, but dull of wit. Men born to join the ranks of warriors, not to lead. Father knew that, he held higher hopes for his youngest three; Conall, Loegaire and me. My brothers and I had been taken from our mother's care to live and train in the boys' hut when we reached ten years.

Older and stronger boys, fostered and hostage alike, looked up to Conall and Loegaire, not because they were the High King's sons, rather because they were clever. No one dared cross them. They protected and cared for their scrawny half-brother with ferocity and kindness. I repaid them by playing the fool, making everyone laugh, defusing arguments. We were a band of three, my brothers cared for me and in return I worshipped them. We tried to make our father proud, make him love us, but he remained aloof. Any sign of weakness in the hostages was ridiculed, as with Fergus. He expected more from his sons.

One morning Loegaire was wrestling when he slipped. Quick as lightening, Conall threw our twelve-year-old brother heavily onto the muddy practice ground. Loegaire landed with a dull thud directly onto his shoulder and it deformed. As he stood we saw his arm hanging limp and useless at his side. He was in agony; fat tears ran down his cheeks.

Appalled, Conall rushed our brother to hound master Finn's hut; as always, I trailed behind. Finn stripped off Loegaire's dirty tunic to examine the injury. I saw a lump protruding out in front of the joint. Finn held sobbing Loegaire tightly between his legs.

'Boys, watch and learn. It is the same with a man as with my hounds and works for any shoulder. This is not an unusual battle injury.'

Deftly Finn placed his thumb on the front of my brother's puny chest, then pulled up and around and pushed the swelling firmly backwards. The bulge disappeared into its place as Loegaire gave a shrill scream; his face told us his terrible pain was over. Wonderingly he moved his limb, up, then rotated his arm.

'It's sore,' he said, 'but much better. I thought it was broken forever; that I'd be maimed, useless. I'd have no future as a warrior.'

Finn began to explain, 'It's a common injury for wrest...,'

He stopped and looked towards the doorway. Our father stood silhouetted there, massive against the light. I gulped with fear watching him stomp toward Loegaire, his face thunderous. Father lifted him by his injured arm and shook him, like a dog with a rat.

'You cried boy. I was told one of you was injured and crying. My sons are above tears. They must be fearless, feel no pain. No one can think you feeble, you must appear strong, always. Hold out your hand.' He glared at Conall. 'You too, you injured him. Let this be a lesson for you both.'

I shrank behind Finn terrified. Would Father notice me? Drag me out for the same treatment? He took a whip from his belt. I heard its sharp whine and slap as he dealt them three stinging blows each; daring a drop of moisture to fall from their eyes. With each clout came a word.

'Never,' swish, 'show' swish, 'weakness', swish.'

If they so much as whimpered, more strokes would follow. Somehow my brothers remained dry-eyed and silent. As he turned his baleful eyes glared into mine with grim threat. He'd realised

I was watching. I cowered, but he stayed silent, compressed his lips and left.

Finn sighed then said, 'Loegaire don't move that arm for a week, I'll bind it to your chest. No bow practice and,' he rummaged in a woven basket, taking out a tiny clay pot, 'here's goose grease infused with willow for your hand.

'Maelon, come and help me with the hounds.'

The youngest of Niall's sons, excepting Ness's twins, I had the freedom of my father's hall. I went everywhere, knew everyone. My brothers and I looked to the young warriors of the fiann to teach us to battle.

In the cold winter months, the men would stay in Tara or return to their family dún. In the summer they'd hunt and take to the sea to raid Wales and lands far away. Full of life and fun, Conall and Loegaire looked up to the fiann. Both had been allowed to join the band on occasion for the last two years; they went out raiding and harrying as often as they could. I ran between these young lords. They teased and tolerated me, teaching me to fight and hunt. I was known to all as Little Lord and Kira as my hound.

My father was the first of the Irish kings to convert to Christ. Bishop Palladius, sent to Ireland by Pope Celestius was delighted with this success. The bishop dispatched a priest to our hall to ensure Niall's numerous offspring were educated in Christ and his ways. That young priest, Sylvester, took a particular interest in me and my little sister Grain, who everyone called Ria.

It was no surprise. Mother may have become the lesser queen of the High King, but her ancestry was saintly and proud.

My half-brothers and sister made fun of Priest Sylvester's hair, head shaved from ear to ear in a tonsure, as well as laughing at his smooth chin. My older brothers wore their hair long, well dressed and oiled, each trying to grow full beards and moustaches to prove their manhood. To us, Sylvester looked absurd with his high bald crown and thin tail of hair at his nape.

My siblings had little interest or time for his lessons but I enjoyed them. By eight I could read and speak common Latin and had started to write on wax tablets. I spoke Briton, using either Welsh or Irish dialects instinctively, depending with whom I needed to speak. I preferred to listen to Sylvester's tales than sit and study, but pride pushed me on.

Sylvester told me, 'Your ancestors would not understand why you can't do what every Roman citizen can; read and write.'

Sylvester, short and rounded with deep-set eyes, was an inspiring teacher. He taught me to be curious about the world around me. I learned Latin script and we studied Ogam, our native Irish writing together, cutting the letters into hazel rods.

'All knowledge is helpful Maelon. You can never know too much.'

Conall taught me to fight with a sword and shield. Loegaire taught me to hunt and ride. They both taught me to swear. They treated Sylvester's stories of Christ with amused disdain and cared for me in the way my father should have. I looked up to them as if they were heroes in return.

On winter evenings my brothers would demand stories of Rome as well as Christ. Sylvester was an excellent story-teller. The thatched great hall would fill with the smoky scent of burning peat and the murmurs of listeners. He regaled us with tales of Christ and his miracles, but also of the Coliseum, of gladiators and mighty emperors, of Romulus and Remus.

Sylvester told his disbelieving audience that in Rome floors were not firmed mud topped with straw. They were made of tiny stones arranged into colourful pictures and heated by hot air on cold nights. Water wasn't drawn from streams but ran into homes, they even had fountains within their halls. In Rome, everyone bathed each week in warm water with scented oils massaged into their skin and hair. Houses in Rome might have a second or even third level, rooms set one on top of another. Most incredible of all, he told us that in Rome the sun shone all year long, rain was rare in summer.

Not to be outdone, Laidcenn, our grey-bearded bard and druid, thrilled us with stories of ancient heroes and battles fought by our ancestors. His poetry told of the defeated enemies, whose shields adorned our great hall's timber walls and severed heads, our palisade.

My brothers pretended to be Christian, but we had been raised to revere the old gods. Rignach had feuded with Niall since his marriage to Ness. Religion was a wedge used to lever her sons away from their father and to her. Sylvester arrived far too late to change what we knew as truth.

440 AC.

Too late because when I was seven years old, I was taken to Knowth; to the Hag. Knowth, the vast burial mound of those who came before, the old ones. Conall, Loegaire and I would never forget that night of the hunter's moon, the day after the autumn equinox and Samhain.

At dusk, we'd arrived at the River Boinne, running sluggish and strong through the fields, golden in the setting sun's light.

Druid Laidcenn chanted from a poem we knew well. "Through water and fire, over stone and under earth to see the future king."

He made us strip to swim naked across the sacred river. As the old man manoeuvred a skin-covered round craft alongside us, I struggled; gulping at the cold, the current dragged at my seven-year-old feet. My head dipped below the surface. I felt a seconds' terror; spluttering, gasping for breath, tendrils of weed stroked my legs and blackness surrounded me. Conall pulled me up. Laughing, he cupped my chin and tugged me forward and onto the bank.

'There, Little Lord, you are safe. We must set you more swimming practice though. When we are out raiding with the fiann, the breakers on the beaches can be fierce. They will sweep you away if you can't swim.'

Giving us back our clothes, Laidcenn ordered us on toward the mound of the ancients. Before the mighty barrow roared a bonfire, its flames leapt high into the darkening skies. His long beard and hair were blown wildly by the wind as he walked to stand behind the blaze.

'Through fire sons of Niall, through fire,' he shouted, 'leap, leap.'

Loegaire and I trembled.

Conall scoffed. 'Don't worry, it is a common test for warriors. Run as fast as you can, then jump, you'll be through it in a moment. It's as if you take cool air with you; I've done it at Beltane. Besides our hair is wet from the river, the flames can't harm us.' He looked down at me. 'Give me your hand, we will run together, Maelon.'

I held on as tightly as I could as we ran, then leapt. He was right, it was a moment's scorching heat. An orange flash of light showed behind my closed eyelids, then it was over. We stood before a mighty stone, taller and broader than any man. It was covered with ancient, carved and painted symbols, spirals and snakes circling around without end.

Laidcenn said, 'Now we must climb over stone to travel under the earth. Listen well. You can never reveal what you see tonight. If you do the ancestors will haunt your dreams and steal your soul. They will bar you from entering the Otherworld. Your shades will suffer alone and abandoned for all eternity.'

Awed we scrambled up and over the boulder, dragging the old druid with us. He urged us forward through a long, low passageway, deep into the heart of the mound. I clung to my brothers, the smell of earth and death in my nostrils. Crouching we crept towards a light glowing in the distance. I stumbled and fell over a rock, my elbow hit the passage wall, the graze stung. I tried not to shout out, didn't want my big brothers to call me a baby. We inched on past niches filled with burnt bones; beside them, gold and silver offerings glimmered dully. As we got closer to the light, I made out engravings; more circles, spirals and lozenges strange to the eye were cut deep into huge stones above my head.

Then we saw the Hag. She was dressed in torn rags which flapped with her every motion, hiding then revealing sagging tattooed breasts and scrawny thighs. The creature wore a mask over her eyes and nose, painted and carved as a death's head, below her wild grey hair. Sharp, pale blue eyes peered from carved slits and long, claw-like nails clutched and beckoned to us. We were appalled and overwhelmed.

'I have Niall's three youngest sons. Two you know, the smallest is the Welsh woman's child,' said Laidcenn.

'Let me see you. Will you pass the test your brothers failed? Who will be the next High King? Who is to be anointed?' the Hag muttered.

She took our chins in turn, staring into our eyes. Loegaire shook so hard I stroked his back to comfort him.

'Drink this. A mouthful each, more could kill.'

She thrust a flask at us. I sipped the liquid dubiously. It tasted bitter yet honeyed, behind it the smell of earth, of mushrooms and forest. The Hag took three long draughts from the pot. Beads of sweat appeared on her forehead, she looked close to retching.

'Sit on those skins. Do not speak or disturb me. Do exactly as you are told,' she commanded.

I jumped as two men carrying drums appeared from a side passage and started to beat out a strange rhythm, slowly increasing in pace. The noise echoed and amplified in the dark chamber; the fire's sparks danced as if in time to the sound. In the centre stood a vast stone basin as long as I was tall, in it a shallow pool of water shook with each pulse. It was hard to think, the drink had made me woozy and the constant drumming dazed and disorientated me. My senses spun, the world shifted around me dizzyingly, my elbow throbbed after its earlier scratch.

The Hag breathed faster, nodding in time to the drum notes. Laidcenn, Loegaire and Conall had started to do the same. I kept still, terrified, waiting, watching.

The Hag took up handfuls of bleached knuckle-bones with rough black markings and thrust them toward us.

'Close your eyes, pick four each. Hold two tight in each hand until I ask for them.'

My hand shook as I tried to decide which ones to choose. Should I pick large or small? Four smooth bones were soon clutched, light and dry within my fists. Clenching my jaw to stop my teeth chattering, I wondered what fate they held.

The Hag took Conall into a long, tight embrace.

'Drop the bones into the basin. The Goddess will foretell your future.'

She stared into the water reading the symbols.

Next, it was Loegaire's, then my turn to be clutched into her skinny bosom. I smelt the sour remnants of the herbal drink on her breath, felt her body shake and heard her mutter incomprehensible words.

There were animal skins on the floor, she pointed. 'Sleep there until dawn draws near.'

Her head turned questioningly to Laidcenn.

'The night is clear, stars and moon illuminate the sky this time,' he replied

I huddled into Conall for warmth and he stroked my arm for reassurance. The Hag's feet were not bare as I'd expected. She wore soft, finely worked leather boots, such as those worn only by queens like Mother or Rignach. That was odd I thought, as I drifted into a disturbed sleep. It felt moments until I was shaken awake. We were dragged to the back of the chamber and told to stand against the wall.

The drumming was frenzied. The Hag stood beside the glowing fire gazing at us fiercely; then came the dawn. A ray of sunlight pierced the darkness, a sliver of light shining along the passageway floor. She stirred embers with a human bone, throwing on a bundle of green herbs. Clouds of acrid fumes stung my eyes and throat, as the sun illuminated specks of soot and smoke whirling in circles up to the roof.

In that vortex I saw a woman's face appear, wise and benevolent, framed with oak leaves and acorns, she smiled at me, then was gone. The light moved fast up and along the chamber wall, passing over Conall in moments, but settled for long seconds on Loegaire. The Hag stirred the cinders again. Ash swirled up from the orange flames and Loegaire stiffened, his expression told me he too had seen something. The beam moved toward me, its rays hit my right arm then disappeared, extinguished.

Disappointment touched Laidcenn's face. 'Clouds have covered the sun.'

The Hag turned to Conall, I detected sympathy and softening her eyes. 'The sunlight shone bright and brief on you. Did you see anything in the flames and smoke my child?'

He shuddered. 'A demon crow with red eyes, in its beak it held a circlet.'

'Macha's gift of kingship. You will fulfil your destiny; you will become High King. Black sorrow will follow.'

'And you Loegaire? What did you see?'

'A dark bearded man, fierce; Lugh of the Long Arm. He held a skull out, then took it back.'

'A warning, a solemn geis; do not betray Lugh and the old gods or those prizes you love most will be lost to you.'

'And you little one, was there anything in the flames?'

'A woman's face surrounded by acorns in the smoke. She... she smiled.'

Startled she gasped, 'The Goddess came to you?' she hesitated, something changed in her voice. I felt a chill tickle at my neck, something was wrong.

'The sun did not anoint, it only touched your arm. You will not be king; your hand will aid others. You have Macha's favour, that may be the kinder gift. The bones foretold you will lead but not rule, and follow a path of twists and turns. They presaged a woman at each bend. The Goddess will watch over you, child.'

She shook me roughly. 'You must repay her favour, always. Do not forsake her.

'Take them away Laidcenn. I will speak with Niall of their future.'

We had looked on the faces of our gods. Priest Sylvester's tales of a forgiving deity who had lived among men, who loved everyone the same, could not reach us. We knew the power of the old ones, could never forget, nor worship other spirits.

When Father told me three years later I was to become a priest I felt confused, torn and angry. Men went to battle, raided and plundered. They didn't shave their heads and preach. I was sworn to the Goddess. I couldn't become the follower of a gentle, forgiving lord who accepted no other gods. I would prove my father wrong.

CHAPTER
4

445 AC

One wet morning in the spring of my twelfth year, grim-faced my father came to Mother's hut. It was unusual, he never approached her door, she went to him when summoned. She guessed why at once; tears filled her eyes.

'Why must you send our son away?'

'I have told you it is for his safety. Anyway you have a daughter to comfort you.'

Holding my face, he tilted my head up with his hand and gazed at me; a tall thin boy, lips quivering, staring back at him, resolute.

'A ship destined for Wales has come to shore. I have paid them to take you to Cor Tewdws, a monastic school. Your grandmother's cousin, Cedric, is Abod there. He has written to Palladius and we have agreed terms. You will leave on the evening tide. Sylvester will accompany you.

'I give you two gifts and a warning my son. The first is Kira your wolfhound, she will protect you and prevent your mother from worrying about your safety. The second is my dead brother Brion's sword, it is not a pretty thing, but it's strong. I hope you will grow to have the strength to wield it if you need to. Brion was a big man, taller than me and it is heavy. You will likely broaden and grow to my height. I remember Anlach, your grandfather, as a giant, although I was young then and all men looked tall.'

He continued, 'Remember my words, Maelon. Be careful in your dealings with your uncles in Wales and Ireland. In Wales Brychan is a danger, be sure not to annoy or antagonise him, avoid his lands. You are an Irish prince and my son. Go! Make me proud in this world or the next.'

He patted my head briefly. I caught a glimmer of sadness in his eyes as he pushed abruptly through the leather hanging at the doorway. Sobbing, my mother hugged me hard and long. She gave me the ring worn at her neck for many years. It was too big for my fingers so I took her woven hair chain and wore it with pride. The ring contained a glowing red stone carved with the imprint of an eagle hollowed out in reverse. Mother said it would protect me. It had been her grandmother's and her mother's before her, so was touched by saints.

On the beach later I said my farewells to Conall and Loegaire. The sea was sooted silver and the sky dark; in the soft mist, it was hard to tell whether it was tears or rain we swept from our faces. We took a solemn oath on that shore; that if any of us were in need then each would come to the aid of the others. We exchanged the ornate arm-rings I had been given the day I saved Nathi's life. I wore one of Conall's raven and Loegaire's boar arm-rings as I made my way across the sand to the boat. My brothers each took one of my hound rings, to wear along with the remaining one my father had given them.

Gulls circled above the ship that carried me across the sea to Wales, their mournful calls reflecting my misery. A heavy lump of pain hurt my chest, but a son of Naill could not cry. The west wind filled coarse woollen sails, as we sped away from Ireland, my home and all that was familiar. Sylvester stood beside me as we looked back over the waves to the Irish shore and my mother's figure dwindling to nothing in the evening sea mist.

Sylvester placed a protective arm around me, his hand squeezed my upper arm comfortingly. 'I am glad we leave Ireland and its warlike, primitive people. It will be wonderful to return to where men of God read books, write and talk of our Lord Jesus. To serve at the monastic school at Cor Tewdws, is a better fate than I could have dreamed. That good Christian Emperor, Theodosius the First, ordered the school founded before the Romans left our shores, it is the oldest in all of Britannia.'

He hesitated. 'I suppose your family has good reason not to view Theodosius fondly.' Then he continued, 'The school is near the vicus town of Bovium on the south coast of Wales. I am going back to civilisation, Maelon.'

I had no idea what he meant; how dare he suggest my family and the kings of Ireland were primitive, and why should they care about that long-dead Roman Emperor? I shrugged off his arm in annoyance and crossed to the other side of the boat. Hunkering between a pair of woven baskets, I gazed back toward Ireland, wretched with longing. The gentle rocking motion finally lulled me to sleep.

The ship beached early in the morning, lurching and crunching on a grey pebbled shore below high golden cliffs formed of strange square blocks. The waves pounded a pavement of rocks extending to a sandy beach at one side of a river. Before us was a wide, flat-bottomed valley, steeply wooded to both sides. Bent trees and bushes, backs to the sea, lined a rough path. No soul in sight, no smoke or huts, just empty green hills with a path twisting away into the distance. The ship's master assured us the school was hidden behind the dunes a short walk inland.

'It is built out of sight for fear of Pict or Irish raiders,' he said cautiously, catching my eye.

Heavy bundles, a twelve-year-old with a huge wolfhound in the company of a priest were landed. Icy waves slapped against my legs, pebbles crunched as the sea sucked and dragged at my legs. As the tide turned the ship left, engulfed by a milk-white sea mist. I shivered, cold and afraid. Sylvester, Kira and I walked alone up the bank path toward our new life.

As we walked Sylvester commented, 'A century ago when Rome controlled the Welsh coast, no raiders would have dared attack. Now towns and villages have good reason to fear pillage, rape and slavery. The fianna talk of a new name, the Saxons, come from the east to join the destruction. Settlements have pulled away from the coast and into dips in the land, or else retreated to ancient hill forts, hoping their smoke and fires won't be spotted.'

At the end of the path stood Cor Tewdws, my new home. I gazed at well-kept buildings, little different to the mighty halls of Tara except for scale. A dozen sturdy wood and wattle huts with neatly thatched roofs were set within stout, timber walls, entered through a high double gate. Inside chickens scratched and women shouted over fires. Beyond them lay an orchard with bee-skeps and pens for pigs and geese.

The buildings varied in size. I soon learnt some were set aside for sleeping, others for studying. One, the scriptorium, had a long wooden table and shuttered windows. It was set aside for the monks to copy the gospels. The largest was the clas[3], a church for daily prayers and to welcome Christian pilgrims.

Sylvester and I were given a hearty welcome and a simple meal of bread and cheese; then I was sent to change. An elderly monk introduced as Johannes, presented me with a rough, brown homespun habit and a simple cord to tie at the waist.

Annoyed I said, 'No thank you, this robe does not demonstrate my status sufficiently. I am a Prince of Ireland, son of the High King.

He snorted, 'All are equal in the eyes of the Lord. You are a novice in our clas now. No one takes precedence over another here; we dress the same.'

Resentfully I handed over my fine linen shirt and warm woollen breeches along with my thick red-dyed cloak. I fumed but did not respond. This was my new life. I couldn't put aside the thought that I was better than these priests. I raged at my father for sending me away; making me feel a nothing and a no-one, worthless. My heart refused to accept I could ever be the same as these men with their stupid shaven heads and beardless chins.

Younger sons of many of the chiefs of south and west Wales and beyond were sent to Cor Tewdws to study. Most of the older monks were considerate; in fact, I was happy in that place for

---

3   Clas Celtic church settlement

the next five years. At the school and church's heart was Cedric, our Abod, my grandmother Marchell's cousin. Small and clever, his eyes penetrated as if he searched inside his boys' souls. In his brown hooded cloak and grey robe, he darted sparrow-like around the settlement, never still. Encouraging, advising, making quips, his round face beaming good humour; we loved him.

Cedric was delighted I'd joined his school and equally pleased with the heavy torc my father sent as payment. We grew fond of each other. He'd spend hours telling me about his home in Powys, of his memories of playing with his cousins, including my grandmother.

Cedric painted a land of marvels; mountains so high they were capped with cloud, green valleys full of game. He talked longingly of lovely Lake Syfaddon, set in a bowl of fertile countryside, rich in fish and fowl; a place, he whispered, of magic.

He told me legends of the lake. 'Pagan nonsense of course,' he said. He'd always agree to repeat those tales anyway. 'Mists cover Syfaddon at night, Maelon. It is then the folk of the Otherworld walk its shores. If you rise at dawn and watch the wisps of mist swirl away, you might catch a glimpse of one walking back into its deep waters.'

He told us of magical hounds, monstrous fish and giants throwing mighty rocks at each other from mountain peaks. We novices dreamt about visiting those lands as he wove his stories; me more than the rest; my ancestors' land. My longing was fringed with trepidation. My father's warning about my uncle echoed in my ears.

As pupils, we spent long hours studying the gospels and learning to write and draw in the scriptorium. Johannes ensured the room was kept immaculate. The tables were scrubbed at the end of each day and ink bottles ordered, fresh straw was spread on the floor each week after a thorough scouring. The hut had a characteristic smell of beeswax and tallow along with a faint, sharp scent of lime used to whiten calf vellum sheets.

Once we pupils acquired a good enough writing hand on wax tablets, we were allowed to practise carefully on parchment and copy the gospels. Those with artistic talent copied verses onto their manuscripts, illustrating capital letters with glorious coloured inks and gold leaf. The pages were kept loose in wooden covers set with precious gems. Our novice, less lovely copies of gospels were sent out as a mark of success to any new church established by our pupil priests. Each church's task to bring the words of the Lord Jesus to local people. Written pages to be venerated, words solemnly read aloud to remind the priests and congregations of Christ's message. Young missionaries were given gospels, along with a sacred or wondrous icon for their congregants to revere.

During my first month in the school, Cedric took Sylvester and me to a nearby villa, Caer Mead. He wanted to introduce us to the owners, Clemens and his wife, Romano-Britons and patrons of our church and school. They owned much of the land along the coast and many slaves. Clemens was magistrate and administrator for the area, acting for King Glywys, who ruled our kingdom, Glywyssig.

Caer Mead was the finest construction I had ever seen; beyond my imagining. A wide gateway led into a cobbled courtyard. Around the yard ranged neat stone buildings, with thick, red clay roof tiles which kept them warm and dry. Cattle and horses were housed in comfortable stone quarters, better than many a king's hall in Ireland. On three sides were farm buildings, on the fourth stood a stone palace. I gawped, as Sylvester had promised, it was

two storeys high, one floor above the first. Cedric introduced
Sylvester to them.

Then in a proud voice he said, 'I would like you to meet
Maelon. He is my cousin's grandson. You have heard of his
father, High King Niall of Ireland, and you will know of his
sainted great-grandmother, Gratianna, daughter of Emperor
Magnus Maximus.'

Caer Mead's owners were as impressed as Cedric had hoped. I
later came to understand those old Romano-British families were
obsessed with ancestry. Clemens reached out to clasp my hand, as
I leant forward, he noticed my mother's ring swing from my neck.

'An imperial seal,' he said gesturing, 'you'll be laying claim to
the Empire then young man?'

I was confused, unsure of what to say. Cedric looked surprised.

'I thought it was my great-grandmother, Gratianna's, ring. It
is old, a gift from my mother, and precious to me.'

Smiling, Clemens changed the subject. He gestured to Kira
asking, 'This is your hound?'

'Yes, Kira has been mine since pupped. She is not fully
grown yet.'

'I keep deerhounds, but they are smaller than this powerful
animal. We must talk of hounds later, for now, I welcome you to
my home Prince Maelon ap Niall. Come in.'

We were taken into a room with a floor of coloured stones,
arranged to depict a goddess pouring wine, the walls smooth,
painted red with black patterns. Clemens invited us to recline on
padded couches. The ceiling was painted as if a starry sky with
nymphs peeping down at each corner. How could rooms of such
comfort, luxury and beauty exist?

Cedric whispered to Sylvester, 'I have never been invited into this room before. Having a prince with us seems to make a difference. I guess Clemens wants something from us.'

Clemen's wife clapped, calling her slaves to offer us light beer served from a beautiful pottery jug decorated with leaping dolphins.

Clemens said, 'My father would have served an emperor's great-grandson Frankish wine from glass goblets, not pottery beakers. Those we have we do not use. They are treasures that can never be replaced, like much you see in this room.'

He shook his head sadly. 'We are taking down buildings to reclaim tiles and stones. You can't make or buy replacements and those with the skills to repair are growing too old to work. Fathers do their best to pass on crafts to their sons, but people die, move away… When your ancestor Maximus left with the last legions, the skills evaporated, like Rome's memory.

'Let us talk of the future, not the past. I will be direct; will you sell me your hound, Prince? I would pay you well.'

'Please call me Maelon, as a pupil priest I am no longer a prince. I will never sell Kira, besides no man could control her. She is trained by me, knows only my commands.'

'I expected that, nor would I sell my best hound. However, I have a proposition. Kira is valuable, worth even more here than in Ireland. She will need to be put to a dog if her womb is to stay healthy. Not until she is fully grown, breeding too early is unsafe, but in a year or so she'll become unhappy if she is not bred.'

Cedric and I nodded. It was true, bitches were healthier if they bore at least one litter.

'I have a fine deerhound, Cai, clever if smaller than your Kira. Their puppies would be choice animals, and valuable. My pack needs fresh blood. If we put Cai to Kira, we could each take half the pups. The church can sell theirs for a fine profit, half Irish wolfhound and half Welsh deerhound, they'll fetch a good price.'

Cedric replied for me. 'We will think about the matter. We would want more than half of the puppies though.'

'No, I insist on half. No better pack exists south of Powys, not even King Glywys's son, Prince Woolos has finer. Prince Maelon will want to see the pups well looked after.'

I spoke up, 'Half, but if there are an odd number of pups then the last is ours, and we pick first.'

Clemens acquiesced, the runt of any litter was unlikely to be worth much; besides I held the power in this negotiation.

'Could I see around your home? Ireland was never conquered by Rome, so I've never visited anything like it.'

His wife was delighted with the opportunity to show off her villa. She led us along an arcade, roofed and open to one side. It enclosed a formal garden of neatly trimmed dark green bushes, with a statue at its centre. Each room we passed was as lovely as the last, most had black and white patterned floors, but their bedroom was tiled with a marvellous picture of gods with horns and hooves chasing maidens. I tried not to gape at the grandeur, act a prince.

As we walked back to the clas Cedric remarked, 'That villa is not a palace Maelon. Most Romans would judge it modest.'

Two years later we bred Kira; she produced a litter of five fine puppies, two for Clemens and three for us. Cedric insisted we sell two, the school could not afford to feed them all. The runt Tipi, he let me keep. Clemens got the hounds anyway; he offered the Abod more than anyone else.

My Tipi was sweet, brindle in colour, smaller than Kira or her sire, affectionate and enthusiastic. She would run up to anyone and everyone, barking and wagging a short fluffy tail. I could not train her, no matter what trick of Finn's I used. She seemed unable to understand she should obey and protect me. She had the concentration of a gnat, always running off to explore a scent or find a stick. I despaired of her ever learning to catch game and return it to me.

After our visit to Caer Mead Sylvester and I, along with Kira for protection were regularly sent out by Cedric on expeditions to barter at Roman villas and temples. Those villas were mostly occupied by descendants of those who owned them in Roman times; two generations and forty years earlier. Ageing mansions that were crumbling, falling into further disrepair as each year passed. We bought glass bottles, chalices and urns, the lovelier the better to adorn our church. Pilgrims came to Cor Tewdws to admire them, the Abod accepting their offerings and praying for them in return.

To my cynical eye, nothing had changed. Druids were paid to offer incantations to the old gods, priests to offer prayers to the new. I kept my views to myself, pretended to Cedric I believed in Jesus and learnt their empty words and prayers. I'd visited an ancient oak grove near the coast and made offerings to the Goddess as each season changed. Satisfied that if I did not accept the truth of Jesus, I couldn't do as my father ordered and become a priest.

We were a happy group of young men in that school. When I was thirteen, I grew tall, whip-thin, like an ash sapling. At fifteen I began to fill, growing in muscle as well as height and the years passed pleasantly. Our teachers rarely beat us; although as chief mischief-maker, I was punished more often than most.

I'd made one enemy with my mischief; old Johannes, the senior monk in the scriptorium. In hindsight, my drawing horns and devil eyes with wood ash mixed with red ink onto his bald head as he dozed, was a mistake. It made everyone laugh, unfortunately Johannes disliked me after that childish tease, he called me the Irish devil. He had no memory of being young, but I was thirteen when I played that jest.

My best friend, the boy we all admired was Maewyn Succat, he who later became known as Patricius, or Patrick of Ireland by some. Maewyn, who we called Wyn back then was six months younger than me. He came from a small town, near copper mines, some thirty-five Roman miles away to the north-west. Wyn had been sent to the school to learn more of Christ and become a priest like his grandfather before him. Tall and fair, he was firm but gentle. There are those in every generation born to lead, Maewyn was one such boy. With a scythe-like nose and warm green eyes, he was not handsome but attractive. Every one of us hoped to become his acolyte when he was sent out as a missionary, we looked up to him. The only person who didn't think he was special, was Wyn himself. He would dwell on his failings and lacked confidence, always worrying he was not good enough.

He was bold with girls however, telling me, 'My mother, two sisters and all our women slaves doted on me, spoilt me. I spent most of my time with women as a child and I love them. Now, well they seem to love me back.'

Wyn was a good friend. One time I was clowning in the scriptorium. Mimicking Johannes nasal whine I'd said, 'Now look here, this letter, "i" needs to be smoother. Upright, standing erect, straight and proud.'

I swung my hand up in a rude gesture and spilt a bowl of black ink over a page of half completed script.

The giggles silenced in horror; then Johannes himself walked in.

'Who did this? Do you know how much vellum costs? How many weeks it takes for calfskin to be made into these precious pages? How long copying those verses took me?'

Incandescent with rage he glared around. His eyes narrowed as they turned to me, the boy closest to the table. My mouth went dry and I swallowed. Johannes often beat me, insisting he was thrashing out Satan. I was regularly in trouble. Everyone knew he disliked me, hit me harder than the rest.

Wyn spoke quickly, 'I did it, Johannes. I'm so sorry, it was an accident. My sleeve brushed the bowl as I passed. I'll work harder to make up for it. I realise how costly the vellum is and how much of your work wasted.'

Johannes called out, 'Come here, take your punishment.'

I felt guilty watching Wyn bear lashes from a hazel rod for my sake. I should have stopped it then, admitted I'd done it, but knew we'd both get whipped, so kept silent.

Another friend was Gastyn, sent from Armorica, over the seas in Gaul. Gasty as we soon came to call him, was too young to have been sent away, aged seven when he arrived. His family joined the wave of the people from southern lands who followed the Romans to Gaul. They hoped they'd be safer there than in Britannia, less at risk of raids from the Irish, Picts and Saxons. Gasty's mother had died giving birth to a sister when he was four. When his father remarried, the new wife wanted the boy gone. Gasty became our little mascot and friend.

He took a passionate interest in plants, learning the uses of each flower and leaf. He enjoyed helping Johannes tend the herb garden beside the scriptorium, a sunny, peaceful spot. The elderly monk bending low to lecture him on the healing properties of the plants. Gastyn nodding beside him, his small face screwed up in concentration, repeating back every word.

Wyn and Gastyn loved my hounds, Kira and Tipi, nearly as much as I did. Wyn had grown up with dogs on his father's farm. Wyn came to the school well versed in the gospels, but his mastery of written Latin was poor compared with mine. He'd no strong leaning to Christ, we were the same; boys looking for fun. After hours scratching away with a quill and ink on parchment, or chanting verses from the gospels, he and I would burst out of the scriptorium and rush away onto the high cliffs or beaches. We two, young Gasty chasing after us calling out, "Slow down, slow down," would spend hours walking, talking and laughing.

We'd watch Tipi snap at moths and butterflies, leap into muddy puddles and chase her tail in the surf. We would plan mischief and fun, wrestle or fight.

As we grew our entertainments changed. We would challenge each other.

'Who will get the first kiss from the brewer's daughter, Wyn? I will, I'm a prince.'

'Nonsense, she won't care about your ancestry. There are far more important things when it comes to pleasing girls. I have already won the first kiss anyway; you are too late. I'm more interested in what comes next, further down shall we say. I want more than kisses. I suggest you try her little sister, rather than hoping for my leftovers.'

Irritated, I accepted the truth of his words. I was better looking than Wyn, my dark eyes, hair and strong jaw got admiring glances. I easily mastered Wyn with sword and sling-shot too, but when it came to girls, they liked him better. I didn't stand a chance, the most I could hope for was to console a disappointed friend.

Each evening Sylvester and Cedric would teach the older pupils oratory: how best to preach the words of the Lord, ways to project our voices loudly but not strain; when to pause in a speech, how to build drama, when to lower your tone to draw people closer, and how to force hallelujahs from the congregation.

Sylvester said, 'I've marked the bards and poets in Ireland, they adopt the same techniques and are masters of telling tales. We must better their eloquence with our stories of Jesus and his miracles.'

I was good, could draw my audience in, speaking out loud and clear in the open air, but Wyn was masterful. At fifteen his words dripped honey and hope, the room would end up in his thrall, thrilled by his speeches.

After the meal, our teachers would argue as to how best to convert heathens to Christianity. The Abod insisted that it would take more than sermons to convince the people.

'We must have marvels to counteract magic. Christian churches to replace shrines. Priests must spread the message, supplant foolish superstitions with the Lord's miracles. Rather than destroy pagan sites, we should reuse them; build our churches within sacred yew and oak groves. People will gradually forget and come to the same places their father did before them. We can show relics of the saints for them to revere instead.'

'Creating false miracles and pretending objects are sacred is twisting the Lord's message,' replied Sylvester.

'If the church is to expand then we should claim saints and wonders. The druids and filíd use every trick they know.'

I was tormented by doubt. What if Cedric and Sylvester were wrong? Macha, Lugh and the other gods had been worshipped for generations beyond memory. Who could say if Jesus, a man from a distant land, was the true God? What did it mean that he was one with God his father when he had been a man the same as me? Just a carpenter, someone who fashioned tables and benches. Were the miracles the gospels taught true? All he'd done was be crucified. I'd seen many men killed by my father as horribly. I couldn't share my misgivings when everyone seemed so convinced, so stayed silent.

Johannes disapproved of my keeping up practice with sword and sling-shot.

'Monks are men of peace; Jesus forbids us to kill. Why is that Irish lad training to maim? I don't trust his motives.'

Cedric supported me. 'These are dangerous times, Johannes. I am afraid monks and priests may need to defend themselves. I agree we must not kill, but the gospels say nothing about not protecting yourself and others. Besides, our boys are full of energy, expending it on something useful makes them less likely to get into trouble in other ways.'

He stared at me meaningfully as he said, "get into trouble". After that, I along with several novices trained each day using staffs, sling-shot, bow, and weighted wooden swords.

CHAPTER
5

450 AD

The spring I turned seventeen Palladius sent a messenger to Sylvester. My father had been wounded raiding. Despite the druids' efforts and my mother's nursing, he was dead. My half-brothers were fighting as to what land each should inherit and who should be High King. My three uncles had been forced to cede land; Ireland was at war. The Úi Neill lands were extensive and my clan strong, no one was certain of the outcome of the next gathering in Tara, or who would be proclaimed High King on the Stone of Destiny.

Palladius letter suggested it was better that I stay in Wales for the present. He complained my seven half-brothers had returned to worshipping the old gods. Palladius's position was more precarious than for many years. I worried for Conall and Loegaire; my mother and Ria too.

Later in the summer, a second parchment arrived with another enclosed addressed to me, the contents of both surprising.

Palladius wrote that the succession was agreed and the country divided between Rignach's seven sons. Conall had taken the carved rod of High Kingship, the largest and richest share; the Kingship of Tara and Southern Úi Neill, as it was now called. He'd divided that land with Loegaire. They had claimed it on the basis that one-third was held for me, Maelon, to be known as King over the Sea; Niall's youngest son.

Palladius added that Ness's twin sons had disappeared and were presumed dead. He asked Cedric to persuade me to return so that at least one Irish king would be a Christian. My uncles and their sons had been forced to give up territory; he doubted the uneasy peace would last.

Sylvester and Cedric exchanged glances and we turned to the second letter.

I read it aloud,

"Beloved Brother,

Conall, King of Tara and High King of Ireland and Loegaire, King of Ireland remember our oath to you. We hold your portion of our father's land safe and will guard it, along with your mother and our sister, as our own.

We wish you well."

Sylvester looked excited. 'You are rich in Ireland, Maelon, a king.'

I shook my head, told them my father had warned me against such a move five years before. He'd thought the risks too high.

Cedric agreed, 'It is your decision, not mine, Maelon. You have not taken the tonsure and aren't bound to the church.

45

However, your father's words were wise. You are seventeen, it would be sending a lamb to slaughter. I notice your brothers do not directly ask you to take the third kingship, instead, they offer to look after your land. They may have used your name as a bargaining chip to keep Southern Úi Neill for themselves.

'Accept their offer, say you are as yet too young to rule. Defer the care of the land to them as your elders. Make it clear in your reply you wish them to hold it in trust for you for the future. Tell them, for now, you will remain King over the Sea. When a king dies and there is a change in the order, a country is destabilised. Let matters lie. Make a decision when you are older and Ireland settled.'

Sylvester interrupted, 'But Palladius needs a Christian king in Ireland.'

'Then the Bishop must work at converting the many kings already ruling there. I am not going to send Maelon to him as a sacrifice.'

Some weeks later Sylvester and I, along with my faithful Kira, were sent on a quest to Moridunum along the old Roman Road. Our task to try again to buy a marvellous black chalice decorated with pink fish, the sign of Christ, owned by a family in the west of Wales. Cedric gave us a heavy bar of silver that Sylvester hid beneath his habit. I wore the sword my father had given me those years ago to deter potential robbers.

At the start of our journey, the weather was fair, blue skies studded with small clouds that rushed along in a brisk wind. We walked from dawn until dusk to reach Nidum, where we were given great welcome by Benignus, a young priest who'd left the school a year ago. We missed Beni's cheerful presence, he'd been a great friend of Wyn's and mine; like me, he was Irish, the son of a chieftain. We sheltered cosy under his church's thatched roof for the night and I set Kira to hunt. To our gratification instead of the usual squirrel or pigeon, she returned with a young boar.

Cutting off the head as the dog's reward; we set the animal to roast on a hearth outside the church. The rich flesh sizzled and popped appetisingly in the heat; flares of flame burst as fat droplets fell on the logs. My mouth watered and stomach rumbled with anticipation as we settled in the deepening twilight to talk of the past. Beni was miserable. A sociable youth, he hated living alone.

He complained, 'In Nidum they look to the old gods and have scant regard for Christ. They are dirty and have forgotten their Roman past. I hate this dark valley and its people. I miss the school.'

Not entirely surprised he was unhappy, we tried to reassure him. Sylvester offered to speak to Cedric and ask if he could return to Cor Tewdws. We rose before dawn to reach Moridunum, paying the fare for a ferry over the river at the old Roman fort at Leucarium, with game caught by Kira. Footsore we reached the town by dusk. Moridunum was impressive, the largest civitas in Wales. Its streets were laid out straight and wide they led to a forum and basilica. What had once been a public bathhouse was filled with small shops, selling everything from shoes to oils from Gaul and beyond. We paid for a room in the mansio, originally built to accommodate visiting officials from Rome or travellers on business. It had provided safe room and board overnight as men travelled around the empire. That night it rained, but I slept comfortably, dry and warm under a tiled roof; on a couch with leather straps.

Sylvester took me through the town's busy streets the following morning. As elsewhere the place was falling to ruin but retained a faded glory. We searched out the owner of the chalice in his decrepit villa, door hanging from one rusted hinge. Yet again he declined our silver, claiming the cup was worth more. His calculating eyes expected us to return and increase our offer. Annoyed, Sylvester told him we would not come again, that the town of Bovium and the Roman villas such as Caer Mead, close to Cor Tewdws, had better treasures.

Disappointed, we trekked back to the school. Near Bovium we smelt burning wood and thatch on the breeze, then saw a distant black haze. Our hearts pounded as we reached the little town, what had happened? We were told the news by the townsfolk; a boat filled with raiders had come to the coast and ravaged the countryside two days before. They had not come as far as Bovium bridge but had pillaged Cor Tewdws and the surrounding area. Buildings smouldered, no one had been brave enough to approach the school. People had heard screams and seen fires turning the night sky red. Some claimed the raiders' boats had sailed. No one knew whether the pillage continued or whether they had gone. Many residents had packed their belongings, some had already departed, others waited, ready to abandon their homes, to hide at a moment's notice.

Horrified we asked some of the younger men to accompany us to the church. We walked with fear in our hearts for the final miles to our settlement. When we arrived the only sounds from inside the school's walls were the calls of gulls squabbling. A blackbird's liquid notes sang a lament. I swallowed and grasped Sylvester's arm.

Devastation lay before us; our buildings were wrecked, thatched roofs charred, fallen in, a thin plume of acrid smoke climbed slowly to the sky. The gate to the palisade was broken, several bodies lay where they'd fallen in the yard, one hung limp and heavy from a tree. I sent in a whining Kira to explore, rooks and crows rose cawing from bodies. She returned tail down, distressed to see men she knew unmoving, murdered. Examining each in turn, we were sickened at the death blows on their corpses. A monk's hands had been cut off and lay, fingers clasped together, in front of his body.

Only old Johannes lived. He rested beside the scriptorium, a purple bruised lump the size of a robin's egg on his forehead, over it a ragged gash trickled fluid from behind congealing blood. Sylvester propped his head up and gave him sips of water.

When the old priest saw me, he made the hand sign to avert evil and spat, 'The Irish, the Irish came and burnt it all. Your kin, you Irish devil.' He pointed to the trees. 'They hung the Abod, killed the rest, took the pupils and women as slaves. They must have thought I was dead from the blow one giant of a man gave me. I was knocked out when they hung poor Cedric on that bough, thank the Lord, but I've had to stare at him each time I open my eyes. They slit his belly. Look… look at him the dear man, hanging there. I pray constantly that he died before they did such a terrible thing.'

I forced myself to gaze again where Johannes gestured. Cedric's carcass hung there, eviscerated, his face swollen and purple. The mound of guts below his feet buzzed with flies. He was suspended from the oak tree we sat under for lessons on sunny days. My amiable cousin, so gentle and good, how could this have happened to him? What sort of god would let his abod die so horribly?

As Sylvester tended Johannes, I walked around the enclosure numb and dry-eyed; the smell of burning and blood pungent, sickening. The scriptorium was destroyed, blackened pages of parchment and vellum smouldered in the rubble, ruined. Not knowing what else to do I tried to salvage what fragments remained; forty years of labour despoiled and useless.

We asked the villagers for help to dig graves and lay those who had died to rest. Four of our teachers, three servants and two of my fellow pupils had been slaughtered. Even poor Tipi, my pup, lay butchered near the church doorway. Kira whined beside her. When I went over, it gave me grim satisfaction to see blood on her bared teeth, along with fragments of cloth. Whoever harmed her had suffered for it; Tipi had finally learnt to protect herself.

Johannes' words rang over and over in my head. "The Irish, your kin, you Irish devil". This was what it felt like to be raided, plundered. I had thought our fiann's exploits so brave. The reality was stealing from the elderly, families with children, priests sworn to peace. Was this brave or proud?

I felt shame flush my body. I prickled head to foot with guilt, swore I would take revenge on those who had done this. I would not turn the other cheek, whatever Jesus taught. I pictured the culprits hanging from trees beside each other as I tortured them slowly; a turn of a garrotte for every friend killed. Macha and Lugh demanded I should avenge them.

We wondered at the fate of the other pupils. My friends, Wyn, little Gastyn and the rest, our poor servants murdered or taken. What would their lives be, sold as slaves in Ireland? Sylvester looked broken and empty as we buried our fellows, the only priest that remained in our happy school. He blessed each body; said they would be remembered as martyrs and saints.

What should we do, should we rebuild or leave? I made a fire in the church under the section of thatch not fallen. Gently we carried Johannes in, his colour had returned. The strike to his head had knocked him senseless and he remembered little of the events during the raid.

'How much warning did you have?' asked Sylvester.

'Not much, the watchers blew their horn about fifteen minutes before they came on us, we should have had longer. We were gathering our belongings when they came.

'I have saved the most precious gospels. I bound them in a pouch under my habit strapped to my chest. The bastard Irish,' he glanced at me malevolently, 'didn't get them. I wasn't searched. I left the precious bindings behind in the scriptorium, they were too bulky to conceal. I dare say they will have been stolen.'

Sylvester gestured agreement.

'The Abod tried to carry away our treasures to safety. Some, the gold chalice and the glass flask containing St Aaron's hair, he had with him. The rest,' his voice trailed off, he looked at me.

'Don't be ridiculous Johannes, this has nothing to do with Maelon. He hasn't been to Ireland for years, has no contact beyond letters with his family. You can admit that we have a safe hiding place for our valuables. Not now, who knows who may be watching but maybe tomorrow night I will check what is left. Eat this soup and let's try to sleep.'

Early next morning we heard Kira barking excitedly as if welcoming a friend. We were up in an instant. I had slept beside my sword and took it up. We heard crying and then Gastyn's voice whispering, 'Down Kira, down.'

I dropped my sword and with Sylvester ran to the broken gateway. Gasty stood there, shivering and wet in the cold morning light.

He ran to Sylvester's arms, crying out a torrent of words and tears.

'I ran away and abandoned them. I hid behind the church. When I saw them killing everyone, I crept away, up the hill. There were at least fifteen men, all wielding swords and axes. They stormed the clas, the Abod and our teachers, once they'd caught everyone, they dragged them to the doorway of the church. Then… then, even though they were on their knees praying and held no weapons they laughed. They told them to hold out their arms…, they cut at them.

'When they realised there was no mercy, some of our brothers in Christ tried to run. It was terrible, clouds of blood, blood everywhere as the pirates slashed at arms and heads. Tipi went for one, gave him a savage bite but they managed to call her off; when they took Cedric, she attacked them again. They stabbed and stabbed, one hit Johannes so hard with his sword hilt, it must have broken his skull. I saw them take Wyn and the others. They tied the pupils and servants together by a long rope and walked them away, toward the sea.

'I didn't know what to do. I followed them a little way and hid beside the shore, watched the boat sail away. I was too afraid to come back, although I knew they had gone. I thought the monk's ghosts would punish me for being alive and a coward. This morning I heard Kira's bark so I guessed you'd returned. I'm sorry, I failed them.'

Gastyn began to cry again.

Sylvester reassured him, 'You did right Gasty, what could a twelve-year-old do against warriors. You were brave not to cry out. Running was the right course of action. Our poor teachers are buried now; safe with our Lord in heaven.'

Johannes in the corner butted in. 'No blow could crack this thick skull of mine young Gastyn.'

Gasty rushed over and hugged him. 'You live, you live.'

Johannes and he clung to each other, crying together. I felt a lump rise in my throat and longed to cry with them as Sylvester did, but could not. Later we fed the hungry boy, cooking a hare Kira had delivered to the church. She had laid it out as an offering at the burnt threshold. My hound understood that something terrible had happened.

I questioned Gasty after he'd eaten as to whether he had noticed any identifying marks on the men.

He closed his eyes concentrating. 'The boat they left on had a white swan on its bow, and two men held shields with swans' necks on them. That's all I can recall.'

Johannes spoke up, 'Yes, now he says it, I saw that too, a swan with a nasty red beak.'

Sylvester looked pleased. 'Good thinking Maelon and well-remembered, Gastyn. It may help us trace who took the slaves and where they may sell them. Do you know whose emblem is the swan, Maelon?'

In fear, I nearly lied but with a gulp admitted, 'It could well be my uncle's emblem, Fiachrae's. That swan is a pun on his name. In the legend of Lir, his son Fiachrae was turned into a swan by his stepmother, a witch.'

If only I'd been there with Kira, I could have stopped it all, or if not the plundering at least the murders. It explained how they knew to call off Tipi.

Gastyn looked worried. 'As they led the pupils away, I heard them asking for you. They were asking for Maelon and what sounded like Mac Neill. They were searching for you.'

Sylvester and I exchanged a worried glance. Had my uncle come for me? Was his plan to use me as a pawn? The memory of my father's words from years before floated back.

"Be careful of your uncles."

Was I to blame for Cedric's death and Wyn and the others' abduction? What was happening at home? Was Conall still High King or were my uncles trying to stake a claim? I felt sick in my stomach, afraid. Was the attack my fault?

Sylvester sighed. 'I'm going to have to send letters to all the pupils' families, some may be able to offer a ransom.'

'My brothers will help, Conall and Loegaire. They have as much reason to dislike Fiachrae as I do. More, if they find out he wanted to capture me; they'd guess his plan at once. If we can trace the pupils they will help, but we should act quickly.'

Sylvester and I wrote short letters on less scorched scraps of parchment to the families of those killed or abducted. We discussed how best to get a message to my brothers in Ireland. We wanted to be sure any letter would reach them directly, could not be used against them.

We had no choice but to write to Palladius and ask him to go to Tara. We told him survivors of the raid suggested, "The swans' men" had taken our beloved friends as slaves. We asked him to trace the captives so they could be ransomed. I made particular mention of Maewyn Succat, son of a deacon; saying I loved him as another oath brother and particularly hoped he might be found.

We visited Clemens and his wife at Caer Mead; the raiders had gone there too. He had been preparing for years for such an attack. He told us they had barred their gates, while his slaves armed themselves with iron sickles and swords. His men fired bows from their upper windows. The attackers had tried to set fires on the roof with brands, but tiles do not burn like thatch. Clemens' pack of hounds had bayed as the marauders retreated, shouting obscenities.

Clemens said, 'We worry they will return. I am sorry we could not go to aid the church, but if we had tried, they would have surrounded and killed us. I will miss Cedric, he was a decent man, a learned, courteous Christian.'

Clemens offered Johannes the corner building in his yard as a chapel if he wished to stay, but Johannes refused.

'I want to flee the coast and those cursed Irish raiders,' he snarled.

'I am likely to follow you, try to move inland. It is too dangerous to stay, every summer the Irish come and wreak death in the countryside. We don't watch for the swallows to arrive with joy because they bring warm weather, but with fear of what will follow. It breaks my heart to think of leaving my father's land and fine home, but I'm not prepared to lie under it before my time.'

Once we'd left Sylvester said, 'We need a protector. Johannes refuses to stay in easy reach of the sea where we can be pillaged. I think he is right. We have to flee, wait for safer times. We will go to your grandparents. Marchell and her son are known as Christian. It is as good as anywhere and there is some connection. We must pray they agree to take us in. You will meet your Welsh kin, Maelon. We will pass close by Wyn's home settlement too. It will be quicker and more certain to give his family the sad news ourselves.'

I smiled, but recalled my father's warning, it not only concerned my uncle Fiachrae but my other uncle, Brychan. Would I would be as safe as he imagined?

Sylvester said, 'We will leave as soon as possible, take the Roman Road up from Nidum to Garth Madron. The road is named for your great-grandmother, Maelon, Sarn Elen after Saint Elen.'

Over four days, we sold what we could not carry. We took two ponies, one for Johannes, who was not well enough to walk. The other carried essential church goods, along with our iron cooking pot and provisions for the journey.

Late one night Sylvester stepped out twelve paces west from the spot where the font had stood. The raiders had thrown the heavy stone bowl over, that was where treasures were concealed in many churches. A fact so well known, that thieves always dug there. Cedric had been wise. He'd left a small hoard under the font to deceive them that they had found our valuables, all had been stolen. The bulk of our wealth lay untouched under the hard earth floor and rushes.

I dug slowly through compacted soil, as Johannes and Sylvester discussed what portion to take and what to entrust to the safety of the earth. They decided to split our wealth in two, leave some for times of future need. We'd take smaller items, the torc my father had sent with me, a cross and plain chalice for any new church, as well as Johannes's precious gospels and coins.

The following day we slowly retraced the route to Nidum taken so light-heartedly days before. The world we knew was razed to nothing, our teachers, those who we looked to guides us, dead. All four of us were tormented by the memory of Cedric hanging from the tree and the bloodied bodies of our friends. The first evening we made a poor camp in the shelter of a fallen wall.

Gasty cried out each night in his sleep, despite Johannes doing his best to comfort him. The two were as close as father and son; sharing that terrible raid had bonded them fast.

I suffered a recurring nightmare. I was back under Knowth's dark mound. The Hag screamed and shouted, 'Macha wants vengeance.' Her long fingernails scratched at my face and mouth. I'd wake, freezing cold, sweating and petrified.

Next morning it rained, we were sodden as well as miserable, my boots leaked and rubbed at an angry blister on my heel. We longed to reach Nidum. At last, we arrived at Benignus's little church. He greeted us with astonishment. He had expected it to be weeks, if not months until he saw another priest. When our tale tumbled out, he was appalled. He hugged Gastyn, then Johannes, who shrugged him off angrily. Leading us inside to a small hearth he threw on two fresh but damp logs, which gave off a black pungent smoke, making us cough. I sent Kira off to hunt. I was not optimistic, in heavy rain men and animals hide to keep dry.

Beni asked, 'What about my fellow pupils? What of Wyn, Bledd and Doch?'

We shook our heads. 'Taken, they will be sold as slaves.'

Beni looked downcast; his hopes to return to the school were ruined.

'At least let me come with you. There is nothing for me here in Nidum. I hate it.'

Kira bounded in, carrying a squirrel in her jaws. It would not feed us, so I gave it to her. We would make do with Beni's barley-meal porridge. If the rain stopped Kira might have better luck in the morning. After prayers for our teachers and friends we ate. Beni had brewed beer which warmed and cheered us a little.

Eyes shining Beni spoke again, 'I've been thinking. I'd like to go to Ireland to look for my friends. You have sent letters, but to a bishop or king, searching out younger sons from this land will be of little importance. It can be my mission to find those lost and return them to the church.'

Sylvester looked doubtful. 'It will be dangerous Beni. You are young and know little of the world.'

'You did it, Sylvester, you were sent to Palladius from Gaul. I detest my life in this damp church, preaching to pagans, who have no interest in my message. I'm Irish and son of a chieftain, my father's name, Sesenen will protect me. It's safer for me than anyone else. Please allow me to go.'

'Very well. I will give you coin for your passage, with a letter to Bishop Palladius; he should help. Go to Moridunum, trading boats bound for Ireland berth there.'

I added, 'Take my raven headed arm-ring. Give it to my brother, Conall, the High King. It will prove to him we are in real need of assistance. He has sworn to help me if I send it to him. It is a geis, one he cannot break.'

Beni nodded, but Gasty looked confused.

'What's a geis?'

'In Ireland, we swear solemn vows that cannot be broken. If they are violated, our gods ensure death and dishonour will follow.'

Johannes sniffed. 'Heathen nonsense, take these two illuminated pages of psalms as a gift for Palladius; that will help better than any foolish oath.' He added, 'The pages are duplicates, there is no harm in them going.'

We laughed for the first time in days. Johannes would never let his gospels out of his sight. It was agreed; Beni would depart for Ireland, while we travelled north to my grandparents' kingdom. I yearned to go with him, home to see my brothers and mother again but had to put the thought aside. I lay on the earth floor and tried to sleep. Kira's cold nose nuzzled my neck, the familiar, comforting smell of damp hound filled the hut as I drifted into fitful rest.

A cold wind blew heavy rain in sheets across the valley. Sylvester looked dubiously at the road and scratched his chin. 'There is no point in starting our journey in such a storm, it is difficult enough without us being soaked to the skin.'

Beni said, 'I must leave for Ireland, whatever the weather. I can't waste time tracing the pupils or the trail will go cold. Besides I itch to quit this dank place. I'd rather risk the storm than stay.'

Sylvester, Johannes, Gastyn and I spent a final day and night in Beni's miserable, leaking church. Once the wind dropped, we set off into a steady, drenching rain. The road over the mountain passes from Nidum to Cicucium was reputedly patrolled by bandits and had fallen into disrepair. To our relief we met a party of traders; they were travelling north too, selling and exchanging goods for woollen cloth, leather, sheep and ponies. Two wore swords and we'd be safer in their company.

The ponies steamed gently in the dank air, Johannes sat complaining and irritable on his mount. Sylvester leant on a stout, iron-tipped staff, its shaft helping him up the steep paths, carrying his heavy backpack. The road was overgrown with brambles, saplings filled side ditches and puddles formed for lack of drainage. Through drizzle and mist, we glimpsed a marshy valley dissected by streams, waterlogged and boggy. Once wolves howled in the distance.

A trader said, 'Wolves are no problem in the day but by nightfall we need to reach Bannavem or build a fire.' Gasty began to tremble again, afraid. 'No, young fella, you don't need to worry. They won't worry us now it is summer, but in the winter and spring when they need food for their young, they can be dangerous.'

He added, 'That hound will keep wolves away.' He looked covetously at Kira.

I warned him. 'Kira will obey no man but me. If anyone even tried to steal her, they would as likely as not die in the attempt.'

He looked dubious, so I proved my point. At two short, high whistles Kira got up and ran toward him, baring her teeth. She crouched ready to pounce.

'Would you like my demonstration to continue? I can get her to knock you down and still not attack, but grip your collar, or I can give an order to kill.'

'No, no she is a marvellous hound, but obviously needs skilled handling,' he stammered.

We walked morosely on. I didn't want to reach the home Wyn had talked of so often. We dreaded telling his parents the tale of his abduction.

After a long, steady climb through dark forests, hearing distant roars of waterfalls filled by the endless rain, we approached Bannavem. We passed mine workings, small pits dug deep in the ground where poor souls dressed in rags, laboured in the wet, cold. They hacked at rocks and handed up green-grey ore in wicker baskets. Some were shackled with heavy chains, slaves, others seemed free of encumbrance. They were all thin and covered in dust and mud.

As we passed each hollow, the men below stopped working and stared. Some spat and hissed at us, but more asked Sylvester for a blessing, which he gladly gave.

I caught the name Niall whispered aloud, followed by, 'Kira and little Maelon.'

Looking down, deeper into a pit, two emaciated men wearing iron collars, gazed up at me. Astonished, I recognised them.

I called, 'Can it be true? Is it Aed and Math of my father's fiann?'

They bowed their heads in acknowledgement.

Math replied, 'Yes Little Lord. We were captured five summers ago…, the boat had sailed back to Ireland when we returned to the shore. We have been suffering in these mountains through the bitter Welsh winters since then. There is little enough food and the bastard overseer whips everyone at the least provocation.'

He flicked his eyes in fear to a burly man approaching us from the road. I threw my pack of food to them before he arrived and they hid it beneath their basket. Math had been a Goliath of a man. I grieved to see him so withered. Aed gave a rattling cough and I felt outrage rise.

Sylvester seeing my body taut, about to explode said firmly, 'Let me speak, Maelon. Do not make things worse for these poor souls.'

The overseer came up, warmly dressed in woollen breeches, tunic and a thick dark blue cloak, which blew around him in the cold wind.

In a belligerent tone he asked, 'Good afternoon, strangers. What business you have with my metal mines and this town?'

Sylvester responded, 'None, beyond kind words and blessings for these poor men. We are on our way to visit Calpurnius of this town. Are you Christian, would you like a blessing?'

Calpernius's name startled him; he had not expected us to be more than passing travellers. With an obsequiousness which sat uncomfortably with his earlier attitude, he replied. 'Our town's magistrate, a fine man. He part-owns these mines. Yes, I am a Christian, unlike these evil Irish sods,' indicating toward the pit. 'I would be glad of a blessing, Father. Have you travelled far?'

Making the sign of the cross over the man's head, he replied, 'From Nidum. How many men work these diggings?'

'We have a dozen or so freemen who labour here in between planting and harvesting, as well as twenty slaves such as these bastards who work all year. They don't last long. Even the stronger ones like those two perish soon enough.'

'They look thin. Would it not be better to try to keep them working longer?'

The overseer scoffed. 'Food is expensive, wretches like these cost little. I work them till they die, then buy replacements.'

'I see,' said Sylvester, pursing his lips. 'Ah well, I shan't keep you, we must reach Calpurnius before nightfall. Could you direct us to his home?'

His hands worked at the pony's strap as he talked. As we set off beside the overseer, the load gave way and fell.

'Bother,' said Sylvester and waving the overseer and the traders on with thanks, he started to reload.

It was a ruse to give me longer to speak with my old companions. I threw down a cloak we had been using as a blanket at night.

'I will do my best to think of some way of returning you home. It would grieve my dead father to see you reduced to this. You were the bravest of the brave.'

Math looked up. 'Niall has died?'

'Yes, my brother Conall is High King now and he will remember you. We must go. I can see what kind of man that overseer is and dare not linger. Hope is good, so you have that at least and you will eat tonight.'

Math asked urgently, 'What of your mother? How is she? She was not made to go with him… to the Otherworld.'

I gasped, that thought had not occurred to me. Could Mother have been sent to the pyre?

'No, my brothers would have told me. They offered to protect her and said they would look after her as their own.'

They might, I thought, but Rignach, could she be trusted?

Sylvester called, 'Come on, Maelon, we need to reach Bannavem. The gates may close.' I hurried on to his side as he continued, 'I hate slavery, that people are seen as no more than animals used by others.'

I was used to slaves, that men and women were bought and sold like cattle or grain. I had never thought of them as people, the same as me. With Wyn in Ireland as a slave and Math and Aed here, I was forced to reconsider. I could easily have been captured with the other pupils and be working in chains like them.

Ten minutes' walk from the miserable mine workings, we reached the vicus. Set with views over the mountains, the small town was neat and prosperous. We were directed to a stone villa which stood beside a wooden basilica. It was a comfortable, but by Roman standards, a modest home. We walked up to the gate and were met by a middle-aged man. We knew at once it was Maewyn's father; he had Wyn's strong nose, green eyes and smile.

Sylvester asked, 'May we come in? We bear sad news.'

Calpernius stood still, and looked us up and down in distress; he'd guessed at once.

'You are from Maewyn's school, but you are here without him.'

Sylvester nodded solemnly. Breathing fast, Calpernius ushered us in.

He turned immediately. 'Is my son dead? Was it a fever?'

'Not dead, but he's been taken captive by Irish raiders. He is gone from our shores.'

Calpurnius groaned. 'Alive, well that is something. Come in, come in. I will call my wife and daughters. You must stay with us tonight.'

It was not a question, but we were footsore and relieved to agree.

He hurried to find his family as we led our ponies away to be fed and watered. Wyn's mother came up, tears streaming down her face, her two daughters supporting to her. I couldn't help notice how pretty the girls were. Shining fair braids, pink cheeks, tall and slim. They reminded me of their brother in their manners as well as appearance. Yet again we recounted the sorry tale of the raid on the school and its destruction.

Glaring at her husband his mother said, 'I knew it was too close to the coast, I told you. He'd have been safer at home.'

Sylvester explained who I was and that we had written to my brothers and sent a young priest to Ireland, to trace the pupils.

He said, 'Ransom is a possibility if they can be found.' Then surprised me by adding, 'You have two excellent bargaining chips that we knew nothing of until this afternoon.'

Calpernius and I looked questioningly at him.

'Who owns the slaves in the mines?'

'I own some of them, not all. Why?'

I realised what Sylvester was suggesting and rushed out, 'We walked past the pits as we approached your town. Two of your slaves are Irish warriors, well known to my brothers, but half starved and one looking close to death. They are good men and have families who would ransom them if they knew where they were. They could be exchanged for Wyn or the other pupils. As long as they are not left to die in those wet pits. If you let them work on your farm and feed them properly, they would be a better currency than gold.'

Calpernius sighed, 'We have little enough gold for ransom, so I thank you for the suggestion. I know the two you speak of. They do not belong to me but if I offer fresh slaves, my partner will be pleased to exchange them. No man lasts long in the mines, as you say they will not work for much longer.'

Sylvester repeated what he said to the overseer, it was poor business sense wasting silver on new slaves. It would be better spent on food and warmer lodging for those they already owned.

Calpernius looked dubious. 'We only buy those deemed un-manageable and consequently cheap. I am not sure you are right.'

Sylvester looked stern. 'But we are Christians, even a heathen slave should be pitied and be treated gently; that is Christ's teaching. What if Wyn is treated the same in Ireland?'

Wyn's mother looked stricken and gripped her husband's arm, the sisters wept again.

We stayed for three days while Calpernius negotiated with his fellow mine owner. On the final afternoon, Math and Aed were brought out to us. They were in a desperate state, so emaciated their ribs could be counted, black scars from whipping showered their arms, back and faces; scarcely clothed, their hair filthy and matted. Aed had a wound in his thigh that dribbled wet pus; both had deep callouses where neck and ankle chains still rubbed. They looked bemused and afraid, but sagged in relief on seeing me and Kira.

'Little Lord, although you are not little any longer, have you saved us? Are we free?' asked Math.

I poured milk into a pottery cup and handed them a chunk of soft bread which they wolfed hungrily. Warned by Sylvester that too much food in their shrunken state might harm them, I held back offering more.

'Eat and I will explain. I cannot free you. I am a novice priest in this country. I'll write to my brothers and tell them you are here. Your new owner, Calpernius is prepared to ransom or exchange you for his son, who was abducted by Fiachrae's war band two weeks ago.

'If you stay in the mines, you may not last much longer. I have asked Calpernius to allow you to work on his farm.'

Math snarled, 'Still slaves then. However, thank you. You are right, we were doomed if we'd remained there.'

He glanced over to Aed, so weak he could barely speak, slumped against the wall, panting with the effort of being brought to the villa.

Aed croaked weakly, 'We are kin you know, Maelon? Your grandfather was my grandmother's brother. I am glad you have done your best for us and so relieved to be out of that hell.'

'I did not know Aed, but I am proud to call you kin.'

Math smiled. 'We missed our little puppies when you left, you and Kira both. Your brothers always spoke fondly of you. You have saved me. I am oath-bound to you now, a life for a life.'

'No, I have done nothing, that vow is for the battlefield, not squalor.'

'Battle or no,' replied Math, 'we would have died this winter, if not before.' His eyes flickering with concern to Aed once again.

'We remain your oath men Little Lord. Did I see your Uncle Brion's sword at your waist on the road?'

Math continued, 'It is a famous sword called Fire Fury and will protect you. Look after it, keep it free from rust and sharp. We will work here for this little man, Calpurnius, but I give no commitment about escaping. I'm going to kill that swine of an overseer. He is stealing from his masters, both ore and food, not only the lives of slaves. He grows fat and wealthy while we starve, the evil turd.'

'Have you any evidence to prove that? If you can, I will tell Calpernius.'

Math shook his head. 'No, but I will find some. Will you return here Little Lord?'

'I don't know, my school was destroyed by Fiachrae's raiders. I am travelling to my grandparents, we are told it is a days' walk away. I have no home. I am no better off than you, other than I am free.'

'Don't speak lightly of freedom. Until you lose it you cannot imagine how important it is,' replied Math. He indicated the milk. 'Can we try a little more and some of that pork? I have dreamt of meat this last two years with such longing, we've been given none. The smell, the taste, its memory has driven me wild.'

'What no meat, but without it men's muscles waste away?'

'None, bar the rats and frogs we caught,' he replied.

'I wonder if Calpernius knows? He is a fair man and Christian. I would be surprised if he wasn't paying for decent provisions. I will tell him about the slave master's thefts before I leave.'

I heard a cough at my elbow. It was the elder of Calpernuis's daughters, Melissa, holding a bowl of steaming water and a pot of ointment. She indicated to Aed's wound and offered to treat it.

She said, 'I heard what you were saying. It is true the slaves are poorly treated. I cannot think my father doesn't pay for his slaves to be fed. However...' Brushing a tear from her eye, she continued, 'Who knows, maybe my brother needs looking after in your country. It is right I should tend to you as I would my brother.'

She bathed Aed's leg, then stirred a yellow salve into fresh warm water. I recognised the scent of sage and elder. Melissa tutted, red and inflamed, the gash oozed a noxious trickle of fluid that smelt horrible. Aed flinched as she began to cleanse deeper, exploring the edges with a screwed-up edge of the cloth.

She called over her shoulder, 'Metella bring me honey from the kitchen and a clean knife, marigold salve is not sufficient; his injury festers.'

Her younger sister was hiding behind a pillar and hurried off.

Melissa ordered, 'Chew on this willow bark. It will ease your pain and help the inflammation.'

Aed croaked, 'Thank you little mistress. If my mother were here, she would have used the same remedies.'

The girl blushed, pleased at the compliment. When her sister returned, Mellissa warned Aed to bite hard on the bark as scraping and honey application would hurt. Their mother came through the atrium and called sharply; but when she saw Aed's thigh, she bent to examine it. Her mother quizzed Melissa on her treatment, nodding as she described her plan.

'Good, what alternatives might you have used?' she asked as if setting her daughter a test.

'Moss from the moor or spiders' webs, but as the wound stinks, honey first, moss later.'

'I agree, but I will treat him. You need not see these two again.'

As the women left Sylvester commented, 'Telling her daughters not to visit you was a tactical error.'

'Tell a girl what not to do and she always does it,' I replied.

Math rumbled a laugh. 'I agree, but this is odd knowledge for a priest, Maelon?' Blushing I muttered, 'novice priest.'

Everyone laughed all the more at my embarrassment.

Aed added, 'She was lovely, so kind and sweet. I'd never thought to feel a gentle hand on my body again.'

'If you are my oath-men, then promise not to harm my friend's family. Wait, so if my fellow novices are found an honourable exchange can be arranged. That may take time.'

Math looked annoyed, but Aed agreed. 'I will need months to recover, even Champion Math is a shadow of the man he was. It is better for us to delay and regain our strength, whether you asked us to or not. I promise no harm will come to your friend's sisters or their mother. As long as Calpernius doesn't take arms against us, he will be safe. I hope that we will leave this cursed place soon. Life as a slave without honour is beyond bearing.'

I spoke to Wyn's father that night, telling him about the overseer.

'Math and Aed told me they have been fed no meat since being brought to the mines. Slaves are expensive and if they are not fed, they cannot work.'

He looked astonished. 'But we pay the overseer well. He demands more money for provisions each year.'

'The man told us that the slaves were worthless and it is cheaper to buy new than feed them.'

Calpernius looked annoyed. 'Now you say that, I've noticed we bought more slaves since we employed him. Male slaves, even difficult ones are costly, those two were bought for twenty ounces of silver each.'

'That sounds cheap. They said the slave-master is stealing ore and selling it on his own account.'

'If that is so, as magistrate I will make sure he is properly punished. I will look into this at once.'

'Good, they will tell the truth; they were sons of lords in Ireland. Accept a ransom or exchange for them sooner rather than later. Both are trained warriors. When they are fit your slave master won't stand a chance, chained or not. I would demand thirty ounces, or better yet two of the Cor Tewdws pupils, for each one of them. I hope Maewyn will be rescued.'

'I will pray every day that my son will be found. Even if he is not, I will agree an exchange. That they were friends of Wyn and are enslaved Christians is enough.'

CHAPTER
7

Sylvester, Gastyn, Johannes and I set out for my grandparents' fortress once more. Calpernius told us we would know our way by passing two huge ancient carved stones set on the road. The road climbed steadily and finally flattened to give views over a vast windswept moor. Above the tree line, the land was good for little but sheep and mountain ponies. Anticipating eight hours walk to Cicucium and safety we pushed on, shivering in the sharp wind blowing through low yellow gorse and cotton grass. No human life was visible on that moor, but in the shelter of the valleys, small huddles of huts could be seen.

As we walked along Sylvester asked whether I knew why Math had asked me about my sword. I shook my head.

'I thought not. Math is more than your father's champion. He was your uncle Brion's natural son. He is your cousin. Fire Fury was Brion's sword, his symbol is engraved on its hilt. Years ago, Brion, was your father's collector of tribute. Fiachrae was jealous of his land and position, so waged war on his brother. Fiachrae was captured in battle and Brion handed him to Niall as a hostage. Your cousin Nathi, Fiachrae's son continued the war.

Nathi captured Brion by subterfuge, pretending he wanted to sue for peace and murdered him along with his legitimate sons when they met to discuss terms.

'Eventually, your father agreed to let Fiachrae take Brion's lands in Connacht as well as his own in Ulster, and become his levier of tribute; although fratricide is a terrible crime. He needed someone he trusted to take the role. Math had been fostered by your father from a little one and showed promise to become a fearsome warrior. Your father told Nathi and Fiachrae he would not tolerate him being harmed.'

Sylvester hesitated. 'Some say your father lived to regret his moment of kindness. Well, anyway Math survived, the last of Brion's sons, but not acknowledged; Math's mother was a slave, a woman from Gaul.

'Math has reason to hate Fiachrae with a passion and Nathi too. He is right to loathe them; they are utterly ruthless. When I think of poor Abod Cedric I weep. If they had captured you on that raid your fate would have been sealed, maybe Conall's too. Christ preaches forgiveness, but I cannot forgive Fiachrae. May he and his whelp rot in hell.'

We rounded a bend in the road and before us ranged the high mountains, sweeping up above us. Majestic, towering, cloud shadows passing over flat-bladed summits that cut the skies. Streams of water, tumbled down over rocks. Gastyn and I gaped, we had seen nothing like this in Armorica or Ireland.

Kira gave a deep growl, from nowhere three unsavoury men appeared, one held a short sword, the others sickles.

'We charge a toll for all who pass,' one challenged.

I drew Brion's fine weapon as Sylvester took up his staff. Ears back and teeth bared, Kira snarled.

'This is the Roman way and free to all,' responded Sylvester. 'If you are hungry, in charity we will spare you some bread, but nothing more.'

The three looked uncertain. 'Priests, we expect gold not bread. Give it to us or we will kill you,' blustered one.

I replied, 'I warn you I am trained to wield this sword. My hound would kill you before you could harm me.'

Half-starved and ragged, they gave way, standing aside sullenly. As we passed, I turned, walking backwards, watching. A hundred feet later as I turned, I heard Kira snarl. She raced back past me.

The three had pitched themselves at us. Kira already gripped the arm of one as I spun around and stood firm. I slashed at the man before he could hurt her. I repeated the mantra Conall had taught when he trained me years before. "Watch eyes as much as arms, parry then swing, keep your shield up, balance is all."

I swung my sword at the man's rusted, insubstantial weapon and knocked it from his grip. As I put it to his neck I nicked his skin to prove I was serious. Kira had the other man held by his throat and waited to see if I would order her to kill. The third bandit dropped his sickle in terror, faced with Sylvester's iron-tipped staff. They were pathetic specimens, crying for mercy on the road.

We had no idea what to do with them. In the end, we took their blades and left them there, wrists tied. I told them if ever we saw them again Kira would be allowed her way; they would be ripped apart and their bodies chewed.

Sylvester glared at them. 'I think you are hungry. Here is that bread I offered you in charity. This is no life, return to your homes.'

We walked on, my heart was pounding but I had enjoyed the encounter. I was elated, delighted with myself. Gastyn complimented me on my bravery and even Johannes looked impressed.

Sylvester deflated me. 'They were desperate otherwise they wouldn't have attacked. There were three of them against we four, and we had a hound. I wish they had accepted my offer of food.'

Johannes jeered, but Sylvester looked at him questioningly. 'Have you ever been hungry Johannes? Do you know what it is to feel such a pain in your stomach that you dream of bread and cheese? If not, don't cast a stone at those poor men, remember the Lord's words.' Gasty outraged said, 'But they would have killed and robbed us if they could.'

'Yes, but they acted not out of evil, rather from need. What they did was wrong but they were starving.'

I disagreed but kept quiet and ran through my moves again; promising to train more often. We carried on, the countryside becoming ever more lovely, barren mountaintops above us, below land as rich as any in Ireland, with cattle, sheep and fields of crops growing tall and strong. Birds sang out mellifluous and sweet, as clouds chased over the sun. I understood why Cedric had said there was no lovelier land in all of Britannia.

It was nearly dark as we passed by the old fort at Cicucium, fording the river they called Wysg. It was another hour before we approached Garth Madron. Scents of wood smoke and roasting meat met us before the fort came into view. We walked into the settlement surprised that the guard looking down over the closed timber gates let us through without question. I heard muttering, the name Anlach being repeated again and again as we were directed to the great hall. As we entered its doorway the room fell silent.

An elderly man, thin and lined sat on an ornately carved chair at the centre of a polished oak table; he had to be Anlach, my grandfather. Beside him a grey-haired woman, her heart shaped face very much like my mother's, undoubtedly Marchell. Beside them sat a red-haired middle-aged man, heavy-jowled and already running to fat; Brychan my uncle. Along the table ranged a dozen or so men and women, wooden trenchers of food before them.

Brychan stood and called out in a deep voice, 'I see four priests, you are welcome. One stands among you who looks familiar.'

The woman stood, smiling broadly, gazing at me with fondness.

Sylvester responded, 'Thank you, yes, we seek sanctuary. Our monastic school near the coast was burnt and destroyed by raiders two weeks ago. We hope to start afresh in a safer land. I bring with me, Maelon ap Niall, son of Inne ap Anlach. He was studying as a novice priest in that school.'

A gasp shivered through the hall as Sylvester continued, 'I bring sad tidings. Cedric ap Tewdric, cousin to Lady Marchell, was slaughtered in that same raid along with several brother monks and pupils.'

My grandmother was already making her way to me. Tearfully she enveloped me in her arms.

'Thank goodness, the news of Cedric's death reached us last week. I feared you dead or abducted.'

My grandfather interrupted, 'What hound is that boy? Tell me her lineage.'

Taken aback to have no word of welcome only questions about my dog, I responded. 'She is Kira, her sires, Cu Braden of Cu Dillan.

'Yes, yes, I gave your mother three hounds. Are any of those in her bloodline?'

I shook my head.

He gave a wide, yellow-toothed smile.

'Excellent, you are twice welcome, Maelon ap Niall and Kira. Come join us, eat. Let go of him Marchell. All of you, move up, make space for my grandson. Maelon, sit down opposite me.'

As he appraised me, I gazed back at him, realising I was looking into a mirror, which reflected an older self. We shared the same long flat-topped nose, heavy brows and chin, as well as our dark complexion and deep brown eyes. Both of us were thin, he from age and I from youth. I did not yet think of him as Grandfather, to me he was what my father always called him, Anlach. He looked as I would in years to come. It was a strange moment; I was young and had never thought to be old until that moment.

'Your mother is widowed now. Is she still fair, or gone to fat?'

My grandmother tutted at him.

'Speak boy... I was sorry to hear of your father's death, naturally.'

'When I left Ireland five years ago Mother was beautiful, still slim,' I responded, confused by his questions again.

'She has sent to me asking to come home. The widow of a dead king is in a difficult position, unless land is settled on her. Your brothers may not think it worth giving her land, especially with no sons left to her, only a priest far away.'

He glanced again to my grandmother as if seeking approval, but she was frowning at his bluntness. I was stung by his words, "only a priest".

'Your brothers and their wives will not regret her leaving.'

I had not thought about my mother's position in Ireland.

I replied slowly, 'My brothers wrote that they promised to care for her and my sister as their own. They will try, but my father's youngest wife has disappeared, along with her twin boys. Rignach, my half-brother's mother is not known for her tenderness. You are right, if my mother and sister could come home it would be a kindness.'

Anlach scoffed, 'You know little of kingship. They will marry their half-sister off to forge a useful alliance no doubt. I can offer to take the girl, but they won't agree. Your mother is a different matter. They will want her gone, especially with you in Wales. I will take her. If she is comely, I will find her another husband. I have heard Cuneglas of Gwynedd's wife has died come to think of it. If Inne is worn out, she can care for her mother when I am gone; Brychan's wife will be pleased not to have that burden. My daughter-in-law arrives with the children tomorrow, your tribe of cousins.'

Those around the table looked uncomfortable at his forthright words, but Brychan had nodded agreement several times.

'You have had a long journey. I will speak to you tomorrow. Take your companions to the guest hut.' I was dismissed. Sylvester gestured for us to retire; no bad thing, we were exhausted.

I rose early, soon after dawn, interested to explore Garth Madron, Kira running at my heel as always. The settlement was set on a flattened rise, a spring at its centre. Dozens of round huts and workshops, along with my grandfather's hall were enclosed within its high wooden walls. To one side it connected with an outer, larger palisade full of animals bellowing and crowing in the thin morning light. There were workshops, smiths, bakers and brewers already at work below us, their hammering and shouts filling the air. The gate to the fortress already stood open. I gazed down over two deep ditches then beyond onto rich farmland, then up to densely wooded hills. It felt familiar, very like my home in Ireland.

At a sharp whistle, Kira loped over to my grandfather, nuzzling his hand as if she had known him all her life.

I joined them. 'That's odd, she's trained not to befriend strangers.'

'She is cleverer than you know,' he replied. 'Marchell says you look very like me when I was younger, the dog can tell we are kin. That is the problem,' he continued. 'Our problem, in fact; I have to send you away Maelon ap Niall. I have a son and he has a son; they expect to rule when I die. Your arrival, especially as you look so much like me disturbs the order of my house.'

He gestured widely. 'Spread before us is your grandmother's land, inherited from her father. The people love her and respect her. Some, perhaps many, might say her daughter has as much right to inherit as Brychan. They think women are less likely to send men to war, and the land grows richer because of it. In truth, they may be right. Your arrival has upset the balance. Neither you nor your mother can remain in Garth Madron.

'We have land further west, on the shore of Lake Syfaddon. Your grandmother thinks it would suit your purpose of establishing a school well. It is a lovely spot, a good place to build a church and settlement. You can keep watch on the two roads into my land from the river in return. The people complain that their cattle are stolen too often. Prince Woolos, my neighbour, refuses to punish his people when they raid.

Brychan will allow you that land as long as you remain a priest. If you do not, then you must leave altogether and return to Ireland, or else marry an heiress far away as I did.'

I sighed, replying with a bitter edge, 'My father warned me of this. I am a landless prince, ever needing to move. My half-brothers have declared me King over the Sea and say that they keep land for me, but I doubt they would want me to claim it when I reach manhood. Here in Wales I am unwanted, grandson of another king, but it is easier for all if I remain a priest. There is no home for me anywhere.'

'Do not feel sorry for yourself and wallow in such thoughts. You are strong and of good birth, you can make yourself a place if you choose. Or you can be weak, whine and complain of the throw that the dice of life has given you. Be glad you weren't born a slave; not sad you were born a prince. This world is hard, accept that and work with it,' Anlach replied brusquely.

I gestured acceptance and asked when we should leave.

'As long as you are going, there is no rush, but summer is nearly over, it would be sensible to start soon. At the very least you need a shelter for yourselves and livestock, be ready for winter.

'May I train in weaponry with your men until I leave?'

He looked askance at me. 'Why should a priest wish to train as a warrior?'

'We were nearly robbed on the road, threatened by miserable bandits, pathetic criminals. Sylvester and I fought them off and left them a meal. Also… well, I cannot forget the Irish raid on Cor Tewdus. I am determined to protect myself and fellows if I need to ever again. I have a sword, but I fear to become rusty if I don't practise. I was twelve when I was last taught to fight; better trained men might have killed us.'

His eyes narrowed. 'You should have executed those bandits, not given them food. They are vermin. I need that road open for trade. You can train with my grandsons, although my son will complain. You look sturdy enough to be useful. Learn to use the battle axe, that was my choice of weapon when I was young; if you become skilled I will give you my father's blade.

'We will breed your fine dog; hounds will be additional protection for your church. Send word when Kira comes into season. Come, your grandmother is expecting you.'

He took me to the largest roundhouse where bread, warm milk and cheese waited, along with my grandmother. Once we had finished, she ordered Anlach out.

'Go view your horses and hounds, fly your hawks. I wish to speak with my grandson.'

As he left, he said, 'Tell your priest to write to ask that my daughter be returned to me. Inform them I do not ask for the return of her bride price. I would like to see Inne's face again before I die.'

'I will write to my brothers, Grandfather, thank you.'

My grandmother held her arms open then held me long and close. Again, it felt as if I were in Mother's arms. She asked me about my mother, Cedric and my life in Cor Tewdws.

Then said, 'Don't mind your grandfather and his manners, he fears being thought of as sentimental above all things. Irishmen prize appearing strong, but when you know him you will find him considerate. He loves his horses, his family and his dogs, the rest he leaves to me. Anlach is very different to our son. Brychan is a godly man, efficient, full of energy, but for all that he views women as objects to trade for power. It is not his fault, as a youth he was sent as a hostage to a king in Powys and learnt their ways.'

She added as if to herself, 'It causes tension between us. We both look to rule.'

The following day my cousins arrived. My jaw dropped to see so many children. They walked in a column and were led by a frail, elderly priest who rode such a small pony that his feet brushed the grass. Behind him trooped perhaps a dozen children, aged from around seventeen to six. Sylvester, Gasty and Johannes joined me to watch.

Johannes, delighting in gossip and scandal told us, 'Yes and five more babes in the hall too; he is fertile is Brychan. On his third wife already, he has worn two out. Last night I heard all the tales of him and his wives, not so godly when it comes to women.'

'What, tell us,' we demanded, amused.

'It seems Brychan started his liking for women young. When he was a hostage, he paid court to the prettiest of the king's daughters, Ban. It is said she seduced him; she was older than him, anyway, the girl became pregnant. Outraged her father threatened to kill Brychan, but after a while he allowed the young couple to return here. Cynog was born and Brychan and Ban married. Ellyw, the dark beauty you see there, came along within the year. Next was Rhain, that red-faced youngster you see leading the priest's pony. He is legitimate and accepted as Brychan's heir, even though he's not the eldest, because Cynog has promised himself to the church. Each year after that, a child; Dwynwen, Gwladys, more and more babies until Ban died. Brychan promptly married a princess of Dumnonia who perished in childbirth after another seven children. Now the new queen is podding more babes; he has an army of children.

His daughters he promises in marriage to the kings and princes over Wales, Dumnonia and Ireland, but apart from Rhain, his sons will go to the church. He wants Brycheiniog, as he has started to call his mother's land, to remain intact, not divided between his sons as is custom. Marchell is not pleased that he is trying to take over. She was the heiress of these lands, and her mother was of Pict stock, where women rule.'

My cousins viewed us with as much interest as we regarded them. First Ellyw; buxom, dark and lovely, white elegant neck, in full bloom. Her brown eyes saw us, then passed on, dismissing us, priests, of no interest. Cynog smiled at us genially, a welcome from him whoever we were, friends in Christ. Dwynwen looked perplexed as she caught my eye, her clear gaze asking questions. Tall, maybe fourteen years old, reed slim with sandy, red-blond hair and foxglove freckles, like her father's.

The old priest dismounted and dismissed the youngsters, the little ones scattering like hedge sparrows. His eyes were cloudy and opaque, he was blind. Introduced to us as Drichan by my cousin Cynog, who gently described each of us to him.

'We have two priests here, one aged, older even than you, he has a purple, healing scab and bruises on his forehead. Another rounded priest in his prime, strong and pleasant-faced. With them stands a young man of my age, around seventeen, taller than most, with long dark hair and well filled with muscle; he looks like my grandfather. Finally, we have a skinny boy of perhaps twelve, hazel eyes with a wide, cheeky grin.'

Drichan embraced each of us in turn, tracing our faces with his fingers, to understand our age and stature as if committing them to memory. Sylvester named us to him.

Drichan sighed, 'It is good to have more priests, I am old and getting weary. I taught Brychan and now his children, but they are so many. Will you establish a school or only a church?'

As the priests talked, I stopped listening to look over to Ellyw and Dwynwen. I so wished Maewyn was with me. He could charm girls and would have stepped up to them without hesitation. I felt awkward and clumsy.

My gaze met Dwynwen's, she came over and smiled. 'So, my cousin the Irish Prince has arrived. Welcome'

"Not so much a prince as a novice priest, but yes I am your cousin.'

"I had heard your father had died, Requiesce in pax."

'Pace not pax,' I corrected her Latin as a reflex. She stiffened, pale blue eyes turned to ice as she turned on her heel and returned to her sisters. I could have kicked myself. I'd wanted to charm her.

To my relief, Rhain marched over. 'Maelon well met. You wear a sword, would you like to practise later, we use wooden ones? Bows too, the girls join us for that.'

Dwynwen called over, 'I like using the sword as well, Rhain, I'm fast. I caught your guard down last time. Let's see if a priest can fight.'

Her eyes challenged mine, my correction had rankled. Ellyw and Gwladys looked at her disapprovingly.

That evening Anlach announced, 'The weather promises fair. Tomorrow I will ride out with my three oldest grandsons. We'll go along the holy ridge above the lake, between land and sky. I want to show this Irish lad my kingdom, point out where he can build his church. We'll take two guards and the boy's dog, along with two of my hounds.'

Grumbling, Brychan agreed; Ellyw and Dwynwen begged to join the party. Cynog declined, preferring to stay and study the new gospels with Johannes; the two had discovered a common interest.

It was high summer on the mountains, bees hummed loud in sweet-scented purple heather, skylarks swooped and darted above the grass. Peaty ponds, oak-gall black, the colour of Johannes' ink reflected the mountains and sky in their shallows. We reached the summit of the Wolf's Head peak by late morning. Around us was spread a vista of wonder. Lake Syfaddon named for its shape, the saddle, shone periwinkle blue far below. Flat-topped peaks ranged to the east, west and south. A bowl of land stretched north, green and lush, my grandfather's domain.

Anlach pointed to a rise at the lake's end. He said, 'This is my gift. Land rich in forests and fields, protected from cold winds by the mountains you see before you.

'The church can use everything within the curve of the lake's saddle up to the ridge top, and fish in the lake. In return I expect you to light a warning beacon if marauders approach. There are two roads into my kingdom from the south, you can see them threading along the hillside over there.'

I nodded and thanked him warmly. It was more than generous, these acres were valuable, almost princely. I wouldn't own them though; they'd remained my Uncle Brychan's land after my grandfather died. As a priest I would own nothing, have no place, I thought with resentment.

The sun shone warm on my back as I admired a serpent's tail of ridges falling to the valley below. I watched Dwynwen as we dismounted beside vast square sandstone outcrops; hungry for the food in the packs. She swept back her tousled and tangled hair, a haze of copper and gold in the sunlight. I was overcome with an urge to brush it from her face. I felt confused, where had that thought come from?

I sat near to my grandfather and played with a scabious flower, picking off its myriad of pale blue petals, one by one.

'Did you ever meet your grandfather, Emperor Maximus, sir?' I asked. 'What was he like?'

'I did but I was three. I only recall his helmet crested with red feathers; a deep laugh and a rough hand turning my chin to his and his tickling me. My mother, Gratianna, spoke about him often. You know his story?

'No, Mother always said she couldn't remember the details, that there were lots of wars and fighting. She said she had enough of that with Niall. I got the impression she didn't want to encourage me. She hated that I wanted to become a warrior, be like my father.'

Grandfather paused, his face clouded; I was unsure if he was irritated or sad. He called Kira over and methodically checked her fur for fleas. As he groomed, he talked.

'It's an old story but you should know who you are descended from. Some called Maximus a Gallaecian usurper. He was far more than that, he came from a line of military commanders, aristocrats. Put down a Scoti conspiracy successfully, saved Britannia.

Maximus was popular with his troops. His own soldiers declared him Emperor. Emperor Gratian was unpopular you see, a weakling and coward. My grandfather accepted the honour and took the title of Augustus.

'He must have been a gifted soldier. I wonder what sort of a man he was?'

Anlach pulled a chain out from under his jerkin. 'This is what he looked like.'

He held out a gold siliqua that hung from it, on the coin the profile of a man with a straight long nose looked out, an imperial wreath on his head.

'My grandfather's downfall was ambition, he decided to take over all of the Western Empire. He was attacked by his cousin Emperor Theodosius, betrayed on all fronts and defeated in a great battle at Save, then executed.

'The Roman Senate declared him a traitor, "Damnatio Memoriae". Do you know what they do when that happens?

I shook my head. My grandfather had become agitated, he was stroking Kira's fur furiously, breathing and talking faster.

'An Emperor's name, his likeness on buildings, every reference made to him in history is obliterated. Every triumph erased, his family are killed, no one dares speak his name.

He glared at me, 'Your mother was wrong not to tell you about him. Blood and honour is everything. Remember that, priest or no. You were born to lead, like me and him, stand proud.'

Kira's ears pricked up, she tensed and gnarled in the back of her throat, low and long; a warning. Her hackles were raised, hair standing erect on her spine, something was wrong. I caught the glint of sunlight on metal some hundred yards away below and to our left. Anlach swore and called his guards attention. Five well-armed men were climbing the hill towards us on horseback. Dwynwen called out and pointed, two more were coming at us from behind the ridge; we were surrounded.

Anlach growled, 'What is their intention? Have I been betrayed? If we live someone will die for this. Girls hide behind those stones deep in the bracken. Maelon, Rhain, stand ready in front of them, defend the girls. I will go forward with my guards. We may be forced to surrender, pay any ransom. A curse on them!'

Dwynwen called, 'We brought our short bows and arrows Grandfather. Ellyw and I can fight. Rhain is better with the bow than the sword.'

He signified agreement with a quick nod. 'I don't want to see my grand-daughters abducted, taken into unknown men's hands. We have the high ground, but only hounds, two boys, and three men against their seven. Rhain, Dwynwen, you insist you can shoot well. Now is the time to prove it. Aim for their horses. Wait until you are sure the arrow will reach. Don't loose them too early, let's not warn them we have bows. If we can take their horses down, the hounds will take the riders.'

The soldiers were getting closer. We could see them clearly, horses sweating and panting, working hard to balance, clambering inexorably toward us, up the steep slope.

One shouted up, 'Yield. We have you outnumbered and surrounded. We will not harm you if you do as we say.'

'Wait, wait,' hissed Anlach, not bothering to respond. 'I'll show them surrender.

'Now, now, let your arrows fly.'

The hounds quivered and let cry on their leashes. The men's horses panicked at the sound, as first one then another was struck, they reared and turned. The riders struggled to keep their mounts in control; the biggest, a fine black steed careered down the mountainside terrified, the rest leapt from their mounts to take cover. Four warriors came at us, swords drawn, shields up, trying to protect themselves from the unexpected attack. Toiling as they climbed, slowly coming closer.

Anlach freed the hounds and he and his men began their rush. Dwynwen took aim again. I heard the thrum of her flight, its point lodged deep into one man's side. He fell with a scream. That left three against three, but we had the hounds, two men were caught in their maws, the dogs savaging them. Rhain let out a call of alarm. We had forgotten the men to our right.

They had ridden up behind the girls and one had taken Ellyw. I whistled to Kira and gave desperate chase. The man mounted ready to ride away, Ellyw held fast in his grip. Kira launched herself at the horse's rear leg. Her bite did not waver, a wolfhound would stay gripping until death. The horse staggered, its rider turning in his seat, letting go of his reins with one arm, he rained blows at her. He slashed at Kira's front leg nearly severing it and kept slicing, his strokes made difficult as he balanced, he had to keep hold of Ellyw and the horse. As I reached them, I realised Kira was badly hurt. In my fury, I put all my strength into my first thrust. He had no chance to parry, feeling the blow's weight to his side, his sword dropped. I lunged at him again, opening a deep gash on his thigh. He tumbled heavily to the ground and Ellyw fell with him.

To my surprise, there was fury in her glare, not gratitude. No time to reflect, I turned to face the final assailant with only my sword for protection, no shield. I tensed ready as his arm lifted to strike. There was a dull thock and he fell forward, mouth gaping open. Rhain had loosed a deadly shot, an arrow was lodged deep in my attacker's back. We were safe.

I looked down the hillside to see if my grandfather needed help but all was quiet, his men were binding their assailants' hands. The man whose horse had bolted sat watching us, some three hundred feet away, beyond reach. He stared at us, his dark face livid, his eyes devouring Ellyw. As he turned to gallop away, Dwynwen shivered. She had recognised him.

'It's Geraint, the young lord of Ystrad Yew,' she whispered.

I fell to my knees beside my whimpering hound; blood seeped from her leg and back. I swallowed hard, desperate to stopping any tears falling in sympathy for her pain. Kira's leg was a mess of sinew, raw flesh and exposed blue-white bone. Dwynwen held my shoulder for comfort and stroked Kira, murmuring gently to calm her. I waited for my grandfather; Would he tell me to put Kira out of her pain?

Anlach came up, his eyes moistening immediately at the sight of my poor dog.

'Kira saved my grand-daughter. Let's see if we can save her in return. Dogs can manage with three legs if they must. We will treat her as we would a man. Bind the leg tight to stop it bleeding with this, Maelon.'

He ripped his fine woollen cloak into strips for bandages.

'We must get everyone safely back to the settlement by the lake. Rhain, you did well with your bow, saved Maelon and your sisters. Ride down to the lake, bring men up to carry our wounded and I suppose, these thieves.' He gestured impatiently to Geraint's injured men. 'Tell them I want six strong branches with leather straps to carry our men and Kira; those bastards we will throw on the ponies. I have no care if they live or die.'

The villagers; men and women came to help their king, eyes huge and wondering. My grandfather looked old, wearied beyond reason after the morning's events. Rhain helped Anlach onto his horse and led it down the slope. Dwynwen held Ellyw's hand on one side and mine on the other. We were in shock, Ellyw silent and brooding. Our guards and Kira were put on the stretchers. Geraint's five surviving men were thrown roughly over the ponies, the dead man dragged down behind another. We made a sorry procession down to the lakeside village.

Anlach took charge. 'Give Kira mead. It will take the edge off the pain and help her sleep. Dwynwen, find a willow branch for her to chew, there is plenty around the shore.'

He patted Kira lovingly as he heated a birch branch in the fire. 'This is going to hurt my girl. Hold her fast Maelon, she is strong and may leap away or bite.'

Kira, weak with blood loss and woozy from the mead didn't move, she understood. The last sinews that held her leg were severed by Anlach's sword, the stump held to the flaming brand; she gave a short howl of pain and collapsed.

'Quickly, while she is unconscious clean the wounds on her back. Use hot water and salve. I must see to my men's comfort.'

There was a commotion when Brychan arrived; furious his children had so nearly been captured or killed. He told off his father at considerable length.

'Enough,' rumbled Anlach. 'The question you should be asking is what traitor told them of our journey. This was no accidental meeting.'

An expression of fear passed over Dwynwen's face, her eyes glancing to a scowling Ellyw.

My grandfather continued, 'Your mother will be worrying, let's return to Garth Madron. Maelon, you stay to tend your hound, I will pray for her. Brychan, set men to guard Geraint's men and then gather your children.'

I nursed Kira all that night, sleeping beside her as I had as a child in Ireland. Next morning, she woke me, licking my face, with a warm rough tongue. I rushed to give her water. The village wise woman came with ointment and gave her willow bark seeped mead to lap. Kira soon slept again so I went out to wash, eat and see to the injured captives.

One sat up. 'Help us, please. Water for the love of Christ. The villagers have brought us nothing.'

In Christian charity, I could not refuse, so I took them barley broth, warm water and bindings for their wounds. Those attacked by the hounds would suffer from the horrible bites on their arms and legs for a long time. The man who'd taken Ellyw and injured Kira was dying.

'Is he Christian?' I asked.

They nodded.

'Would he like a blessing? I'm a novice priest. I can pray with him.

The man gripped my hand in supplication. I said the words and dipping my finger in the water, made the sign of the cross on his forehead.

He sighed and slipped from this life. I felt a pang of remorse. I had been the one who had wielded the sword that had slain him. He deserved it, but I had killed a man for the first time; a sin according to the new religion.

The other man spoke again. 'Two of my comrades are dead. How could it have gone so wrong? You were supposed to surrender, give up the girl.'

'What do you mean? I am a stranger here. I don't understand?'

He shrugged downheartedly. 'We expected a couple of guards and an old man, along with a few children. How could Geraint know you would fight back and even if you did, prevail? We were told not to harm anyone. Geraint planned to capture his betrothed and flee. He was a fool; her grandfather would always have come after her. It was lunacy.'

He put his head in his hands and moaned, 'What will happen to us. Will we be sold as slaves?'

I asked dry lipped, 'Which girl was his betrothed, the dark one?'

'Yes, fair Ellyw. She sent her maid with a message for Geraint.'

'But if they are to be married, why would they do such a thing?'

'The agreement was broken by Brychan this spring. He found a richer suitor, a king not a petty lord. The girl is to be his second wife. She loves Geraint and he adores her; does everything she asks. Please help us. Priest have pity on us.' He clawed at my habit.

'I'll do my best. I will try to persuade my grandfather to offer you for ransom. I am no friend of slavery. Don't tell him what you told me, whatever you do. They'll be less likely to agree if they know who planned it and why.'

I wondered at the consequences if my uncle or grandfather discovered Ellyw had betrayed them, that she was the traitor.

Kira improved steadily, in four days she tried to walk, she wobbled but seemed to manage well enough on three legs. Sylvester borrowed a pony and came to visit, beaming and excited.

After commiserating and making a fuss of Kira, he burst out, 'Great news, a letter has come from Beni. He went to your brother and was sent on to your uncle Fiachrae's dún at Emain Macha. Three of our pupils were working there as house slaves. They are safe.'

'Your letter about Math and Aed must have arrived too. Your brother ordered Fiachrae to agree an exchange; the three pupils for Math and Aed. Fiachrae had no choice. I shall leave for Ireland at once and bring the boys home while the weather holds.

'That is wonderful news, Sylvester. Who is found?'

'Bledd, Doch and Dingad,' he grinned. 'Only Maewyn and Llyr left to find. Such good news, I can't decide if it is better to tell their families now or later.

'Have you seen the land your grandparents have given us Maelon? It is a wonderful spot. We can fish as well as farm sheep and cattle. I'll keep bees again. Would you begin building while

I am gone? We need shelter for the winter and a small church for worship.'

'Leave me a dozen coins from our hoard. I will buy grain to exchange with the villagers for labour, wood and thatch. I liked the people in the lake village. They are loyal to my grandfather and were very kind when Kira was injured.'

'I showed Anlach the finely worked gold torc your father sent when you came to Wales. It is worth many swords, slaves and loans of labourers. He lusted to own it and said it belonged to an ancient Irish king, one of his forefathers. He told me it would be perfect for his funeral and if it were placed with his grave goods, he'd be recognised as a king in the Otherworld. I wanted to reply that Christ welcomed all into Heaven, but thought it wiser to keep silent. Anlach is Christian, but like many prefers to appease the old gods. I'll ask him to provide an escort and weapons for Math and Aed, as well as workers and materials for the school in exchange for that torc. If your mother still wishes to return to Wales, I will bring her back along with our pupils.'

'I am happy my friends will be freed, although I do wish Wyn and Llyr were with them. Calpurnius said he would let Math and Aed go in exchange for other men's sons. He seemed generous, but you may need to offer to pay for replacements. It feels so strange to think only weeks ago we were returning from Moridunum to Cor Tewdws, with no care other than we couldn't buy a chalice.'

Kira was soon well enough for me to return to my grandfather's hall in Garth Madron. All the way there I found myself thinking of Dwynwen and her smile. Her proud walk, the lift of her chin. I was eager to see her again, but what did she think about me? I need not have worried, as I arrived, she ran up.

'Kira, you are recovered, thank goodness,' she laughed and touched Kira's head as I bent to catch her collar.

Our fingers brushed and I felt a tingle course up my arm. I caught Dwynwen's blush. It was at that moment I fell irrevocably in love with my cousin.

'Has your grandfather found out who betrayed us on our trip to the lake?'

She shook her head. I watched her soft hair glisten, wanting to caress it the way she stroked Kira.

'I need to speak to you and Ellyw about it. I think you already know what I have discovered,' I replied.

She looked afraid. 'Tonight,' she murmured, 'please, don't tell my father until you have spoken to us.'

My grandfather and uncle were welcoming when I walked to the hall.

'My other brave grandson,' boomed Anlach, 'and Kira limping beside you. I am relieved she survived her wounds. Sylvester has left to bring your mother home Maelon. He will arrange the exchanges of those Irish slaves for your friends while he is in Ireland.

'Thank you for your actions when Geraint and his men attacked us. I don't understand why they came there. I wonder now whether they'd planned to raid the settlement on the lake for cattle and took the high road to surprise them.

I noticed that my grandmother was watching Ellyw, gauging her reaction.

I replied, 'I did what I could. Your guards deserve the thanks, as well as Rhain and Dwynwen. It was their arrows that saved us.'

Rhain went pink with pleasure as Brychan looked proudly at his son.

'I have promised Sylvester to start work on our new clas while he is away. Could you spare some skilled men to help? Johannes is old, Gastyn is only twelve, and I know nothing about construction. The harvest is a short weeks away; unless we start at once, men will be too busy gathering their crops.'

Brychan spoke for his father, 'You are right, you must build before winter. We can start tomorrow. I will come with you.'

He launched into a list of suggestions, more enthusiastic than I had seen him before. His eyes shone with enthusiasm, telling me how to dig ditches and sink posts. My grandmother smiled fondly and winked at me.

He caught her glance and laughed. 'Yes, Mother, this is what I like best, making our kingdom safe and building churches to celebrate Christ. I hope my children will do the same; that there will be many churches across our land.'

I left for the guest hut calling Kira to heel. As I went Dwynwen beckoned from the shadows. Ellyw waited for us in a quiet corner, close to the stockade.

'What were you suggesting to my sister earlier?' Ellyw asked.

I stared her down. 'Don't pretend. Geraint's injured men told me everything.'

She put her hand to her mouth and started to shake, mumbling, 'It wasn't supposed to happen that way. It all went wrong.'

Dwynwen touched her hand comfortingly and looked at me fiercely.

'Don't judge her harshly, she was desperate. She is to be married in two months to a man of thirty, old, widowed with two daughters. She and Geraint were sweethearts from childhood. Then Father got a better offer from north Wales, from King Einion. My sister will never see home again.'

I glared at them both.

'Two men died. Rhian and I could have too. Kira lost her leg. They would have had to kill your grandfather. Was Geraint worth that?'

Ellyw narrowed her eyes defiantly. 'Yes,' she spat back, 'if it meant I could marry Geraint, yes.'

'You can't believe that?' asked Dwynwen.

'I do. Don't you see, are you so blind? How would you like to marry a man you don't love and be taken to his bed? Grandfather and Father–I hate them. They control us, what we think, what we do. I'm older than Rhain, but will this land be mine, no. Even though it was grandmother's; it will go to Rhain.

'You, you are free Maelon, you are a man. You can choose to marry or not. Women have no choices. I made my bid for freedom and I would do it again.'

I shook my head, looking at Dwynwen, whose pale eyes had clouded at her sister's self-absorption.

'What are you going to do? Geraint's man says unless he is allowed to go free, he will tell your family.'

We heard a rustle behind us. It was our grandmother, her expression furious; she had been standing out of sight, listening.

'You think your father and I haven't guessed,' she hissed at Ellyw. 'Only your grandfather is fooled and that's because he thinks the best of everyone. You two go, I will take charge.' Grabbing Ellyw by the wrist she pulled her away.

'I'm sorry,' I whispered to Dwynwen. Unsure whether I was commiserating with her for the secret being found out or for discovering how self-centred her sister was.

Next day I left for the lake and our new home, taking the ponies, Gastyn and the goods we had brought from the old school. Johannes would stay in Garth Madron until our shelter was ready, although I was glad to leave that place; I'd had enough of its intrigues. Rhain promised to visit. I told my cousins that I hoped they would all come, but it was Dwynwen I wanted to see.

After an hour and a half we reached the lake, the spot Anlach indicated the week before. We were entranced, it was beautiful; the view across Syfaddon to the mountains beyond glorious. A sacred grove of hawthorn and mountain ash grew beside a bubbling spring that trickled to the lake's shore. The land was good; rich, red earth, fields of green pasture close by. The woods around were oak, ash, alder, and sycamore. An abundance of oak for posts, as well as ash for the roof timbers and to burn in our hearth over the winter.

Late morning Brychan arrived accompanied by four craftsmen, skilled in woodworking. He took up a branch, paced and marked outlines in the dirt. I was annoyed at first. I'd wanted to build the clas, take the credit. I quickly realised how little I knew as he assessed the slope to ensure water ran away, not into the huts and was glad of his advice. We agreed on three buildings; a church, a school but first we'd build the small hut to sleep and eat in, along with two pens for sheep and pigs.

'You'll need a fence to keep out raiders and keep the animals in.

'No, we don't want a palisade. It didn't help when the raiders came for us in Bovium. A church must trust that people will do no harm, be open and welcoming.'

That first moonless night we slept under stars shining bright as embers fanned in the wind, they dazzled against the black sky. I sighed, the soft sounds of night surrounding me. I felt safe at last, after weeks of fear and sorrow.

The men felled sturdy oaks all through the following day. Iron axe heads sang and thudded as they bit into trunks, sharp cracks and shouts sounded as each dropped. After each tree was down, their iron blades were placed in the fire and hammered sharp again, the noise ringing across the lake. Villagers paddled over in canoes to watch, the men delighted to be offered payment to work for us.

Gastyn was set to cooking for us in the heavy iron cauldron brought from Cor Tewdws, adding fish and grain, along with green leaves and herbs he'd gathered from beside the lake.

Meanwhile, I oversaw the work, ensuring as Brychan had advised, each post hole was dug deep, a quarter of the length of the trunk. I placed handfuls of small pebbles at the very bottom of each hole to keep the wood from rotting.

While the men dug and pulled, I went to the lake to cut reed for the roofs, a back-breaking task. I hacked at armfuls of reed, my feet squelching in the deep, stinking mud as I tried to keep upright. Bare-legged, leeches clung and sucked at my calves and thighs, stones and stems cut into my feet. Water and mud would have ruined my leather boots and my wooden clogs had been abandoned in my burnt school; we couldn't carry all our possessions. The reed was ripe and ready, the more I collected while the water was warm from the summer sun, the less poor-quality stems we would have to gather later in the year from icy water.

We constructed a simple roundhouse five paces wide. Eight posts were set firmly in a circle, the two thickest at the doorway to take the weight of the lintel and sprung walls, woven using stout hazel rods. The craftsmen put up light branches of ash ready to support the roof. I suggested a small hole to allow smoke out at its centre.

Brychan arrived and laughed at my idea. 'The first brisk wind would make a fire roar and flame up, the thatch would catch. You priests will have to learn to live with smoke.' He relented. 'My halls are high to let the fumes filter away slowly above us. In time you will find taller oaks and build a larger home. Use year-old willow and ash logs to burn on days you cannot cook outside. You may even be able to cut and dry peat if the weather stays warm.'

By the end of the day the roof supports were finished, ready for my bundles of reed and then a layer of turf. The roof extended well beyond the walls, to ensure rain would drip into a gully we'd dug, with an outlet at the lowest point of the slope.

Village women tramped a shallow pit full of mud, manure and soot with sheep's wool, then pressed it into woven wattle walls to proof them against the Welsh rain and wind. Their feet squelched and they sang softly as they worked in the sunshine. We started on the church, I'd wanted a rectangular building, like the Roman ones I'd seen in Caer Mead. I said it should face south, with the door looking west to the setting sun.

Brychan was doubtful. 'Round huts resist the wind far better; you may lose your roof in winter gales.'

He'd paced the site and threw strands of dry grass in the air, watching as the wind took them. Staring at the hill behind us, Allt Yr Esgair, he nodded saying it protected us from the worst of the west and north winds. Maybe my idea would work.

Six massive oaks were hewn, each took two men a day to fell and ready. Smaller timbers were set between strong main supporting posts. Brychan's men took care crafting the high joints ready for the roof, which would need to survive winter storms. The villagers brought a horses' skull cleaned of flesh, bleached and shining white in the sun. They'd expected it to be placed deep below our threshold. Brychan thanked them and shook each man's hand but declined firmly.

'This is the house of the Lord Jesus. He doesn't need any protection. He is powerful, kind and cares for us all. Come back when my nephew's church is finished and worship here, you will understand then.'

Gastyn and I were happy. We worked hard, our muscles burned at the end of each day, but we made good progress. My body hardened with the work, I revelled as my strength grew, felt alive. After two months labour, the church was taking shape and most days one of my cousins would arrive to help or distract us. Cynog came often, envious of our task, interested to understand every detail of the construction.

Rhain followed, he wanted company and to practise with sword and shield, and enjoyed helping chop ash and willow branches into logs ready for winter. I was surprised how easily I bested him with the wooden staff and sword.

Rhain grimaced, 'You've grown stronger over the autumn, Maelon. You look different, older.'

'It's the lifting and felling. I've never laboured so much. It's a different exercise but useful, the strength of my blows has improved. If I were at home… and a warrior I'd be coming into my full strength in the fiann. As Niall's son I'd be giving orders to men, not working in a grubby habit.'

Rhain could see I was downcast at the thought. He understood I had no wish to become a priest.

'Let's borrow a boat. I'll show you how to fish for pike and perch with baited hooks. Eels are easiest for every day. Use rotten meat and you'll collect plenty. Look, here is an old trap.' He dragged a decrepit willow basket with a woven tubed entrance from the shore. 'If you pay them the village women will make you more. Dry the eels high above the fire in the smoke on your rafters, they stink at first but in a winter stew they're delicious.'

Then at last, she came, the girl I had longed to see since that accidental touch in Garth Madron. My heart sang at the sight of a sturdy pony trotting towards the church with Dwynwen; straight-backed, her glorious tousled hair the colour of a fox's brush streaming behind her. I beamed a welcome. Gastyn ran to her as she dismounted.

'Maelon, Gastyn, greetings, I've heard you have been busy. I would have come before but Ellyw and I are not allowed beyond the gates. Father's guards will arrive in a second, I gave them the slip.'

Sure enough, in the distance, two exasperated men followed; looking relieved as they spotted Dwynwen.

'We've had word that your mother and Sylvester will return tomorrow. Grandmother sent me to ask you to come back with us ready to greet them.'

Her face fell. 'That's not all, King Einion is on his way from north Wales to wed Ellyw. She is distraught and looks to elope with Geraint. My father has two men at our hut door at all times. Ellyw's angry, insisting she will insult the king, so he won't want her. My father has beaten her three times this week, but she will not give in. Grandfather is miserable. He hates to see us unhappy. He pleaded with Father to let her marry Geraint. Father says he has given his oath and cannot be seen to break it or men will not trust him. Grandmother agrees with Father, she insists thirty is not old,' we exchanged incredulous glances, 'and that we are honour bound to make Ellyw marry Einion.'

Dwynwen looked so forlorn, I took her hand in sympathy. Soft and warm, a fledgling nestling in my grasp, a wave of emotion shook me. I looked at her wondering whether she felt the same. Glancing up at me through her lashes she gently took her hand away.

'We must go back to Garth Madron, Cousin. Gastyn, will you join us?'

He nodded agreement at once. Since the raid on the school, Gastyn hated being left alone. He suffered nightmares, shouting out in his sleep, the least noise startled him. He'd told me he would never be the same after that terrible day.

Dwynwen's hand brushed mine again, this time it was her doing. I felt the warmth of her body next to mine and rejoiced at it.

On the journey to Garth Madron I thought about my mother. Five years had passed, but it felt as if it was yesterday, she last held me on the Irish shore. Now she had made the same journey to Wales; would we even recognise each other?

That evening Kira barked, then loped off on her three legs toward the road. I looked up and saw the familiar rounded shape of Sylvester, walking beside a woman, two men and a youth. They had come, it was my mother. I ran after Kira, who was bouncing between my mother, Sylvester, and a boy I recognised; Bledd. Mother held her arms wide and I felt her hold me again, smelt the scent of her hair. I looked at her face, more familiar than my own, how could I think I might not know her? I turned to see who else was with her, it was Math and Aed, sent as escort to ensure her safety.

I embraced them, turned to Bleddyn, my old friend. 'You are home Bledd. I am glad to see you safe.'

He laughed, 'Yes free, thanks to you, Math and Aed. We went from being slaves working in your uncle's kitchen in Emain Macha to honoured guests at the court of the High King. We couldn't believe it. We were saved.'

I led them toward my grandfather's home.

Mother was tearful. 'It is so good to see Garth Madron. I have pined for this place since I was your age, Maelon. It is even lovelier than I remember.'

As my grandparents came closer, she began to sob, her voice ragged as she called out, 'Mother.'

My grandmother's arms encircled her as they had me that first evening I arrived, my grandfather couldn't restrain his tears. It had been seventeen years since their daughter Inne had left, now they were reunited.

Tomorrow we would celebrate her return, but that evening she rested and told me all that had happened since I left home.

'Your father got grosser with age, but he was shrewd and of course an old goat, still liked his women. Rignach would have none of it, I too refused him. He accepted our decision, ashamed of his girth and rotten teeth. He became ill, weak, his feet and legs swollen and cold. He had no breath; he should not have gone on that last raid. He said if the clans thought him weak, he would be made to relinquish the High Kingship. I nursed him as if he was my father at the end. Ness had no care to and Rignach argued with him; it had to be me. In those last months before he died we often talked about you and your mischief. We'd wonder how tall you were and whether you'd got your first beard: he regretted sending you to Wales, saying perhaps he sent you away too soon.'

She paused. 'I came to respect his decision. Maybe it was early, but I have to admit he was right. You might be dead now if he hadn't.

'Sylvester told me Fiachrae came looking for you.' She shuddered. 'Of all your uncles, he was the one I feared most. He should have a snake for an emblem, not a swan.

'After Niall died, I was treated with respect but Conall had married. His wives and Rignach plotted, planned and schemed constantly. I didn't feel safe. The dead king's comely young widow had no place in Tara. Your sister Ria has married a few short weeks ago, she was pleased, ready. She is hand-fasted to a chieftain to the west, in Connacht. That man is bound to your brothers, their sons kin to the Úi Neill's. There was nothing left for me there. I was relieved when they agreed to let me come home. They'd have married me to a lowly prince or chieftain, to diminish my status, and yours…'

'I won't be allowed to stay. Brychan won't want his sister here. Better a queen than the old king's widow.' She patted my hand and looked out to the hillside. 'I'm going for a walk, to revisit my best-loved places. Who knows how long I'll be allowed to remain?'

I found Sylvester sitting alone roughing Kira's fur. I noticed how he had aged since we left Ireland five years earlier, long hair greying behind his tonsure, his face deeply lined.

'How is the building work progressing? I am impatient to see our new home.'

'Very well, I can't wait to show you. We have a sturdy shelter ready and the church is half finished. Tell me about your trip.'

'I'm glad to say it went as planned. There was no problem with the exchange. High King Conall was pleased to see Math and Aed return. He was already annoyed with Fiachrae, knew he'd raided the school, but presumed it a coincidence, that Fiachrae didn't know you were there. When I told him, they had come in search of you, Conall was furious. He called Fiachrae's grandson to court, Nathi's eldest boy; fostered he called it, but they knew why he'd demanded it. The boy was a hostage. Fiachrae got no gold in exchange for the pupils either. Conall told him he'd profited enough and that he wanted the other two boys found.

'Conall told me he was relieved to see Inne leave, that it would stop his mother and mother-in-law making nonsensical salacious claims about her liaisons. Math and Aed offered to accompany us as guards, claiming it was because they spoke Welsh now; they had their reasons.

'There is a sadder tale to recount I'm afraid. As we had Aed and Math's protection, I took the opportunity to return to the school, to collect the remaining treasures buried there. It was horrible to see our old home abandoned and decaying. I collected the hoard. We can make it safe tomorrow.

'I decided to call into Caer Mead to see Clemens and his wife. When I reached it, their villa was utterly destroyed. A terrible sight, I cried to see what had been done to that lovely home. Two boats of raiders had returned weeks after the first raid; the same ones; a swan emblem on their shields. They'd realised Caer Mead was a ripe fruit ready for plucking, and came in greater numbers. It is possible they thought you had taken shelter there after failing to find you the first time. They didn't bother taking slaves, they murdered the whole household. Twenty people slaughtered. Clemens' hounds were stolen, not killed, before you ask. The villagers showed me the grave dug within their walls for those poor souls. I blessed it and said prayers for them.

'Clemens left leaving too late. We made the right decision. I'm so glad we didn't leave Johannes with them.'

I was appalled. Our amiable friends had been murdered by my uncle.

Sylvester continued, 'We travelled back through Nidum, up the old Roman Road. Math and Aed had unfinished business there. At the mine workings they asked for the overseer. He was no longer in charge; he was labouring in the pits. Calpernius had found plenty of proof that he was stealing. I argued with that was punishment enough, but Math hates him and has sworn to kill him. As we left Math sneered, telling him to enjoy the next weeks, they would be his last. Math will not relent. I have pleaded for mercy but he is unmoved.

'Then we returned to Calpernius's villa, sad to report we'd found no trace of Wyn. Aed is restored to his lands and he asked to marry Melissa. Her father agreed, although he said he had hoped not to see her go so far away. Aed Ruad is a prince in Ireland, it is a better match than that family could have imagined. You could see from Melissa's face that she loved him. The two will marry on Aed's return journey and travel on to Ireland. There will be many eyes looking for Wyn in Ireland, his sister, Benignus and Palladius.'

The following day I took Sylvester and Bledd to our little church by the lake, proud of the progress made in their absence. Kira leapt in the lake chasing mallard and geese, pleased to be home. Gastyn and Bledd stayed there, while Sylvester and I returned to Garth Madron and my mother for the evening's celebration.

As we arrived, I heard the guards calling to my grandfather and uncle. "Be aware, strangers approaching from the north."

I walked to the gate and watched a finely dressed, clean shaven man, of middle years, leap from a grey horse. It was King Einion, arrived to take Ellyw in marriage; accompanied by a dozen men, who he ordered to make camp outside our stockade.

Walking back into the settlement I overheard my grandmother speaking to my mother.

'Harvest hasn't begun. We can't manage a marriage feast and your welcome meal, Inne. We need to be sure we have enough for the hand-fasting. Anlach's lords and King Cuneglas and Glywys will all come. We want to impress them with our hospitality. Your brother aims to bind the Welsh kingdoms and our allies together.'

Mother rubbed my grandmother's arm. 'I understand, don't fret. I'm glad to feel the grass of my home beneath my feet. I'm relieved to be back, away from Ireland and Niall's poisonous kin.'

That evening preparations reached fever pitch, organised chaos reigned: cooks screeched and complained, men swore, children squabbled and cried and dogs barked. My cousins bathed in the river and put on their finest garments. Cynog wore a bronze and silver neck ring he had been given at birth. Shining brightly around Anlach's throat was the massive torc my father had gifted Cor Tewdws.

Envy made me wish to match them. Why should I act as a priest when I was the descendent of kings? A kingdom waited for in Ireland…probably. By right the torc my grandfather wore should have been mine. I tore off my habit and put on a tunic of red-dyed wool under a yellow cloak held by an enamelled brooch. I pushed the boar headed arm-ring up over my elbow. It felt satisfyingly tight on my muscled right arm. I thought back to the time I'd won the rings for myself and my brothers. That day I couldn't have imagined it fitting my arm so well; nor how saving

Nathi would cost me so much. I was stronger and taller than my red-faced, red-haired cousin Rhain. I look like a prince, Rhain doesn't, I thought. We assembled before Anlach and he nodded with pride.

Brychan introduced his eldest children to Einion: Cynog, Rhain, Dwynwen and Gwladys first, then me. 'This is Maelon ap Neill, son of the old High King of Ireland, Niall, and brother to the new one, Conall.' His eyes narrowed. 'He is a novice priest, despite his clothing. You will meet my sister, his widowed mother, Inne shortly. She is recently returned to us. Tonight was to have been her home-coming celebration.'

We waited for Ellyw, as horns of ale and mead circulated. Musicians played harps and pipes, singing of love in the flickering rush-light. My grandmother led in my cousin. Dressed in fine cream wool, a garland of hedge roses on shining deep brown hair, Ellyw looked a plum; but young, very young. Einion smiled at her. She pouted in response and looked down, avoiding his eye.

Brychan stood up. 'This is my daughter Ellyw, betrothed to you in spring.'

The music paused and the room hushed as my mother walked through the doorway. She looked wonderful: serene and regal, her dark hair simply dressed, her glass-beaded necklace and earrings glinting in the fire's glow. Walking up to the high table, she bowed to her father and brother, smiled politely at Einion, then came to sit at my side, touching my hair as she sat. My heart was swollen with pride. I had never thought of her as a woman before. To me, she was my mother, lovely yes, but that was how she had always been. Every man in the hall looked at her in admiration. Math looked moonstruck. Aed glanced sideways at him, an anxious expression on his face.

Einion said, 'My lady, I apologise, this banquet was for you. Please take my place. I should not wish to detract from your day.' He looked to my grandfather. 'You have a beautiful daughter and your grand-daughter is a graceful child.'

Ellyw stiffened, slighted at being called a child, her expression thunderous. Anlach gestured for the harpists to resume. Einion insisted my mother take his place at the centre of the table beside her father, coming over to sit beside to me. The company was astonished at his courtesy, that a king would travel so far and then relinquish his place of honour to a woman. I read my mother's face; he had impressed her.

As he sat, he whispered, 'I can watch the room more easily from this seat.'

His view of my mother is better and less observed from here, I thought.

Succulent odours of meat roasted with rosemary and sage made my stomach rumble in pleasurable anticipation. The servers brought in roast mutton, then smoked fowl, along with a huge pike from the lake stuffed with pork. It was followed by curds and heather scented mountain honey, all accompanied by gallons of watered beer and mead. Throughout the meal I noticed two pairs of eyes watching my mother intently: Einion's and Math's. Einion smiled once at Ellyw, who turned away with a scowl.

He shrugged and spoke to me, 'So, Maelon, do you have brothers?'

'Many half-brothers and sisters,' I laughed, 'but only one full sister. She is married and in the far west of Ireland. Conall and my six half-brother's rule, but my father had plenty more children.'

'I have two daughters aged five and two. I've been widowed for two years. How old are you?'

'I'm nearly eighteen. I came to Wales aged twelve to train as a priest.'

'So tall at seventeen, your mother has bred a fine son. My youngest brother Siriol is a priest like you. Your uncle seems godly?'

'Yes, very, it is his obsession. He was taught by blind Father Drichan, that white-haired priest sitting near the doorway. All Brychan's children have been taught the gospels and can read and write, even the girls. My cousin Ellyw can too, of course. She is beautiful don't you think?'

He nodded, but, as we turned to her Ellyw frowned, drumming her fingers on the table looking bored.

He sighed, saying as if to himself, 'She is very young, pretty enough, but hardly a queen. His eyes moved back to my mother, as she presented a bronze spoon to the harpist.

'I need a queen and consort, a mother to my children, not an older sister for them to squabble with. That girl, Ellyw is in need of firm management by the look of her. I wonder should I speak with Anlach tomorrow?'

He looked at me questioningly. 'Does your mother still grieve for Niall? Do you think she might marry again?'

I saw a way out for Ellyw. 'Father was old when they married, he had seven sons already. Mother disliked him at first, although she came to respect him. She nursed him when he grew ill and loved him like a father, but never a husband. My uncle will marry off my mother as quickly as possible. Mother has already told me she expects it.'

'I understand why Brychan might wish her wed and far away. Watching her scowls, I have little doubt that Ellyw would be glad not to have to marry. To a young girl's eyes, I will seem an elderly. How old is your mother?'

"Thirty-two I think, still young enough to bear many sons.'

I understood what was required, this was the art of kingship. Working out what men wanted and needed. I'd have made a good king, I thought with resentment.

Ellyw slipped out of the hall. Dwynwen's eyes followed her departure and she frowned. It was late so I excused myself and left the older men carousing, as a priest I was expected to be modest in my drinking. Mother and my grandmother came with me and we walked to the guest hut.

Grandmother raised an eyebrow at Mother, who blushed.

'You always knew how to charm. You get it from your father, I have no such skills.'

Mother laughed. 'Einion is rather handsome; his giving up his place was gallant.'

'You liked that he only had eyes for you. Everyone noticed; I don't wonder Ellyw left in a huff.'

'My niece is surly whenever I see her. Was that really my fault?'

'The girl sulks constantly, no wonder Einion said she was a lovely child. It's how she acted, like a spoilt brat,' replied my grandmother.

I interrupted. 'Einion questioned me about you Mother. He wondered if you still grieved for Father. He asked if I would mind you remarrying and told me he plans to speak with Grandfather tomorrow. He said he needed a mother for his daughters, not another child to care for. I'm guessing he will ask to be released from his betrothal to my cousin, and take you instead.'

She hesitated, 'Mother I'm afraid I must leave here if he does ask?'

It was half question, half statement, but my grandmother nodded. If Anlach and Brychan agreed, my mother would have to do as she was told.

We said goodnight and went our separate ways. I had thought to tell Ellyw that she may not have to wed, but the women's hut was dark and silent. I decided to check Kira, who had been bred as Anlach had suggested. As her time got closer and the litter grew, she was uncomfortable and slept poorly. She woke when I looked in and pushed her muzzle into my leg demanding a walk. I gave in and we headed toward the gate. Passing Mother's hut, I heard angry whispers. I called my dog to heel and crept silently toward the door, worried for her. I heard Math's voice; he and Mother were arguing.

'You plan to marry that man, Einion. Everyone could see he wanted you not his betrothed. It was shameful; you encouraged him with your eyes.'

'I have to wed. I have no choice.'

'You could marry me.'

'No, Math, I cannot, you have no land. No man would take you to his household as a warrior if you married me. They would fear my father's wrath in Wales or my nephew's in Ireland. Neither family would tolerate the alliance.'

'Because I am Brion's bastard,' he said bitterly.

'Yes, it would cause outrage in Ireland. My father would see it as an assault to his pride. He will expect me to marry where he chooses, like last time. I am a woman, a commodity. This man may not offer for me, but if he does, I will take him. I am used to being a queen. I cannot cook and tend cattle and am too old to learn.'

Math growled, 'Not even for love?'

'No, not even for that. I can live without passion. If you are a woman in this hard world, affection becomes less important than survival. I endured Ireland, and will carry on because I must.'

Her tone softened. 'You should marry Math. I saw the way that girl looked at you in Bannavem. She was devastated when Aed offered for her sister and you stayed silent. Marry, have children, live a happy life. Don't hope to be tied to an ageing widow, running scared we might be found. Conall would give you land. He is your friend and loves you. It might be that Calpernius will ask you to stay in Wales, he is well off and the girl his last remaining child. It would be a good match. Math, you must forget me.'

I crept from my mother's door, whispering for Kira to follow. I felt sick and confused. How dare Math speak to my mother so; and yet a part of me knew they loved each other. Everyone in my father's dún had whispered of it; their shame, and what Niall would do when he found out. I'd blocked it out, but had always known.

CHAPTER
10

At dawn Sylvester shook me awake, Brychan demanded to see us. I went smiling, guessing he would want to speak of my mother and Einion. As I entered his hut, everything changed. My uncle's face was white, lips thin with strain, he looked sick. A shaking peasant wearing a thin dirty tunic stood in front of him, hands twisting in anxiety.

'Maelon, would you fetch your friends Math and Aed? Bring your hound.'

We led the horses out of the settlement without a sound, perplexed. Math's face was drawn and weary.

We traversed a pleasant valley, a sparkling veil of dew covering cobwebs and grass in the chilly morning light. Our ponies breath left a steaming cloudy trail behind us, as we followed a sunken path lined with rowan and blackthorn, a stream gurgled beside us. At the summit of the lane, I looked down to a cluster of huts, thin wraiths of grey smoke hanging heavy above their mossy thatch. Beyond on a rise stood an enormous yew. The peasant gestured silently toward the tree.

Brychan told us to wait; we stood mute, wondering what would happen. I heard Brychan howl then saw him collapse to his knees. Sylvester and I ran to him. Beneath the yew lay Ellyw. Wild rose petals were scattered around her head and feet, but across her stomach was a dark stain, drying blood and a deep wound. Her hand gripped a slim knife. Sylvester reached over and pulled her arm up toward the wound, the knife slid up and matched the entry exactly. She had stabbed herself. What we saw made no sense.

Brychan had watched Sylvester's action and shook his head firmly.

'My daughter would not kill herself; it was not in her nature. She loved life. Indeed, she took care of herself above all others.' His face gazed at us urgent and intent. 'No one must know she was found like this.'

He told the man to fetch his wife; when the woman came, he asked her to check if Ellyw had been violated. We turned away in horror. To our relief the woman told us there was no indication that she had been molested.

Aed asked, 'What of the roses? Who would place rose petals at her feet?'

Brychan replied, 'Geraint. Geraint would.'

I whistled for Kira to scent. The dog quickly found a path up beyond the yew. In the mud were horse and foot prints. Math bent examining the tracks.

'One horse had a rider, the other did not, they came and returned from the mountain path. The mud has not dried, it can't have been long ago.'

Brychan sighed, 'Yes, Ystrad Yew is only an hour from here if you follow the mountain ridge path. She was running away to Geraint.'

He turned back to the trembling woman, who told him the girl had been coming for months to meet with a dark-haired youth. She had seen nothing the night before, but her husband remembered the dogs barking in the early hours.

Brychan looked at Math and Aed. 'Will you come with me to Ystrad Yew and Geraint's hall. I can't tell my father; he dotes on my daughters. I need time to accept what happened before I can face him. I don't want my men with me. I can't bear for them to see her or him, they will be too angry for sense.'

He looked down at Ellyw's body and grimaced, agonised. 'She is with her mother Ban in heaven now. Please stay with her Father Sylvester. I will send her grandmother and my wife to you.'

Leaving Sylvester kneeling in prayer beside the girl, we returned to Garth Madron. Later Math and Aed and I rode out. I had not been asked to join Brychan, but hadn't been told to stay either. I went with my sword belted at my waist, incensed, appalled at the sight of Ellyw's body. Her young blood spilt; life drained into the soil.

Geraint and his men would pay a heavy price for this. I remembered the mountainside ride when Kira had lost her leg and I'd killed my first man. I shivered; would I be called to fight for my life again?

Along the roads, it was more than two hours out of one valley across and up the Valley of the Yews to Geraint's hall. When we arrived at the settlement the gates were open but everything was eerily silent. A lone guard waited, he saw us draw our swords, but laid his own down. He held his arms above his heads, gesturing for us to enter.

The dark hall was empty, deserted, no movement within, its hearth was cold, a central table stood bare. Math and Aed walked around the perimeter, moving benches and blankets. Then Geraint appeared from a small doorway in the corner, face ashen, streaked with tears, his tunic covered in drying bloodstains. He seemed bemused and shocked. He ran to fall at my uncle's feet; as Math drew out his sword.

Brychan gestured him to hold back.

Sobbing Geraint spoke, 'It was not meant to happen. I loved her, longed for her. We planned to marry in secret, but Einion came earlier than we expected. We had to hasten our plans. My Ellyw was so lovely…. I had waited so long. I tried to persuade her that it was our real wedding night, we should make love there.

'She refused, insisting we must marry in the sight of the Lord before I took her, that I must convert, become Christian. I began to shout, then she drew a blade. It was so sharp and she was so angry. I felt afraid for her and myself. I grabbed for it and she pulled away from me. She slipped in the mud, fell against the tree and the knife slid deep into her belly. She gasped and called out in terror. I held her close but there was so much blood. I couldn't stop it. She moaned, asked for you, then as I said I would always love her, she…she.'

He rasped hoarsely as he sobbed, 'She died in my arms, I felt her leave.' He stared fearfully up at Brychan. 'I didn't know what to do. I laid her down, took the roses from her hair and spread them at her feet. Then I ran. I know you will kill me. I am ready for death, glad of it. I adored her. I can't bear to live without her.'

Brychan sighed and put out his hand, then stroked Geraint's dark hair comfortingly.

'I'd guessed how it must have gone from the wound. She was like her mother, all passion. I was five years younger than Ban and yet she made me hers, she'd decided you see. I believe you

Geraint. I know,' he choked… 'knew my daughter, she would have done and said all that. Once her mind was made up, she would not waver, not for anyone or anything.

'Go, flee. When my father discovers what has happened, he will want you punished, tortured. Do not call for death. You are young and will recover from this blow, time is on your side. You have perhaps half a day to make your escape. Never return, Ellyw's death is punishment enough for you… and for me.'

He turned away, slumped, despairing and signalled for us to follow. Math and Aed were open-mouthed that he allowed Geraint to go free.

He looked at us sadly. 'You don't understand, do you? I cannot kill a man when I know he was not to blame. It would be against the law of Christ and honour. I knew how Ellyw was with him; she called it love but it was not. Geraint was weak and in her thrall, she could control him. I love… loved my daughter but I know in my heart she brought this on herself. It was an accident. She did not intend to kill herself; she loved drama, like her mother.

Killing Geraint, when I know he speaks the truth, not forgiving him, would condemn me to a life of regret. More than that I would have sinned. I hope you three will keep this sad truth secret. Please say nothing of the circumstances of her death.'

Chastened we rode back across the mountain. The weather was fair and the ride beautiful, but not one of us could think of anything other than Ellyw's body crumpled and bloody under the yew. For the first time since we'd met, I respected Brychan. My father and the old religion would have demanded death for Geraint. He'd admitted trying to seduce my cousin. Christianity and honour had stopped Brychan's revenge. I felt perilously close to admitting that Christ's teaching was right, but irritated that should be so. Surely Macha demanded a death to appease the stain on our family honour? But in reality, that would achieve nothing, it would not bring my cousin back to life. I turned away upset and confused.

When we arrived back at Garth Madron, Cynog, Dwynwen and my grandparents stood waiting at the gateway. Sitting leaden on his horse, Brychan knew he had to speak.

'My beloved daughter Ellyw is dead. There was an accident. I know you will grieve with me. We will bury her where she died, near the ancient yew at the head of the valley. I will build a church in that place in memory of my virgin daughter.'

My grandparents walked away clinging to each other. There would be questions later, but I resolved to keep my promise of silence. That evening Einion spoke quietly with Brychan, a contract agreed. He would marry my mother later in the winter. In the circumstances, they agreed the wedding would be held in his kingdom on the Llyn. I would attend her, accompanied by Cynog and Rhain. Brychan and his family were left to grieve. Math and Aed departed for Ireland the next day, closely followed by Einion and his men. Johannes offered to take charge of the new church.

'I've had enough of teaching, of young scamps teasing me.' He looked at me with a hint of wry affection in his eyes. 'I'd like peace in my old age. I will pray for the lovely child each day, until I join her with the Lord.'

I was left to work in the school each day, to study to join a priesthood I had come to despise. I'd hoped the church and school I'd worked so hard to build would start to feel like my home, but it didn't, it felt like a cage. I could see no way out, my family and friends expected me to follow their chosen path. I didn't want to betray them, abandon them. Besides, where would I go? It was too late for me to become a warrior like my father and brother's, that training took years. I was desperate, longed to escape my life.

CHAPTER 11

Spring 453 AD

I turned twenty and again delayed shaving my scalp for the tonsure. Every year Sylvester asked if I wanted to give my life to Christ, and each time I declined, saying I did not feel ready. Bledd had shaved his forehead two years before. Gastyn was impatient to become a priest when he was older, but I couldn't bring myself to agree. Sylvester reassured me, said I would know when and if the time was right. Old Johannes nagged at me to repent, change my wicked ways. Benignus had returned downhearted from Ireland, he'd found no traces of our last pupils, Llyr and Wyn.

Math married Metella and stayed in Wales running the mines with Calpernius. Older, in his mid-thirties, he was starting to grey, but still fearsome, strong as a fine bull, compact and muscular, hard as rock. His appearance belied his nature, he treated everyone well, especially the slaves working his mines.

To my astonishment, he had converted, become a Christian. He insisted it was not his wife's influence. His workers were well fed, given decent huts and warm clothes. He freed slaves who'd worked hard and consistently. Most stayed working for him, either in the mines or if they were older on his farm. Calpernius and Math became wealthy as the seasons turned. Men walked the road to beg for work, his miners better fed and housed than many free men.

The roads between Garth Madron and Bannavem were safe to travel. Neither Math nor my uncle tolerated bandits on their territory. When we met Math teased me, called me Little Lord, although I stood taller than him and grown stronger. We practised with sword and spear and I'd bested him twice.

The second time he'd thrown down his weapons and said, 'I'm proud of you, Maelon. You remind me of Niall when he was young. I remember him as he was when I was a boy, before my father… died. Before the clan started fighting over who should be High King. He was a good man then, brave and strong. You are taller than Niall, darker too, but the way you handle your weapons reminds me of him.'

The three years had passed productively for our little church and monastery by the lake. It was making its name as a safe place of learning for good Christians, away from the coast and raiders. Protected by Brychan, a champion of Christianity. A number of wealthy families sent younger sons to us.

It helped that we were on a pilgrim's route. People walked to Johannes' church now called Llanellyw; they travelled to the tall Fish stone beside the river, then followed a path to a dolmen built by the ancients, then downhill to arrive at our lake. We sheltered them for the night and blessed them as they made their way on to Garth Madron. Many believed praying at St Ellyw's grave would cure their ailments, young women hoped the virgin martyr would make them fertile. Johannes encouraged that belief as they left offerings at his church. Sylvester told us it was the pilgrim's faith that cured them; so not to be too concerned that Ellyw had not been martyred. More hypocrisy, I thought with disgust.

My grandfather had died the winter after Ellyw's death, weakened by his heartbreak. True to his promise, I was gifted a fine battle-axe, forged by Irish smiths and wonderfully engraved.

Brychan ruled in his place, although to his annoyance the people still turned as much to Marchell as they did him. He half joked; half complained that it would have been better if she had retreated from the world to be looked after by my mother. He'd repeatedly ask why wasn't Mother fat and lined as he'd hoped. Cynog left Garth Madron and journeyed across Brycheiniog, as Brychan insisted his land be called, as a priest. Cynog walked the countryside giving blessings and as often, sensible advice on how to cure common ailments, teaching about Jesus.

Brychan's younger children still attended their little school in Glanddwr, but now the older ones came to our school; elderly Drichan could not manage so many children. Dwynwen no longer studied, she was being taught to manage a royal household by our grandmother. My eyes yearned to see her, Dwynwen. I looked for her everywhere, saw her in every shadow.

In truth, Ellyw's death had changed her. I caught glimpses of the girl I first met three and a half years earlier, but she was often sad and sometimes angry. She was no longer slim but painfully thin. I thought her angular face was more beautiful, but many criticised her appearance. She spent long hours on her knees, praying beside Johannes, in the church named for her sister. I overheard Sylvester and Johannes talking about her one evening.

Johannes said, 'I'm uncomfortable with how much time Brychan's daughter spends with me. I've never had to debate about Jesus with a woman before.'

Sylvester replied, 'You must be gentle, she has taken her sister's death badly. She is heartbroken. Worse she blames herself for not noticing Ellyw leave that night. I imagine she looks for comfort in the Lord's words. Treat her no differently than you would any other pupil.' He paused, 'Well maybe more tolerantly than with them; she is our benefactor's daughter after all. You can be, a little harsh on occasions.'

Johannes tutted. 'It's not that. She doesn't eat, she's always fasting. Sometimes she looks … well inspired, as if she has visions. It's disconcerting and I don't see why a woman should receive messages from the Lord if I don't. I've given my life to him.'

'The Lord knows of your service, Johannes; you have no need to be jealous. But I agree, for a girl of her age to be so thin can't be right. She's skin and bone, her grandmother is desperately worried about her.'

It made no difference, to me Dwynwen was breath-taking. Seventeen, long old enough for marriage, her smile melted my heart each time we met. A novice priest what could I say? I had nothing to offer.

Her father was negotiating her marriage, discussing with kings and princes across Wales and Dumnonia who would take his eldest daughter, a rich prize. Rumour was he favoured Glywys, widowed king of the rich lands across the River Wysg stretching many miles to the sea. Brychan hoped the alliance would bring peace to his borders. I had never dared ask Dwynwen what she thought, but Rhain had shaken his head when we spoke of it. He told me Glywys's grown son, Prince Woolos opposed the match.

Woolos had enough siblings, without his father siring more on yet another young wife.

When I saw Dwynwen, we'd take long walks and talk of Kira and her puppies. My hound loved her nearly as much as I did. Kira produced two final litters of puppies before I decided she was too old to be bred. I'd kept one from each, Beah, a dog and Tas a bitch.

I never knew what to expect when we met. Sometimes Dwynwen would seem warm and her eyes would meet mine boldly, she'd tease me. More often she would be distant, speak of doing the Lord's work and avoid my touch. I dared not speak of my feelings, nor hope for anything from her beyond fondness for a cousin.

CHAPTER
12

A letter arrived for Sylvester from Palladius. He had word of a young Welsh slave, known to be Christian, who might be our friend Wyn. The slave was working on the Irish mountain where the old god Lugh's sling-shots were found. It was a sacred place, forbidden to Christians and foreigners. Sliabh Mis Mountain, was in the land of the Dal Riata tribes. The king, Milchu the Bloody, was pagan and renowned for killing priests who dared preach in his kingdom.

Sylvester and I talked long into the night. 'I have to go and rescue Wyn, Sylvester. Only Benignus and I speak Irish well enough. Beni's tonsure would take months to grow out, he wouldn't be safe. It has to be me.'

'No, it is too dangerous for you to go alone if this man is a priest killer. The Dal Riata tribes have a fearsome reputation.'

'Math will come with me, after all, he is Wyn's brother-in-law, and also…

Also, what?

'He's my sworn man, if I ask, he will come. We might be able to buy Wyn. Offer a good price. It may be simple'

'I suppose there is no other option, but stay in Wales for as long as possible. Take the shortest sea crossing from Mona.'

Mona was known as the isle of druids, until the Romans killed every man, woman and child. It was in Einion's kingdom. I had only seen my mother twice at gatherings since her marriage. I was glad to have the opportunity to see her again and meet a half-brother and sister I had only heard of. I wanted to give her one of Kira's pups too.

Sylvester and I took the news to Bannavem. Math agreed, insisting he was oath-bound to come with me if I was going into danger. Seeing Ireland again was another attraction. I borrowed a faded black tunic and woollen breeches, topped by a cloak. As I changed out of my habit I felt relief to look and feel a man again. Calpernius was delighted that there was a chance we might find his son, but Metella was anxious for her husband.

Math reassured her. 'It's a strange thing, chance. No one will think it unusual for me to go there. I am sworn to Lugh and bear his mark.' He showed us the black tattoo on his shoulder. 'All of the brotherhood is expected to visit that place at some time in their lives. We are expected to collect smooth green stones from Sliabh Mis's summit: Lugh's sling-stones hold powerful magic. It was fate Maelon found me working in your mines, that same fate means I can go without fear to a mountain forbidden to outsiders.'

We were ready in two days. Calpernius's eyes were filled with tears of hope as we set out; Beah and Tas bounding joyfully beside us. He'd thought carefully about we would need to free a slave. He pressed on us a bag with a file for the slave chains, gold for any ransom and fresh clothes for Wyn.

He called out, 'Farewell and safe journey. I will pray morning and night you will return with my son. His mother and I long to see Maewyn's face. We will go to our graves happy if we can speak to him once again.'

The journey north would take a week. I strapped my sword to my waist, hidden beneath my warm, worn clothing. It was a wearisome journey, but I was glad to be seeing new places, travelling again. After two days on the road, we heard a sharp whistle. Tas, the younger of Kira's pups, ran off, her tail wagging furiously. Perplexed we stopped. A piebald pony trotted out of a copse of fir trees, on it rode a tall youth, a quiver of arrows at his back. Math and I drew out our weapons, ready in case he had companions waiting to attack us and was a decoy. Who could it be? Why wasn't Tas barking?

Then I recognised Dwynwen, her red hair hidden beneath a woollen cap. She was wearing a man's breeches and shirt.

Shocked Math asked, 'My Lady, what can you be doing here? Who is with you?'

She shook her head defiantly. 'No one, I have been following you. My family think I am in Glandwr with Drichan; although they may have realised by now. I am safe with you two though.' She smiled at us persuasively. 'And Maelon is my cousin. It is perfectly proper.'

'When they find out you have disappeared there is going to be trouble for us all,' I replied.

Frosty blue eyes glared at me. 'No, not for you, I will bear the chastisement if I'm caught. I don't want to marry. Father must have misgivings after Ellyw. This was my first chance to escape. I hope Aunt Inne will give me sanctuary. If not, I will become a servant or a nun. It is my life and I will live it as I choose. I refuse to submit to my father's demands.'

My heart sank, she was not going to return home willingly. Our only option was to take her with us, or else return to her father. Knowing Dwynwen, we'd need to tie her up to do that, she would run if we opposed her. In the wilderness of Powys, with bandits on the roads, she would be in terrible danger as a lone woman. I kept silent but knew we could not allow her come with us without her father's agreement.

At the nearest settlement, a town built around an abandoned Roman fort, I found someone prepared to act as messenger. I wrote to Brychan, suggesting it was safest for us to escort her to my mother.

My father's last words to me sounded in my mind, "Be sure not to annoy or antagonise your Uncle Brychan."

We made camp outside the town, a villager agreed to let Dwynwen sleep in a thatched shelter with their hens and sheep. I gestured to her to come and walk with me away from the huts. Math shrugging in irritation as we left.

I tried again. 'Are you sure about this Dwynwen? If you leave home your reputation will be destroyed. To live dependent on my mother and Einion's goodwill could be hard, even if they agree to take you in. To be honest, I doubt Einion will risk Brychan's wrath for you. Why should he? Unless your father agrees, he will have nothing to do with you. Life as a servant or nun is very different from that of a noble woman.'

She looked at me mutely, her eyes sad but also disappointed. I felt a weight in my heart. I realised she had hoped for more from me. What did she want?

'I, well I care for you, but I am a priest and one dependent on your father's favour. I am going to Ireland. When I'm there I will find out whether my brothers really hold land for me. Abod

Cedric thought they might not be enthusiastic about giving away territory; said the offer was a ploy to hold the kingship. I cannot say anything, offer you anything. Your father will never agree to a match between us. Anlach would have disapproved too.'

I felt sick as I spoke. I was speaking the truth but my soul told me the opposite, to take her and flee to Ireland.

She nodded thoughtfully and leant forward kissing my cheek. Warm and soft, her lips made my spirit soar. I made to pull her toward me but she shook her head and drew away.

'You are right, Einion probably won't agree. It changes nothing. I will become a nun. I'm not sure I want to marry anyone; not even you, dearest cousin.'

I heard her words, but her earlier kiss dismissed them from my mind. It was Glywys she didn't want, I thought. She'd have kissed me properly if I could have offered her marriage.

We three ate then settled to sleep. I was restless, tossing and turning, my dreams were haunted by the Hag. The woman shook my arms, she smelt of strange herbs and kept telling me not to betray Macha. Short hours later I woke, it was still dark. I heard the sound of distant riders cantering toward us. Brychan had arrived.

Seeing where Math and I slept he asked grimly, 'Where is she?'

With mixture of trepidation and relief, I indicated to the hut.

'When did she join you?'

I started to explain but Dwynwen came out into the night.

'Yesterday afternoon, Father, they didn't know I was following them. When you told me of my betrothal, I had to go. As we got deeper into the countryside, I realised it was too dangerous to remain on my own.

'You were putting your safety and that of others at risk. I am disappointed and angry with you.'

He slapped her face twice, with the back then the palm of his hand. I heard a crack as he hit her face, saw a drop of blood swell out and fall from her lip. A red flare appeared on her white skin where she had been struck.

'Kneel, beg my forgiveness. You are my daughter, you'll do as I say, always. You are promised to Glywys. He is rich; it is a good match.'

Math held my arm in a vice-like grip as I tried to move forward to protect her. I should speak, say she could marry me instead, but fear froze the words in my mouth. Tears of rage filled her eyes.

Through her swollen lip she spat, 'I don't want to marry anyone, Father. I sat with Mother when she died giving birth to my sister. Saw what she went through, so much pain and blood. I watched her die trying to get little Tydfil out, being cut when she wouldn't come. I held mother's hand. You didn't; men can't bear to, can they? You went hunting, away from her screams.

'I was there with your second wife, Prawst. She died the same way after five agonising births. I don't want to go through that, not unless I truly love someone. Even then... well, I'm not sure I can face it. Please let me go to my aunt.'

My uncle slumped, Dwynwen's words had shocked him.

'My men and I need sleep; we have been riding all day and night. I will be at your doorway, go in. Math, Maelon, rest elsewhere. I will guard my daughter.'

They left the next morning. Brychan holding his tearful and furious daughter in front of him on the horse.

She scowled down at me, 'You could have spoken up for me, cousin, betrayer. I hate you.'

As they left Math tried to console me. 'Arguing with Brychan would have achieved nothing. You were right not to dispute, or try to stop his chastising her. It would have made him suspicious. Even your note will make him wonder. All of Garth Madron watches you moon over her. He would have thought you'd planned it together.'

I was taken aback, I'd thought my feelings for her were secret. Worse, I'd let Dwynwen down, I had betrayed her. She was right, if I cared for her I should have supported her. Told Brychan he should release her from her betrothal. I hadn't thought about Glywys, beyond resenting that he was rich and powerful and I wasn't. When I thought of an old man touching Dwynwen, exploring her body with cold hands I felt nauseous. I had failed her, broken faith with love. I tried not to think about what she'd said about her mother and step-mother's deaths. Rignach had seven sons, Mother two sons and three daughters now, most women survived childbirth.

Math gazed at me, concern in his eyes. 'Maelon, I'm the last person who should advise on love; but don't hope for too much from that girl. There is something…'

I shook off his arm, didn't want to hear more. 'Come on, let's move out, the day is passing.'

I noticed little and thought of nothing on that journey except how useless I was. If there were bandits, that we were big men and accompanied by two wolfhounds was enough to deter them. We reached Einion's borders in three more days, to be told his court was gathered near the forked mountains, at Tre'r Ceiri; the town of the giants.

We toiled wearily up a steep slope to a strange settlement; magnificent views in every direction. From its heights, we could see Ireland far away; home. It was a weather-beaten, forbidding and windblown place. We entered through first one, then a second high double ditch; each entrance had a bored guard on duty. Dozens of round stone huts were set among purple heather and yellow gorse.

Math muttered, 'I can see why there is only one guard; you'd see any attacker for hours before they climbed this damn hill, and they would be exhausted by the time they reached the settlement.'

Einion was waiting, he had recognised us and bid us welcome. Embarrassed he shuffled his feet, wanting to explain.

'The Picts and Irish raid my shores. Many of my people have retreated to the old places, built before the Romans came. This is a poor home I know, but Inne insists she and the children are safer here for the summer. She says she likes it, that she feels free of worry and can watch the kites fly above and dream. I'm usually defending my halls and cattle down below. I miss Inne and the children, so when I am on the Llyn I stay here.'

He gestured to the wide country laid out before us and over to the island of Mona across the sea. It looked prosperous, but having suffered the horror of an Irish raid I knew the risks those farming below were taking.

My mother rushed up; arms open wide. It was a comfort to feel them around me again. She looked older and had a sprinkle of grey hairs but was still slim and fair. There were three children at her skirts, two were Einion's daughters along with my sturdy half-brother, almost three now. She carried another child, my baby half-sister in her arms. I was pleased to meet them and spent time chucking the little one's chin and tummy. I wrestled with my half-brother; to his delight I let him win.

Mother and I walked away from Einion, who was pointing out all of interest on the wide horizon to Math.

'How are you really Mother?'

'I am well, very well. I never thought to be happy in this life, but Einion is kind, we are a good match.'

Her dark eyes searched mine. 'And you, my son, why are you here? You are still not confirmed as a priest?'

'No, I don't feel ready. I'm not sure of my faith. I don't know what I want of life Mother. Math and I are travelling to Ireland, to try to find my friend Maewyn Succus; a pupil from the school. We hope we know where he is held captive.'

My mother looked thoughtful and asked, 'Why is Math here with you, as your friend?'

We started as Math replied from behind us, 'Yes Inne, but also because I took your advice. I married the girl as you said. Wyn, the boy we seek is my brother-in-law.'

She turned. 'Are you glad you wed?'

'To my surprise I am. I never expected to be content, after, well everything. It was good advice and I am glad I listened. I have two sons and our mines are thriving. I am a wealthy, satisfied man, running to fat. And you Inne; you have more children?'

Looking at Math not me, Mother replied, 'I have. I love them dearly, but on the matter of children, I have a favour to ask. I have had no word from Ria for many months. It is odd, there must be a travelling priest who could write for her, she scribes herself come to that. I would not expect much, but to have heard nothing feels wrong. I worry. Ria married Fionn, a chieftain in Connacht. Please could you go check all is well with her?'

Mother looked tearful as she asked her favour. I put my hand on hers.

'Of course, we will. I'd like to see my sister too.'

'It would be such a relief. Ria is a woman now, seventeen. She may have children of her own.' Her voice trailed off but I noticed her hold Math's eye.

We rested one night in that strange fortress among the stones. Before we left, I tried to give Mother my hound, Tas.

She refused. 'Take both dogs; the Dal Riata tribe are fierce and who knows what perils Connacht may hold. I will rest easier knowing you have them to protect you.'

Her little son's face was so disappointed I had to laugh.

'I will send you a puppy of your very own to train, little one. Tas will need to be bred soon.'

Einion offered to accompany us to the port on Mona. He travelled his lands constantly and would have visited in the following weeks, with or without us. We would have an easier trip with him. I'd listened with interest as Math and Einion discussed how to deter the Picts.

Math said, 'The only thing that will stop war bands coming, is if the trouble and risks are so great that they can find easier picking elsewhere.'

Einion sighed, 'Our problem is that for raiders from Ireland, the Picts and Scots, we are that easy place. The south of Wales and the lands beyond are better for plunder but further. My coastline is long and my warriors are few.

I half suspected Einion escorted us because he wanted to show me that he did have comfortable palaces. That my mother was not forced to live in a stone hut on the windiest mountain in Wales. We descended into fertile green countryside to see Wyddfa, mountain of legend, in the distance. Lakes glistened at her feet; her head hidden then revealed as clouds chased across the sky.

Wyddfa was said to be the burial place of giants and was the haunt of fairy folk and a dragon. Few cared to climb the steep slopes, else they were caught and eaten by that monster serpent. Her peaks were still capped in snow, although midsummer was near.

By late afternoon we reached the remains of a fine villa with far-reaching views across the water. It stood outside the vicus surrounding Roman Segontium, an abandoned army camp. Once a beautiful home, it crumbled, rooms barely kept up and furnished, only shadows of its past glory remained.

'Your mother loves this palace Maelon, but when the May trees blossom, we know raiders will come. That we have to retreat inland or to the hills.'

There was still daylight after we ate, so we rode east to view Mona across some straights. The tide had turned, there were eddies and whirlpools and a rush of water between the shores. It looked so close, two hundred paces away but we could see the dangers of attempting the short crossing in the fast tidal race. Safer to travel from the harbour near Segontium, across still waters and around the island.

Next day we journeyed to a town set below a headland at the far end of the Mona. Einion negotiated our crossing to Ireland on a ship leaving on the morning's tide. We spent an uncomfortable night in a steady drizzle on the little craft's deck, using its sheep-fat soaked sails as blankets. I wondered what dangers the future would hold.

A brisk wind pushed the craft north west. I felt nauseous, then vomited miserably, much to the crew's amusement. They said most who were new to the sea were affected by such sickness. The ship's master insisted he would land us at the very limits of the Úi Neill territory. He refused to put into a port, saying it was a pagan place and cursed.

Late in the day, the boat drew close into a sandy shore; breakers pushing the craft ever landward. A stone anchor was thrown over the side to hold against the tide, the master was keen to turn back. He threw our baggage down to us as we stood waist-deep in a cold swell and pointed to a settlement in the distance, Latharne.

'Good luck. You'll need it,' he called over the widening distance. The boat sailed away as we stared inland.

'Come on then,' said Math. 'Let's get to the town before dark, and see if it this tribe are as fearsome as they say. I'm guessing they will be men much as we.'

He whistled cheerfully as we set off; we'd agreed our story on the ship. He might be remembered, even here, as Niall's champion.

He had fought Dal Riata warriors in Tara's tournaments in the years before his slavery. There was no chance I would be known, so I would play at being his servant. It would help find Wyn. A slave was more likely known by other servants and slaves. It is best to lie as little as possible when spying, so we agreed to say my mother was Welsh, try to tempt people into talking of others of our nation hereabouts.

As Math predicted, Latharne was a settlement much like any other. A dozen or so fishing boats were pulled above the tide line up, their fields were well kept, spread with seaweed manure. People seemed fearful and hurried inside their huts, until Math called out greetings in Irish; then they looked suspicious and unwelcoming.

We explained we wanted shelter for the night and to buy horses if they had them, mules if they did not. We were directed to a hut of a surly middle-aged woman. Her red chapped hands gutted mackerel at lightning speed, scales and guts falling into a fly-blown bucket. Beside it, on a hazel frame were dozens of fish carcasses, split ready for smoking.

She reluctantly agreed we could buy bread, ale and fish soup. When Math produced a silver bar and grudgingly cut off slivers to pay, she cheered up.

'Your accent told me you were from the Úi Neill lands. The Úi Neill's take what they please and leave. I didn't believe you'd pay, until I saw your silver. We hate those southerners. Our lords demand more and more for the Úi Neill tribute. We have hardly enough left to feed ourselves.'

'Of course, I pay. Why wouldn't I. The Úi Neills are fair kings. Don't they protect you from raids and take their reasonable portion in recompense?'

'Huh, we have to protect ourselves from the Picts, they do nothing,' she scoffed.

Wiping her hands on a sacking cloth, she disappeared into an adjacent hut to return with warm flatbread and steaming wooden bowls of delicious fish soup, flavoured with wild garlic. There was even honeyed mead. Not as badly off as she claimed, I reflected. We asked for directions to Sliabh Mis and where we might buy horses.

'I'll find horses if you will recompense us.' She was smiling, more friendly now she anticipated a fine profit. Calling to a thin lad of twelve years or so, she said, 'Boy, go to the smith. Tell him I have strangers who will pay well if he wishes to sell his mare and pony.'

We were forced to agree an exorbitant price for a mangy brown horse, long in the tooth and well past its prime. We also bought a scrawny black and grey pony. Crotchety, it tried to nip me each time I came close. The burly smith was interested that Math planned to visit Lugh's Mountain.

'Fewer warriors come each year to visit the sanctuary. More worship the new god, Christ, the one some call Jesus. People hereabouts pleased that he was a fisherman, like them.'

Math didn't comment at this interpretation, but said it was the same all across Wales and Gaul. The man told us of his burdens, his complaint was the same as the woman's, the extra tribute asked for by the High King, Conall.

'Who tells you how much tribute is expected?', asked Math.

"Our chieftain Milchu, and he is told by the High King's tax collector, his Uncle Fiachrae; he of the swan,' came the reply.

Milchu's court was on a plain, a day's walk away. We stayed in the woman's home overnight, sleeping on pallets that stank of fish and set out next morning. We agreed a plan, to say Math was looking for new blood for his sheep stock in Wales. He'd offer an excellent price, but insist on a shepherd to look after them and as he was a countryman, we hoped to buy Wyn along with the animals.

We arrived at Milchu's dún at dusk, busy with the work of the evening meal. Above the gateway, I shivered at the sight of two fresh heads nailed to the timbers by their hair. Math shrugged, it was normal for enemies and thieves' heads to be displayed like that.

On asking for lodging, the traditional welcome for strangers was offered. Math, a warrior given a place at the chieftain's table. I was sent to eat with the servants.

I did my best to sound Welsh, making my voice lilt and sing; sounding different to the flat tones I heard around me. Sure enough, one of the men tending the evening meal was pleased to gossip.

'We have a troublesome shepherd out on the mountain from your homeland, a slave. Milchu loathes him. The boy has tried to run away three times, he keeps making for the sea. He'll be maimed or worse if he tries it again.'

Trying not to sound too interested, I asked if they knew where the shepherd came from.

'No, Dana may; she was fond of him. That's another reason he's disliked, he was too appealing to the women. When he first arrived, they doted on him. We don't like our women smiling at foreigners. Take a look at those heads on the gateway if you don't believe me.'

He glared at me as he spoke.

'I'll be gone soon, so I'd have to work fast,' I quipped.

The joke got a hard stare rather than a laugh. I left the cook to stir his juniper and mutton scented cauldron and went to search out the herdsmen and stable boys.

Two riders on sturdy black mounts trotted up to the dún. I stopped in my tracks. Both men carried a shield on which was painted a swan's neck. I followed them to an enclosure for the horses and saw them fling their reins to a lad standing at the gate. Clearly, they were well known. I was invisible as a servant; the two brushed past me to make their way to Milchu's hall.

I asked the boy, 'How is my master's horse? You're busy, do you want me to lend a hand?'

He replied, 'Yes, please. Those two bastards often come here and act like they own these stables. They never reward us with coin or thanks. Expect their horses to be fed, groomed and watered; as if we are their slaves.'

'Arses,' I sympathised. 'Who are they? It's an unusual sign on their shields?'

'Fiachrae's men; he's the tax collector for the new High King. The bastard who squeezes the country dry with his demands.' I nodded and kept on brushing. 'I've been told I have a countryman living nearby, Welsh like me. Maybe I'll meet up with him later. Talk in my own tongue for an hour or two.'

'There is a Welsh slave, but he's alone out on the Sliabh with his sheep, miles away. Lord Milchu doesn't like him here.' He grinned. 'That's because the lad flirted with the king's favourite. Lovely girl, the king preferred her to his wife, but Dana smiled back at the slave! He keeps trying to escape. Our chieftain hates him. Say's Mae is going to rot on that hill until he's old and grey.'

I was delighted. Everything I'd been told about this shepherd sounded like Wyn. Even his name, Maewyn, had been shortened but to Mae, by the clan. It had to be him. I searched out Math, who I found sitting in the hall plying the newcomers with beer. He filled their cups filled more often than his. Listening, I gathered he'd told them he was a warrior from Connacht, in Aed's service.

Towards the end of the evening, one drunkenly threw an arm around his shoulder.

'You seem a brave man. Might you and Lord Aed be interested in joining us, do you think?'

Math replied, 'Joining who? Not sure I understand?'

'Would you want to take part in Fiachrae's uprising. He is a better man than his nephew; older, wiser and stronger. We have the North with us and many Connacht chieftains. Your master would be welcome. We will be dividing the spoils very soon and have been promised land.'

'I will certainly tell Lord Aed of your offer. How would he let Fiachrae know he will support him?'

The other slurred, 'Tell him to meet him before the summer gathering at Tara, and swear his loyalty.'

He burped and fell asleep, head slumped, a thin dribble of saliva running from the corner of his mouth. The other man was already lying flat on the table, snoring gently. Math signalled to me and we made our way outside.

'Troubling information, we can't talk about it here, we'll wait until tomorrow. Have you discovered anything of my brother-in-law?'

'I'm certain Wyn is here, they even call him Mae, short for Maewyn. He's herding sheep on Sliabh Mis.'

As dawn broke Math shook awake the stable boy and told him we were off to Lugh's shrine at the top of the sacred mountain. The boy called out that we might see the famous shepherd and winked at me. Once alone, we walked beside our mounts and exchanged information. What was this about the demands for more tribute from my brother Conall? It didn't sound at all likely. What was going on?

Math made a guess. 'Fiachrae is keeping back tribute and stoking discontent. He is a treacherous bastard. We have to journey to Tara and warn your brothers. I was bound to Tara, as captain of the household warriors. I can't, in all conscience, let my old comrades down; allow them to be surprised and slaughtered.'

Sliabh Mis was a strange sight; a lone conical mound with a flattened summit. It rose from a windswept plain, its peak covered with vast grey boulders. Gnarled hawthorns, fairy trees, circled the dark summit and deep gashes ran down its slopes. It would be a cold, eerie place to live. A cutting wind from the east circled and swooped, making us shiver. There was no sign of sheep as we climbed, but once we reached the peak we saw white specks on the sheltered western slopes, but there was no sign of a shepherd.

As loudly as I could I sang out an old Welsh goat song Wyn and I had sung together as youngsters:

"Oes gafr eto;

Is there another goat?

That's not been milked?

On the craggy rocks

The old goat is wandering

To my relief, a faint response came floating back on the cold wind.

Gafr wen, wen, wen,

White, white, white goat."

I ran down the slope to find a painfully thin young man with a slave neck ring standing in front of me. He was dressed in rags, barefoot, black hair matted, a thin beard reaching his chest, flea-bitten skins were slung over his head and back. He stank of sheep. It was Wyn and he looked desperate.

He blinked up at me; speaking slowly, as if he'd lost his use of his tongue. 'Who is it? Are you Welsh?'

'Wyn, it's me, Maelon. Don't you recognise me? We have been searching for you all these years, at last, you are found.' I beamed with delight and relief.

Wyn looked bemused. 'Maelon, from school? Maelon?'

He seemed to stumble. He had fallen to his knees and was weeping, his hands clasped together in thanks. I put an arm around him and shortly he looked up.

'I have prayed to the Lord for this moment. My pleading has been answered. I am looking at the face of a friend.'

I was taken aback and saddened to see him so reduced. I struggled to think of what to say.

'I have your brother-in-law with me. Your sister Metella has married, this is Math her husband. We have come to take you home.'

Wyn shook his head doubtfully. 'It won't be easy. Lord Milchu hates me. He won't let me go free. He hunched with fear. 'Milchu promised I would lose a hand if I try to escape again.'

'Would he sell you to us? We've brought gold from your father?'

'No, he dislikes me too much. I made a mistake and injured his honour. Pride is everything to the Irish.'

Math spoke, 'We don't have time to negotiate and insufficient gold to make a ransom irresistible. Milchu has no idea that we know you. We should run; we have two horses and can travel fast. Once we reach Maelon's brothers' land we will be safe, it's not so far. If we leave tomorrow, we should have a day, maybe more, before they notice you are gone.

'We'll rid you of your slave collar, cut your hair, shave you, and dress you in proper clothes. You must not be recognisable. If you speak Latin, rather than Welsh or Irish we can say you are sent from Gaul to Bishop Palladius. We will change your name. Until we return to Wales, we'll call you Patricius, the priest. Once we are out of Dal Riata territory, I'll shave your head so you look like a man of god. You'll be unrecognisable.'

Wyn looked scared but agreed it was his best chance. His sheep would have to look after themselves until Milchu discovered he was gone.

I took food out from my bag, along with the metal file his father had packed. I offered bread to Wyn, now to be called Patricius. Gaunt and famished though he seemed, he reached for the file.

'Please remove my neck ring. I am hungry, but have dreamed of freedom for long years.'

He blinked at us. 'There are so many questions, so much to tell, but I don't have words. I am so glad to see friendly faces at last.'

Weeping, he gestured to his shackle. I started to file away at its thinnest point, handing over to Math when I tired. It took over an hour, the rasping, screeching made me wince. What Wyn felt with that sound so close to his ear was unimaginable. Finally, it fractured. Math put out a hand to stop Wyn ripping it off.

'Wait, if anyone sees you without your iron collar, they will know. Leave it until we are ready to depart. Maelon and I will go back to Milchu's hall overnight. Be ready to leave early.'

As I led our horses and my two hounds back into the stable, the same boy asked if I had found my countryman.

'No, the flock was spread far from the summit. My master wouldn't let me search for him. Made me stay with the horses while he went to the shrine to collect his sling-stones. We leave tomorrow at first light.'

The boy grimaced sympathetically and agreed to have our horses fed and ready at dawn. I'd told him Math would reward him well for getting up early.

There was no sign of Fiachrae's men at the table that night. Math casually asked Milchu whether he was going to the summer gathering.

He replied with a grin, 'Oh yes, I wouldn't miss that for anything. All the lords hereabouts are planning to be there; with as many warriors as they can manage. We will give him his just tribute.'

My heart beat with trepidation for my brother at the veiled threat in his words. We had to get back to Tara to warn Conall, but first, there we had to help Wyn get away from his captors.

We set off early the next morning. Math flicked the stable lad a decent sliver of silver; likely more than he had ever seen before. We told him we were going east to the coast, following the road past the holy mountain. We hoped if we were pursued, they would search the wrong road, the boy was unlikely to forget what we told him.

Wyn waited impatiently on the mountainside. The farm overseer had called to check on the flock the evening before, so it was as well he had not removed his slave collar. Two sheep had been taken to feed Milchu's dún. Wyn doubted anyone would look for him for at least a day, maybe much longer.

'It is isolated here. I speak to no one for days at a time. I have nothing to do but watch the skies and listen to the animals.

You'll laugh Maelon, but praying to the Lord has been my only consolation these last years. The dolt who never took Cedric's preaching and lessons seriously. I found myself remembering Christ's words. I was comforted by repeating them.'

As we spoke, he pulled at his neck ring, throwing it into a deep peaty pool. He took off his filthy clothes and was about to throw them in after it. Math stopped him.

'We will take your clothes with us. If they find them floating here, they will guess you had help. The sheepskin will be good to sleep on anyway. We handed him clean robes. Wyn and I rode the brown horse for as long as we dared without exhausting the old animal. Math the heaviest, rode astride the bad tempered pony. By mid-morning we had covered several miles, so alternated, either Math or I walked. Wyn was too weak to stride out.

Once we had crossed the River Bhanna we were in safer territory. Math shaved my friend's forehead and crown, leaving a traditional long lock of hair falling at his nape, then Wyn's unkempt shaggy beard. The young man before us was finally recognisable as the boy I had known so well years ago.

We travelled south and then east, straight to Tara to warn Conall about the planned attack at the summer gathering. Each night as we sat around a small camp-fire, Wyn told us his tale. I found it hard to think of Wyn as Patricius back then.

He said, 'That night… the night the Irish came was terrible. It was dusk, we had finished vesper prayers. I was looking forward to supper, the cooking pot wafting a flavoursome scent of game when I heard a menacing rumble in the distance. It was as if drums were being beaten but with a flatter note. I'd never heard anything like it before.

Math and I exchanged glances; hilt on shield, drumming to sound attack.

'Then there were shouts everywhere, torches lit the sky; huge, bearded men brandishing axes and swords surrounded us. They came from nowhere; it was so sudden.

'I saw two brothers in Christ kneel to pray for mercy. The Irish showed no pity, both were struck down. They skewered them as they knelt, their lifeblood spurting everywhere. Then they looked for more monks. Johannes was struggling out of the church with his gospels. His brains must have been knocked out by the blow one gave him using an axe handle as a cudgel. I saw the raider laugh as he fell.'

He shuddered. 'I was lucky. I'd taken up a staff and was trying to defend two of the servants when I was grabbed from behind. An iron grip held me, I felt an arm around my neck, I could barely breathe. There was more laughter as I struggled. Someone kicked my legs away and trussed me with a rope, tied my hands tightly behind my back.'

I watched as Wyn rubbed his wrists. His face twisted in horror at his memories.

'I saw Cedric being dragged towards the oak. They were beating him, asking him questions, demanding to know where someone... was.'

He looked at his feet, there was a pause. We both knew who the raiders had been searching for that awful night. Tortured green eyes stared into mine. I dipped my head to tell him I already knew.

'They put Cedric's head in a noose and threatened him again. I heard him begin to pray, ignoring their blows and threats. They began to cut at him then started pulling at the rope. He was teetering on tiptoes reciting the Lord's Prayer. I heard one shout that he'd heard enough nonsense about Jesus and he kicked away Cedric's feet. They hauled him up, as he strained desperately for breath. Their leader, a slim man with a pox-scarred face and long moustache, went over to him. He offered the Abod a last chance to tell him where... where you were. Cedric shook his head on last time. Enraged, the cruel bastard cut at him with a slim blade, ripping open his habit and belly in one slash. I saw a splash of dark red spill out, then couldn't bear to look.'

He turned away from the fire, trying to sleep, overwhelmed by his story. I didn't attempt to rest. After I'd seen Cedric's body hanging from that oak all those years ago, I hadn't thought anything could make that memory worse. I was wrong. Now I knew; Cedric had died refusing to tell Nathi where I was. My body flushed with anger and shame. Guilt that I was to blame for so much misery engulfed me.

The following night Wyn took his tale up again. 'Most of the pupils and some servants were captured and tied up. They slaughtered the oldest priests and servants, who were worthless as slaves. Then we were marched to the beach. I stumbled along the path, trying to keep upright, roped at the ankle to someone behind and in front. There were three boats on our shore. We were made to walk into the sea, hauled up and thrown onto the deck. Llyr and I were separated from Bledd and the other pupils and put on a different craft. My boat headed north and put into a bay many hours later.

'We were thrown into the water, hands still tied behind our backs. As Llyr tried to scramble ashore, a huge swell hit. He and two others were sucked out by churning surf. Their balance and strength hampered by the ropes that tied them together. Llyr fell, he hit his head on the side of a boat and was swept away deeper and deeper. I caught glimpses of all three struggling to keep their heads above the waves. The raiders tried to reach them but couldn't. Llyr perished in that bleak place. I was left standing alone on an Irish beach, abandoned by God and everything I knew.

'In the slave market we were stripped naked. Humiliated, I cowered with embarrassment, cold and fear in front of crowds of people coming to buy or to enjoy our shame. I was inspected and prodded by several men, but bought by a greasy, fat warrior, Milchu.

'I worked with the cooks at first and life was comfortable enough. I picked up the Irish dialect and made friends, but knew I had to get away.

'My first attempt was a disaster.' His face showed irritation. 'I got lost and headed the wrong way, inland! I only got as far as Sliabh Mis before I was caught. My slave collar marked me instantly. I was dragged back to Milchu, who ordered me beaten. I got such a thrashing I couldn't walk for a week. When I could move, I was sent to the stables as punishment. It was there my real troubles began. I looked after Milchu's horses and his wife and concubines liked to ride.'

I realised an eyebrow at him. Of course, Wyn would not have been able to resist charming them.

'Yes, you are right Maelon, I did always flirt, didn't I? The prettiest, Dana, started to warm to me. She would wait for me to finish my work and meet me returning to the dún, or come out to watch me groom the horses. We became,' he coughed, 'friendly.'

'Milchu noticed Dana smiling at me; one time she gave me a little wave. She was smitten and I was flattered. I was stupid, we were caught kissing one summer evening. After another thrashing he sent me away to herd sheep on the mountain. People were forbidden to speak to me, I was left to rot. It was so miserable that I tried to flee once more, and was retaken. I was warned I'd be tortured, then killed if I tried again.'

As the fire crackled, Math and Wyn spoke of their shared experience of slavery and Christ. Math described his time in the mines and how much satisfaction it gave him to spare others now. How good he felt when he gave a man his freedom.

'In those pits, I knew Lugh did not care for me and I despaired. He loves only warriors, there is no forgiveness for the weak or even the unlucky. I came to need a gentler god, one who would accept everyone. Who would let anyone enter his otherworld, heaven if you like.'

Math talked of Wyn's parents, sister, and nephews; said there would be land and wealth waiting when Wyn returned to Wales.

'No, I shan't return home for long. For years, I saw only one mountain, in snow, frost and rain. I decided long ago if I regained freedom, I would travel.' He hesitated. 'Help people find Christ perhaps, but I want to see towns and cities, visit centres of learning. There was nothing to do but watch over sheep day after day. It gave me time to pray, to search my heart.

'On my hillside, I experienced a vision.'

He glanced at us, as if checking we wouldn't ridicule him. Math nodded encouragingly.

'It was a cold night and the stars were bright. I saw a tall man approaching carrying a bundle of letters. I understood instantly it was Saint Victorius; it was as if his name had been spoken aloud. The saint rummaged through the sheets of parchment, extracted one and handed it to me. On it was written, The Voice of the

Irish. As I tried to read, I heard as clearly as I hear you, hundreds of people calling out from the Wood of Focluth many miles away by the western sea. They called, "We entreat you to come and walk amongst us."

My friend stared at us earnestly. 'So, you see I have no choice but become a priest. To do as that vision commanded. One day I will return to Ireland, I'll keep the name you have given me, Patricius; it fits somehow. You can stop calling me Wyn altogether. I'll have to give up women and that will be hard. I like their company as well as their pleasures.'

I had always been troubled by Math's conversion to Christ and was even more discomforted by the change in my friend. That Wyn of all people was proposing giving up women, to become chaste, seemed impossible.

One god didn't seem any better than another to me. Victorius may have appeared to Wyn, but as a child, I'd looked on the Goddess Macha's face. I understood Math feeling comforted by helping others, but Lugh of the Long Arm would think it a weakness.

Was Christ so different from our old gods? I couldn't accept that, despite my years with Sylvester and Cedric. I wasn't sure if I envied Math and Wyn their certainty, or despised them for being fools. I kept silent. I had little to contribute, but my soul wavered. If the two men I liked and respected most, as well as Abod Cedric, were convinced, was I wrong? Was Jesus the way?

CHAPTER
14

It took over two weeks, but at last, we reached Tara and were safe. When the familiar walls and hills appeared, my heart sang. Home, does anywhere look quite as welcoming? How would Tara be with my father gone? Tara without the fearsome force that was Niall within its turf and timber enclosure was unthinkable. Would anyone recognise me? It had been ten years since I'd last walked through its forbidding gateway.

I swallowed and took a breath. The grizzled guard didn't recognise me, but he greeted Math at once.

'Math, can it be you after all these years? Welcome, welcome.'

He shouted to his fellows, 'It's Champion Math, returned to us.'

Math grinned, 'Good to see you too, but don't you recognise my companion?'

The guard stared at me. 'Lugh's blood, it is Little Lord grown to a man. When your brothers told us, you were King over the Sea, we doubted them. We thought you murdered like Ness's boys. We resented our little mascot and his hound leaving us at Niall's command. We believed your brothers' hands were stained with your blood.' He glanced briefly at Math and continued, 'Murder of brothers runs strong in Niall's line.'

Men were crowding around us. The words "Little Lord," "Niall's youngest" and "Math" circulated around the dùn, like a ripple from a pebble thrown in a pond. Someone was running, he flung his arms around me. It was short legged Finn, our hound master, stooped and older now. The sounds and smells of Tara enfolded me; I could hardly speak for happiness.

I called Tas and Beah to heel. 'Look, Finn, here are two of Kira's pups. I've never forgotten all you taught me. Soon I will tell you how Kira saved me from brigands, not once but twice.'

He shook his head in wonderment, speechless.

The crowd quietened and parted. Loegaire and Rignach were walking towards us. I looked at my brother, a man now, when I had left him a youth. He appraised the child also grown to manhood. We embraced, overcome. I turned to Rignach, frail, white-haired, iron and desolation in her eyes.

To my surprise she whispered fondly, 'It is good to see you Little Lord. Had you heard? Did you come to say farewell to Conall? He speaks of you often. He will be glad you are here.'

I looked questioningly at Loegaire.

'Conall is dying,' he sighed, 'a stupid accident. We were hunting last winter and he speared a fine wolf. It was lying under a tree, crows gathered cawing above, waiting for their share. The hounds had savaged it and we assumed it dead. The shrieks of Morrigan's birds should have warned us. As Conall bent, the animal turned with the last of its strength and snapped at his leg. A small injury, a scratch, but the wound festered. With each month it worsened; first redness climbing the limb, then pus and ooze. The poison has reached his groin, red boils inflame his body, he is weakening fast. We have tried every healer but none have helped. We try to keep hopeful, but...' he shook his head a second time.

'Can I see him?'

Rignach interjected, 'Yes, at once. He has a fever, when he is hot, he raves, but he has asked to see you many times. I thank sweet Boann you are here. I hope he recognises you; you have grown so tall. I will call you Little Lord as I always did, even though you're the same height as your brothers. It was the name my sons and I remembered you with. Your colouring is your mother's, none could miss such dark eyes, but I see Niall in your mouth and chin.'

She took my arm and led me into a dark corner of the hall. Set apart behind coloured woollen hangings was a raised bed. At first all I noticed was the appalling smell, foetid and sweet, of rotting meat and death. Then in the dim light I saw my brother, the High King. I would not have recognised him; horribly thin, his waxy skin showed outlines of bones beneath as if he was a skeleton already. Conall's cheeks burned red, a slick of sweat covered his brow. Holding his hand gently was a beautiful woman with hair the colour of ripe barley. She wore a necklace of golden bees, their red glass wings shimmered in the guttering light. She tried to make way for Rignach; who pushed her aside impatiently, reaching over to wipe her son's face. Loegaire looked irritated. I saw him bite back a complaint.

His eyes were adoring, as he said, 'Maelon this is my wife, Princess Lanthchilde, daughter to the King of the Franks. You will meet her properly later; spend time with our brother first.

'Conall, wake up. Look who is here. It is Little Lord, grown into a man.'

Conall stirred. With effort, he opened watery eyes and raised himself on the bed.

'Maelon, is it you, after all these years? My favourite younger brother; the puppy we cherished and spoilt.'

'It is me Conall, here with my hounds, grown older but no wiser. You must get better, so I can play more tricks on you. I will find some frogs for your beer horn.'

His laugh turned into a cough, then he collapsed back onto the skins.

'Your voice hasn't changed Maelon, deeper but it's you sure enough. I am glad to see you one last time, brother mine. I am sorry but you must make Loegaire suffer your toads and rose-hip itching seeds, my end is near. Let me give you back your hound arm-ring, I cannot call you to my side from the Otherworld.'

I suppressed a sob. My throat ached, closing with heartache. 'No, you must get better, you must. Keep that with you.'

He smiled but said no more, exhausted. It was hard to tell if he was awake or not in the half-light. His open eyes were rolled upward, unseeing, but faint breaths moved his chest. Rignach wept silently as I stroked his arm. I reminisced about our childhood; of riding across the countryside, him teaching me to make a fire, skin a deer, saving me from drowning in the River Boinne. I told him the truth; that he and Loegaire had taught me to be a man. He heard some, twice he gripped my hand in response.

After a while Rignach beckoned to me. 'Don't tire him too much. One of his wives will sit with him through the night. Come and eat, people are waiting.'

After she left, Conall roused and gripped my arm.

Hoarsely he begged, 'Protect my son and daughter, as our father protected you. They will not survive long unless you do.'

'I will, but Loegaire would too...'

'We sons of Niall breed children like dogs, there are too many of us feeding from the same bowl. My memory will fade. My children will not be safe. Mother is old, she has dozens of grandchildren. Please Maelon, you are my anum cara. Promise you will take them from this place, keep them safe until they are adults.'

I gave my oath as he lapsed back into unconsciousness. How could I refuse when he had called me soul friend?

I emerged from that dark fetid space, into the torch light, to the sound of cheers. Horns of ale and wooden drinking bowls were lifted in toast.

I was led to Loegaire who stood tall and proud. 'King over the Sea, Maelon mac Neill, we welcome you back to your brother's hall.'

There were many familiar faces, men I half recognised as well as strangers in that room. The chant, "Maelon, Maelon; Little Lord, Little Lord," filled the space.

I was overcome. I had felt abandoned and forgotten for over ten years, but I was remembered and fondly. As I sat and ate, I picked out familiar faces: Laidcenn our bard, the tall Brehon judge, face as impassive as ever, Finn my friend and hound master, hearth warriors, hostages and foster brothers.

The sounds of harp and drum, then soft voices, started to fill the air. Tunes and words half-forgotten flooded back, and with them came a sharp sadness for the loss of my home. I realised I'd never see my father presiding over the dún again. The knowledge of his death hit me hard. The loss became real. Niall, who had seemed all-powerful and everlasting was dead. How could that be? My grief surprised me. I thought I hated my father for rejecting and deserting me, but if I had, it was mixed with love and admiration; and now he was gone.

Once the meal was well underway I recovered my composure and spoke to Loegaire. 'I am afraid I have come on another matter entirely. I had no idea Conall was ill. I bring warnings of an uprising at midsummer. Math and I hoped to tell Conall, but now we must share it with you...'

'What, more trouble? Damnation, but I am relieved you had not heard of his injury. I have tried to suppress the tale. It weakens us. The death of a king is a time when others try to seize power. We can't talk here. Tell me about it tomorrow.'

In the morning, Loegaire and I returned to my poor brother's bedside and Patricius came with us. Conall was little changed, sweating, muttering and shouting to himself. The gagging scent of rot filled the room. Patricius offered to sit and pray for him, only to be roundly sworn at by Loegaire.

'We have no place for Christians in this court. My brother and I worship Lugh, not that soft and gentle foolishness you priests spout. Conall will join our warrior kin in the Otherworld, not slaves and peasants.'

Patricius bridled. I touched his arm warningly to prevent any reply.

As I sat beside my brother he woke. 'Was that a priest I heard you speak of?'

'Yes, well nearly. In truth both I and Patricius are novices. He has spent many years in prayer.'

'I would like him to bless me, we have no priest here now. I sent Palladius's man away. Since my injury, I have thought on all Sylvester taught us as children. I hope there is an afterlife, and there are many gods. I see no harm in asking for the blessing of Christ as well as the others. Do you?'

He looked so ill and frail; I told him I could see only comfort in a blessing.

Math, Loegaire, and I rode out with the hounds that afternoon; alone and far from Tara, we dismounted. We outlined the mood in northern lands and our suspicions that Fiachrae was raising taxes and fomenting discontent across the land. As we'd guessed Conall had not demanded, nor received additional tribute. Someone else was taking it, in all likelihood our uncle.

Loegaire looked thoughtful. 'The summer gathering you say? His timing could not be better, with Conall likely as not dead. The High Kingship was due to be confirmed at the Stone of Destiny then. Lugh strike Fiachrae dead.'

'I am certain our uncle was trying to find me when the monastic school was razed. A pox-marked man murdered my cousin the Abod, it had to be Nathi. I believe he sent a second party to search for me and killed more friends. It was no coincidental raid that destroyed my school.'

'There have been persistent rumours circulating that Conall and I ordered you dead. That we sent that raiding party to kill you. It made us unpopular, even in Tara; especially after the twins.'

'I heard they and Ness had died.'

'My mother, I'm afraid. She insisted Father had ordered her to do it. None of us knew what to think. Ness was sacrificed with Father, so he had comfort in the Otherworld. She went with him on the pyre, then the boys were poisoned.'

'I don't disbelieve Rignach. Father could well have told her to kill them. That night before I was sent away, he implied Ness and the twins were not important. That his marriage had been tactical. He married Ness to protect my mother and stop his sons fighting each other for the kingship. He was a wily fox.'

'Wolf more like, but that's what it takes to rule. I must be as ruthless as our father to survive. It seems you may need to be too. I'm relieved you think Mother was doing as he bid her, that it was not for spite.'

I shivered. Niall had warned me to be careful of Rignach. If she considered me a threat to her sons, she'd not hesitate to act. I had to make sure she thought me an ally, not a foe.

We returned to Tara in low spirits. As we rode towards the gates, we heard the wailing notes of horns and slow beat of drums. Conall was dead.

In the hall Rignach stood dry-eyed, ashes on her face and hair, desolate. She smiled weakly at Loegaire's approach.

'He is gone. It is a relief, as well as a knife to my heart. He has suffered so these last months. You are High King now, Loegaire. You two will wish to see your brother one last time.'

We passed through the hangings. Conall lay still in his eslene shirt, looking younger, at peace; little changed from the day I left ten years earlier.

Rignach said, 'He wanted you to have these,' handing me his pair of raven arm-rings, 'said you must take them to confirm your geis to him. Do you want this one back?'

She made to take my hound-headed ring from his arm, lifeless and limp on the furs.

'No, that hound ring must stay with him for the after-life, be placed with his grave goods. I will know him by it in the halls of the dead, as I will know Loegaire by its pair.'

I thought back to that Samhain tournament long ago when I'd won our arm-rings; how invincible and eternal I'd thought

Conall then. He was gone from this life too soon. I fought back tears. Niall's son could not cry in front of others, especially in Tara.

Loegaire nodded in agreement then ordered, 'Prepare to mourn the High King. Make ready the funeral games and feasts. My brother must be welcomed into the halls of the dead with honour. I will send to my uncle Fiachrae first. He and his family must come to pay respects, as Conall's chief levier and right hand. A little later, I will inform our uncles and older brothers. I'll deal with Fiachrae first.'

He bent towards Rignach to explain.

The intervening seven days were spent preparing. Conall's women stayed at his feet keening, afraid. Any or all of them might accompany their husband on his pyre. Conall's body was closely guarded so no evil spirits could harm it; rushes were lit throughout the night to keep them away.

Loegaire and Rignach decided that the mothers of his son and daughter were to be spared. Two lesser wives along with two concubines were prepared for a final journey with their husband. Patricius was outraged. He and Loegaire clashed again.

'How can you kill four young women? It is cruel beyond imagining. Conall had a good life, he will be blessed and go to heaven.'

'This is our custom. We follow the old ways in Tara, priest, the right ways. We do not bury bodies and let them rot. Shades haunt this earth and find no rest if not released.'

'You will be damned and go to purgatory if you murder those women in cold blood, Loegaire.'

'My brother needs women to please him and wait on him in the Otherworld. I'd happily send you to join him, if your constant whining wouldn't make the afterlife a misery,' growled Loegaire.

I pulled Patricius away. Told him not to anger my brother or he might be flayed, for all he was my friend.

Over the next week, I spent hours with old Finn who reacquainted me with the pack. Forty of the best hounds in Ireland, trained to hunt, maim and kill. We took them ranging out across the woods and hills each day. Game would be needed to feed the Irish chieftains, kings and their retainers coming for the funeral rites.

Finn complimented me. 'He's a grand hound Beah, ready to become the leader of this pack. If you were not leaving that is what I would ask. I am proud of the way you have trained him. You're as skilled as I was at your age. You could be hound master and take the dogs to war if you wished. Your sister Ria, she loved the pack too.'

Instantly, he had my attention. 'How was my sister when you saw her last?'

'I'm glad you asked. I wanted to talk to you about her. Your sister, well, some speak ill of her. Don't give what they say credence. It is true she behaved badly at times; especially with Rignach, who loathed her. She was young and wild. If she'd been a boy, they'd have admired her for it. Rignach was afraid she'd steal one of her precious sons' hearts. Ria had no interest in those men, her brothers. She knew it for a sin. She was lonely when you left. She wanted to leave this place and her kin. She was right to go. She was not safe here once Niall died.

'Don't accept everything Rignach tells you as the truth, that's all I'm saying. Ria's tough, difficult even, she had to be, but at heart, she is a good girl.'

In two days time horsemen arrived; Fiachrae, with his son Nathi and two grandsons. The youngsters Loegaire sent to the boys hut to await the funeral. He went to the round guest hut at the corner of the settlement. Math and I had been asked to wait outside, to hide in the shadows. The foursome had left their swords at the guardhouse, as was customary. They were unarmed and unprepared.

'Welcome Uncle, Cousin,' said Loegaire. 'It is a sad day, but I am pleased you have come to say farewell to my brother.'

'Sad indeed. Conall lived barely twenty-seven summers, he was many years Nathi's junior. Kingship is a heavy burden for a youth, and you, Loegaire, are younger yet.'

'Indeed Uncle but command is a weight I intend to continue to bear. I will be High King, as my brother and father would have wished. I will need an honest levier.'

'If the chieftains and kings of Ireland confirm the high kingship at Tara at the summer gathering, I will be pleased to continue in that role,' replied Fiachrae smoothly.

'Honest, the word has many meanings to you then, Uncle?'

Loegaire drew out his sword, spinning it slowly in his hand.

Startled, Fiachrae barked, 'What do you imply by that? Put that weapon down. Are you trying to intimidate me, your elder?'

'Word has reached me that the tribute demanded from the north and west has increased year by year. That was strange news because my brother had not asked for, nor received additional tribute or cattle. More than that, I am informed that at this summer gathering you plan an uprising.'

Fiachrae blustered back. 'Who could have suggested such a thing. How can you believe the word of spies rather than family?'

'Ah, but the news comes from family. It comes from my brother, Maelon, King over the Sea. Who should I believe? My blood-sworn brother or an uncle renown for treachery?'

I stepped forward; Fire Fury hissed menacingly as I pulled it from its sheath.

'Fiachrae, Uncle, I imagine you must be pleased to see me. You sent ships to Wales in search of me. Now I stand here before you.'

'Why is it you Maelon, son of the Welsh Queen? Yes, it is. You have the look of my brother about you.'

A bead of perspiration formed above his left eyebrow. Nathi's fists and jaw were clenched, veins standing out on his temples. Muscles twitched on his upper arm bringing his tattoos to life.

'After Father's death there was a raid on my school, pupils were taken as slaves. I found my Abod cousin hanging dead from an oak when I returned. The same story was given by every survivor; men with white swans on their shields came, murdered and stole. They asked for Maelon mac Neill. A pox-scarred man killed my cousin, slit open his belly.' I stared down Nathi.

Math emerged from the shadows.

'Death stalks you Fiachrae. You talk of family but what have you to say to me, son of Brion, the brother slain on your orders?'

'Math,' whispered Nathi, his face drained of colour, his anger deflated.

'It was good of you to bring your sons to us,' said Loegaire conversationally. 'My father was levier of hostages, now I have two more boys to join their number.'

He smiled menacingly. 'Here is what's going to happen. This year there will be no summer gathering. That is because you have been skimming our tribute already. The country is groaning and complaining, so you will pay the entire amount for them. The people will only know it is good King Conall's last gift. That is the story I will announce across Ireland. I expect no rebuttal. You have stolen more than enough from the Úi Neill's to cover it. You will support me when I claim the High Kingship or else you will have no grandsons, no son either.

'You are not required at my brother's funeral. You were plotting to kill Conall. My cousin will represent you and stay awhile with us; he'll be very secure. He will enjoy every comfort a small hut can bring.' Loegaire gave a thin-lipped smile, 'Oh and if you try any uprising, your lands fall forfeit. I will share them between Math; your murdered brother's son and Maelon.'

Fiachrae turned, eyes unrelenting, burning with hate. 'Nathi killed Brion and his sons on Niall's orders. Their blood was not on my hands alone. He felt guilt too, why do you think he let Math live after Inne was unfaithful? Niall punished Math for it, but not with death. He preferred dishonour. He ordered me to arrange for Math to be left behind on that raid, so he'd be killed or taken as a slave. He didn't want to look on his treacherous seducer's face any longer. Niall couldn't bear to be the cuckold but he was soft. I'd have killed Math straight off.' He snorted, 'None of us are truly innocent, are we? Except maybe for that boy, Maelon, but given his parentage, I doubt he'll stay so.'

He strode out. Math looked at us mutely, then walked away.

I turned to Loegaire, 'You knew all this didn't you?'

'That Father sent Math to slavery? Yes, Mother told me. Math bedded your mother. Lugh's breath, most men would have killed them both. It was lucky for her the child was a girl.

'I didn't know he'd ordered Brion and his sons killed, but I'm not surprised. You have to be ruthless to be High King. You know that, but you don't have that heartlessness. People in Tara love you for being genial, a clown; it's why you were sent away. You are fortunate, Conall and I, we have to suffer and rule, we can't stop. We are rich, powerful and …afraid, always afraid.'

We parted; Loegaire to oversee his kingdom, me to wander my old home in a daze. I called to Tas and Beah, trying to think straight.

Math emerged from a copse of trees. 'We both discovered dark secrets today, Maelon.'

I shook my head, 'You and Mother? I knew you loved her, but not for how long. You may be Ria's father? That's why Mother asked you to see her and check all is well?'

'Yes, I'm sorry Maelon, it seems long ago now. I loved Inne more than life back then. She loved me too. We knew the risks. We thought Niall unaware; we should have known he would find out eventually. Guilt over my father's death can be the only reason he spared me. I was the last of his brother's line. I don't blame Niall for abandoning me to slavery. To order the death of your own brother though! The gods will not forgive that crime. What will he say to my father when they meet in the Otherworld?'

I sought out Rignach later that evening. Sitting alone in her hut she looked old and defeated. I held her hands as she cried for Conall, watching tears track slowly down deeply wrinkled skin, wetting her skirts. Eventually, her weeping stopped.

'Thank you, Little Lord, my sons would not think to comfort me. They will expect me to bear this loss with pride and be strong.'

'I am sorry Rignach, for you and Conall's wives and children, but also for myself. He was a wonderful brother, he protected me, taught me and loved me when we were boys. I pined for him and Loegaire when I was sent to Wales. At times like this, I feel closer to Christ, a god who gives comfort to those who are left. Would you like me or Patricius to pray with you?'

'Thank you,' she patted my hand. 'No, the old gods are a comfort to me, not this new Jesus. He's too soft and kind for an Irish Queen... I have done things your Christ might find hard to forgive, but Lugh and Macha would understand. I will feast with Conall and Niall, made young and comely again in the afterlife.'

I nearly said Christ would forgive all but knew it would not please her, so changed the subject.

'Can I ask you about my sister, about Ria?'

She raised an eyebrow in query, agreeing.

'Mother is worried about her. She's had no letters, nor word, nothing, for months. She is anxious something is amiss. She asked Math and me to look for her. I learnt Math may be Ria's father.'

Rignach sighed, 'So the truth is out..., you know. I'm afraid that's why I took less trouble with her marriage than I should. If I'd been certain she was Niall's child, I'd have insisted she married a king and ensured her safety. Ria was young and impetuous. She married a Connacht chieftain warrior called Fionn. He came at Beltane for the spring tournament and was the first to ask for her. Ria was nothing but a nuisance in Tara, so we agreed. Princelings and chieftains fight in Connacht all the time, lands are constantly won and lost, it is a wild place. He was a wild man, needed to be, to tame that girl. If Ria had been my daughter, I'd have made her wait; be sure of her mind.

'After Niall died nothing mattered to me; when the girl insisted, it was a relief. Everything was grey. Many days I wish I'd gone with him to the pyre, not Ness. I should be with him in the Otherworld, not her. I wouldn't have had to watch Conall die if I had been. I loved Niall, as well as hated him. I gave him seven sons and then he took that child Ness to wife.

'I am sorry, I should have done better for Inne, she would have for me. I don't know what's become of your sister. Well, since you know now, in all likelihood your half-sister. I will find out. Many people will travel to Tara for Conall's wake.'

The kings, princes and chieftains of Ireland arrived at Tara over the coming days, to send off the young High King to his next life. My brothers and remaining two uncles were among them. I worried that one would try for the high kingship but they seemed content to allow Loegaire to remain in Tara.

I heard that Milchu arrived, but as a minor chieftain, he camped far from our walls. Games were held in Conall's honour, with the bards singing tales of his valour. Most verses recounted our father and grandfather's deeds. Conall's reign was too brief for glory.

Patricius tried again to persuade Loegaire that Conall's wives should live. The argument ended with Patricius cursing Loegaire and his descendants.

'I swear that God will punish you. No son of yours will rule this land if you send those women to their deaths.'

Loegaire had scoffed, laughed in his face; but late that night one of his wives, Angias had come to our guest hut. She begged Patricius to relent, holding out her sleeping boy, Lugaid, crying for mercy.

My friend acquiesced. 'If you raise this child in the way of Christ, there can be no curse. Jesus is a forgiving god. He will not harm your son.'

Patricius railed at me because I refused to even attempt to persuade my brother not to burn the women.

'Abod Cedric instilled in me never to fight battles I stand no chance of winning Patricius.'

It was true that nothing would change Loegaire's mind and it shut him up, but I felt ashamed. I knew perfectly well Cedric had not meant a battle of this kind. I did not dare admit to Patricius that I would light the pyre, standing beside my brothers. How would I'd feel knowing living women would die at my hand? If I refused, I'd disrespect Conall. Everyone would think me a weakling. That thought, that they'd say I was too soft for a warrior, for a son of Niall, was unbearable to me.

The seventh day following Conall's death dawned bright and dry. Flocks of sheep and two white oxen had been slaughtered, then set to roast; rendered fat set aside to feed the pyre. The plaintive sounds of drumming and wailing carried over Tara's halls at sunset. Conall's body was taken in slow procession to a mountain of kindling and logs. Closest kin took up positions of honour. We tried not to choke as the breeze blew over the bier of oak branches and skins towards us. His leg and body had continued to putrefy; the corpse stunk horribly of death.

Conall's two barren wives and two concubine slaves followed him; dressed as if for marriage, wearing bright fabrics from over the seas and fine linen; garlands of ivy adorned each woman's head. They had been fed poppy juice with mushrooms and sloes soaked in Gaulish wine as a final meal; told they would live a life of ease and pleasure in the king's hall of the Otherworld with Conall ever after.

Druids and filídh led by Laidcenn chanted incantations and lamentations over my brother. His favourite hound and horses' throats had been slit and bodies placed beside him, along with bread and honey for his last journey. The women clambered clumsily up onto the wood pile, taking places at the head and foot of his corpse. They were set to kneel, gagged and tied firmly into position. One made a pathetic attempt at flight, fluttering like an injured bird from a cat. She was clubbed down and set in her place unconscious. Laidcenn threw jars of precious scented oils from lands far away, onto the pyre.

My brothers and I each lit a sacred gorse wood torch and threw them into the mound. I winced as seven flames took hold. The bonfire cracked and sparked in the trembling twilight. The women's dresses caught light, then their hair; its acrid smell stung our throats. Finn set the war hounds to howl. The blaze's smoke danced higher, obscuring then revealing glimpses of bodies.

To my wonder the women straightened, their heads raised back as if in worship. Conall appeared to sit up, arms flexed, fists clenched ready to fight, head thrown back to the sky in triumph. His shade had been freed of this world and was travelling to the Otherworld to join the gods. A cheer coursed the crowd. I thought of Loegaire's words, "Who would wish to be left to rot in this world, their soul never to rest, if they could have a place of honour in the Otherworld?" I tried to convince myself I'd had no hand in those women's deaths. That the torch I'd thrown was not the only reason they'd died.

Math had met up with Aed, his fellow slave from those years before now a chieftain in Connacht. I joined them at the feast, to be crushed by Aed in an embrace. Math made the usual inquiries as to the health of Aed's wife, Math's sister-in-law, and children. We asked him if he'd any news of my sister.

Aed shook his head. 'Bad affair I'm afraid. Ria's husband Fionn was stealing a neighbour's cattle, as men in Connacht love to do. It's pointless, they are always stolen back, but it keeps fianna occupied over autumn and winter. He was killed and his brother Diarmuid inherited his land and title. No one has heard anything about your sister for months.'

He looked at me hesitantly. 'It is said his brother tried to take her as part of his inheritance. She was distraught at Fionn's death and refused him. He violated her anyway and she stabbed him. She didn't kill him; it was a flesh wound.'

I stared at Aed. My poor little sister; I remembered her playing in the stream singing to herself, legs muddy, her hugging Kira whenever she saw us.

'We must find out if she is all right. I must go to her. How dare he treat the High King's sister like that?'

Aed replied, 'He would say she tried to kill him, as the wound bore witness.'

'But he had raped her.'

Aed shrugged. 'She's a woman and his brother was dead. That makes her his property. Even Conall could not have punished him.'

I turned on my heel as Math asked where to find her. I sought out Rignach, she'd know how to handle this. She sat in her roundhouse; her son's grave goods spread before her. I was relieved to see the hound arm-ring with them, not destroyed in the flames. Conall would take a sword, knife, bow and provisions with him into the afterlife as well. These would be buried with the funeral urn containing his ashes. Rignach was deep in thought but turned as I entered, brushing more teardrops away.

'It went well did it not? My son went bravely into the afterlife. Did you see him call to Lugh as he burnt?'

'I saw him rise up. He was a good man, a wise king; no one had a better son or brother. His son will carry his legacy down the generations.'

'That's not why you are here though. You are troubled?'

I outlined all we had learned of Ria.

'If she lifted her hand against Diarmuid, as his brother's heir even if he killed her, he acted within the law. We have no need to call on the Brehon to give judgement.

'Tell him Loegaire demands his sister return to mourn her brother's passing. They cannot refuse the High King's command as a client, or Loegaire can punish him. He might forfeit his land. Diarmuid won't refuse, why should he? When Ria is back, we will negotiate, find her another husband. Although she cannot stay in Tara.'

Rignach hesitated. 'My son loved you and you have been loyal. You deserve to know the truth about your half-sister. You already know in all likelihood she is not Niall's child, that Math is her father.

'Sit back I will tell you more; Niall loved your mother. That a wife has been unfaithful is a bitter draught for any man to swallow. Niall did not take insults well. I expected him to kill them both along with the child at once, but he didn't. He knew there was more than one way to mete out punishment, to make a man suffer. To a warrior, slavery and death by starvation with no hope of the Otherworld would be a terrible fate; to die without honour. Niall had been shamed, so he made sure Math was too.

'It would have diminished his status to be known as a cuckold, he would have been mocked, the wooden staff of the Kingship could have passed on to one of his brothers at the summer gathering. Niall knew any suggestion Inne had been adulterous would threaten your legitimacy. People might have said you might not be his son. He loved you and your mischief, although he tried not to show it. Said you reminded him what it was to be carefree.

Inne had hurt him but he still adored her. His marriage to Ness and Math's enslavement was Inne's punishment. He told her where Math was; said he'd die in a mine digging in the dirt for what she let him do to her. He twisted the knife to make her suffer.'

Rignach sniffed. 'That marriage to Ness was my punishment as well, my bed was abandoned by Niall as I grew older. We were the same age he and I; childhood sweethearts. I loved him before he became king. He was a younger son with an uncertain future when I took him. My sister had already married his older brother, they'd expected him to become High King, not Niall. My family believed I'd been unwise; after one year they sent a Brehon judge to check I was happy. The law allowed me to leave him, along with my bride price then you see. I gave Niall seven sons, but he cast me off for younger women. First for Inne; but she was a princess, and brought prestige along with a rich dowry. I understood that. Anyway, she didn't love him, she was fifteen, half his age, but was respectful towards me.

'We were both furious when he took that chit, that nothing, Ness, as his bride. She used to order me to obey her; gloated that she was his Christian wife and I a lesser wife. We were born royal your mother and I. Ness got what she deserved. She burnt with Niall on his pyre. Revenge smelt sweet as she cried out and cooked. It was as well for your mother he had lost trust in her. He was afraid she'd betray him if she burnt. That she'd be unfaithful in the halls of the dead and bring shame on his manhood. He left instructions that only Ness and the concubines were to go with him.

'Well, let me tell about your sister. A child when you left, petted and spoilt. Ria could charm scent from the flowers, her smile sweet as honey from the skep. Your father used her to hurt your mother. He praised her when she teased and taunted men, sat on their laps and flirted. He'd reward her with a bracelet or hair bead when her behaviour was particularly outrageous. As she grew older Niall would watch your mother's face as he encouraged Ria's wanton behaviour. He'd turn to stare expressionless at Inne. Ria grew used to being obeyed in all things and admired. She even tried to place herself above me and Ness.

'Ria was passionate about everything. If anyone didn't do as she wished there was trouble. One time, after you left, she was playing with the other children and a girl had a wrist braid she took a fancy to. She demanded it and when the girl refused, her face darkened. That night the child's mother was found crying, the girl was vomiting, close to death, poisoned with nightshade berries. Ria insisted that they'd been playing and the girl had eaten them, despite her warnings, but I was not convinced.

'When Ria reached womanhood, she was lovely, took after your mother. A face and body to make the bards sing; hair black and glossy as a raven's wing, skin of cream, lips red as blood. She used her beauty as a weapon. It was disconcerting. Neither Inne nor I could influence her, make her act modestly. If men were near, she affected a sultry charm that drew them to her, entranced. She would enter a room and all eyes would be drawn to her, she'd toy with and tantalise men.

'Ria revelled in her new power. I worried for your brothers,' she hesitated, 'your father even. I knew she was probably not Niall's child but no one else did. It would have caused outrage if she took one of them to her bed. Your mother did her best to protect her, but she was shocked by Ria's provocative behaviour. I was relieved when the girl insisted on marrying. She was too young; her husband was much older. Ria was adamant and I didn't care.

'You will think I'm being unkind and exaggerating, but there is something about Ria that is chilling, malevolent. I am ruthless but only for one reason, to protect my sons and their sons. I never harm for spite or make enemies unnecessarily. Ria would calculate who to beguile and who to ignore, how to set one man against another. The fiann were at each other's throats over her; my sons' wives wary and irritable. She took pleasure in causing chaos.

'I'm sorry Maelon, when you return, with or without Ria, neither of you can stay in Tara. I remember you fondly, as does everyone else. That is precisely why you cannot stay. Niall inherited despite being youngest, his older half-brothers did not. The parallels between you two are clear. The High Kingship needs to be confirmed at the Stone of Destiny this year. I cannot permit there to be any competition. Loegaire will give you land, but it must be far from here. You understand what I am telling you?'

'I do Rignach, that your sons and grandsons come first. It is a clear warning, thank you. I had already planned to ask Loegaire to grant me land. I don't mind how far it is from Tara. I'm not certain what to do now. I don't want to become a priest, that much I know. I have business in Wales which will help me decide.'

'A girl then?'

A vision of Dwynwen rushed into my mind at that second, the memory of her brief kiss before I'd left overwhelmed me.

'Yes, but betrothed to another, a king.'

'Go carefully, kings and princes go to war over women. It's about pride as much as the woman. I am glad we two do not need to be at odds. I know you love Loegaire and he needs allies. That he stands by the old gods is more of a problem as each year passes, Ireland is becoming Christian. It annoys me to admit it, but Niall was right to convert. The people want a Christian king like themselves, but Loegaire is stubborn. You and that priest of yours, Patricius, need to help him understand.'

'We are only novices, but Patricius is clever if anyone can convert Loegaire, it will be him.'

In two days a second procession led by an ox-drawn wagon left Tara for the day's journey to Knowth. Laidcenn sang his dirges before it as the chieftains and princes of the tribes of Ireland followed behind. Pottery vessels containing Conall and his wives' ashes rattled alongside his grave goods on the wagon. As the moon rose, the urns were interred deep inside the dark mound I had last seen on that terrifying night so many years before: a night when I'd held tight to Conall's warm hand. When I'd met the Hag.

M ath and I set off into the western wilderness, Connacht, to find my sister. Patricius chose to stay in Tara, busying himself helping people, praying with them, listening to their worries. The little church, abandoned since Niall's death three years before, was busy once more. Hymns praising Jesus as the true god rang out morning and evening. He gave lessons in the scriptures about a god, who was kind and gentle, loved every man, woman and child and forgave all.

Loegaire had only sour looks for Patricius, but one of his wives asked to be baptised. Rignach was right, my brother needed to be in step with his subjects. Like me, he had to bite his tongue and stay silent. Try not to remember his visit to Knowth as a boy, when he looked on Lugh's face.

Patricius and his messages were popular. I wondered what dry old Bishop Palladius, sent by Rome would make of this upstart novice having so much influence in the High King's court. It might not end well if he was jealous. Patricius might make enemies within the church if he tarried here long.

After a week of riding by day and camping at night, we arrived at Aed's sturdy hall, glad to find that Melissa well and happy with her children, she was delighted to hear her brother was safe. A small church with a young priest ministered to their neat settlement. Their people looked well fed and content, unlike many we had seen on our journey. Aed ruled his chiefdom well, he was accepted by his people.

The land of Connacht was often bleak and there were few settlements, instead people spread across the land in small groups of huts dotted across the landscape. It was very different from the fertile valleys of southern Wales. The Welsh complained that since the legions left the land had gone to ruin; but in Ireland such prosperity had never been dreamed of. Irish kings and princes were rich in treasure, gold from the Avoca River, copper, bronze and silver, but most lived in huts of stone or turf and wood, barely surviving, eking a living from the land.

We journeyed to Cruachan, only to be told Diarmuid their chieftain was not there, but at Erris near the ocean. I thought of Finn's words as well as Rignach's. Who was right? What sort of woman had my sister grown into? The countryside was harsh with a desolate beauty, the settlements smaller with each mile; finally, we reached the sea. On a windswept coast stood an ancient fort, high on a rocky headland. Too many thin cattle and sheep grazed the short grass of its enclosures. Inside the walls were dozens of turf-covered roundhouses. Stone abounded on that coast, trees did not. I wore my old cloak, ready to play servant again if needed.

As we rode up the people looked at us warily, a warning shout came from inside a sagging gate. Two elderly guards appeared demanding to know our business. They looked scared as Math and Aed loomed above them, fearsome on their horses.

'The High King orders us to visit his sister, the Lady Ria. I am Math, this is Lord Aed.'

A shadow passed over the men's faces. They seemed lost for an answer. After a pause one gathered his wits.

'You must speak with our chieftain. We expect him tonight.'

'I see no reason to wait, we would like to see the lady at once.'

This caused consternation. They ushered us into their hall, insisting we would have to wait for Diarmuid's return.

I spoke in Welsh to Math. 'I will try to discover why they don't want us to see Ria. Order me to stable your mounts.'

I took the horses to the enclosure to feed and water them. I was soon joined by servants intrigued by our arrival.

'I'm Mael, servant to Math, High King Loegaire's Champion. I need to feed and groom the animals and then make up my master and his companion's accommodation. Where shall I put our baggage?'

'If Diarmuid lets you stay, you'll sleep in the hall.'

'He can hardly refuse shelter to the High King's champion, now can he. The King seeks word of his sister. He has heard she is widowed. Once we've seen her and ensured all is well, we'll be away.'

The man sighed, 'And if all is not well?'

'She is King Niall's daughter. A princess, why would it not be?'

The two exchanged glances. 'She is a comely woman. Such women bring trouble on themselves.'

I raised my eyebrow as if asking for more gossip, took out a leather flagon and offered them a sip of ale.

Softened, one continued, 'She is fair and full of life, gracious to all the warriors, if not to us servants. She treats us harshly, as you'd expect of a king's daughter, but is charming with any man who might be useful.'

He hesitated, so I offered him another drink from the flask.

'That was the problem, our chieftain's younger brother fell in love with her. Diarmuid was used to coming second. Until the Lady Ria arrived it had never troubled him. He would fight, rustle cattle, drink and enjoy life in the fiann. Neither her husband, nor Diarmuid could do anything but think of that damn woman, they were obsessed. They started to argue and show off in front of her. Fionn would walk her to their bed each night gloating at his treasure and every man in the room envied him. The lady seemed amused at first, taunted them, teased and played with their emotions. Diarmuid is young; handsome and vigorous, Fionn was older. The brothers became suspicious, jealous of each other.

'Some months ago, our fiann went to retrieve cattle stolen by our neighbours. Fionn and his brother rode out together and gave chase to a rustler. Only Diarmuid returned alive, no one knows what happened. Diarmuid said the rustler swung his axe at Fionn who died and then he'd killed the rustler in revenge. It's odd though, when men ride out to steal cattle they travel light and fast, don't usually take heavy weapons.

'Diarmuid was a savage when he returned, tormented. He had his brother's torc and arm-rings brought to him that night; before the funeral rites, before Fionn had been sent with honour to the Otherworld. He called the lady and told her she belonged to him. Lady Ria stormed away, saying she had to grieve for her husband. Diarmuid picked up a flagon of wine from Gaul and followed. No one is sure what happened. All we know is after that night, he nursed a flesh wound and is morose and embittered. The lady keeps to her hut.

I said, 'To provoke one brother to kill another, she must be beautiful. Can I see her? My master will expect to speak to her soon, tonight or tomorrow.'

'I didn't say Diarmuid did kill Fionn. No one dares say that, but we wonder. I don't see any harm you looking at her. You'll see she is perfectly healthy, as lovely as ever. Don't speak to her unless she speaks to you. Don't even look directly at her. She expects to be treated like a queen. If she tells you to do something, do it straight away, no delay or she'll have you whipped.'

Ria's stone hut was pointed out and I walked over. I sat whittling a stick opposite its doorway, watching as daily life went on around me. Some time later a woman emerged through the low doorway. She was very beautiful; long black curls, curving at breast and hip, neat straight nose, like mine. My little sister grown up. I wondered if she'd recognise me but shook away the thought; it was ten years since we'd seen each other. I'd changed as much as her.

'You, why are you gawping? Get me water from the stream,' said Ria nodding at a pail. She looked sharply and none too kindly at my face.

'You look familiar. Why do I know you?' I started to reply but she held up a hand. 'No, don't bother me,' and turned away.

When I returned a remarkably pretty maid stood at the threshold.

She smiled winningly. 'Thank you, you have saved my back toiling up the hill with that weight. I would normally have fetched it by now, but we were gossiping about your master and his demand to see the lady. We are not sure how Diarmuid will react.' She lowered her voice, 'He is turned mad over this one.'

'No problem sweet one, I'll carry you up more later. When do you think your lord will return? My master won't wait. The new High King expects her return to mourn our...his brother.'

'Tonight, if all has gone well and the cattle are found. Then we can travel back to Cruachan; leave this summer pasture.'

She fell abruptly silent. Ria was standing at the doorway.

'What are you two gossiping about? Who has come? Tell me at once.'

The maid looked scared and stammered, 'Warriors, lady.'

'Shush Frid, I was asking this one, not you with your empty head. You boy, I haven't seen you before. You must be with them?'

'I am. Your brother, King Conall is dead my lady. The new High King, Loegaire has sent his champion, Math to bring you to Tara to mourn his passing to the Otherworld.'

She looked nonplussed, shaking her head as if in a dream. 'Math here? I remember Math; he played with me when I was tiny. He was killed in Wales, wasn't he? Mother cried and Father shouted at her, then laughed. Math must be old. They said he...' her voice trailed off.

'He is not so old, my lady.' I replied.

She showed no hint of grief at Conall's death. Ria's thoughts were for herself.

'Frid, come inside. I must prepare. Find my antler comb.'

Ria ignored me. I was no more than a house-fly on a twig, beneath notice.

I made my way back to Math and Aed, who sat relaxed on sheepskins outside the main hall, competing at throwing smooth pebbles into a pot placed some paces away. I told them I had seen Ria. Math's shoulders dropped in relief. I didn't know what to tell him about her behaviour, so grunted in response to his query as to how she seemed.

'Not very charming to servants, ordered me around at the moment she saw me. Looks healthy enough, glowing.'

He laughed, then we heard hooves and cattle lowing in the distance. Diarmuid' and his men had returned. Horsemen leading a couple of dozen scrawny cattle appeared at the gates of the settlement. At their head rode a straight-backed, handsome warrior, athletic and powerful, fair hair streaming behind him. A man women would sigh after, but not one to be trifled with; I knew him to be Diarmuid.

Later that afternoon as I sat in thin sunlight with Tas and Beah dozing at my feet Frid joined me. She handed me a fresh flatbread, hot from the bake-stone folded over tasty mutton. I smiled at her. Unlike many servants her face was washed and bright, her dress and shoes clean and neat. With brown braids, dimples and sparkling amber eyes, she looked a treat.

I thought back to when Wyn and I would woo the local girls with sweet phrases.

'This bread smells tempting, as delectable as you.'

Frid blushed pink, pleased. I moved up, gesturing for her to sit on the log beside me.

'Thank you for thinking of me, it's delicious. I guess they are preparing a meal for your chieftain's return. What's he like?'

'He's wonderful, or at least he was until that woman from Tara came. He'd make time for every one of us. He'd tease us and treat us like people, not servants. He was especially considerate towards me.'

'I'm not surprised, you are the prettiest girl in the settlement.'

'Thank you. She's changed him though. Men, they all like her. We women see through her wiles, she's a witch,' replied Frid with unexpected venom.

I nodded encouragingly, and she continued.

'That woman may have married Fionn, but she was always making eyes at Diarmuid. She wanted both brothers to adore her, and so they did. She was Fionn's wife, he should have beaten her to keep her in line, but he was afraid to. He was older you see, she was his third wife, the other two in their graves and Fionn desperate for a son.

'He loved his younger brother but longed for a child. This girl from Tara was supposed to give him one. There are stories that Fionn had been ill as a young man. His, you know, well his balls, his neck and cheeks were swollen and sore from that illness. It was said he was unable to father babies because of that time. Seems to me the story was true. She didn't produce a son any more than his other wives, for all her wiles.

'The lady saw herself growing old in this place with an angry, resentful husband, and no babies. She tempted Diarmuid time and again. We saw her drop something if he was near, then pick it up slowly so he could see her bosoms. She has a smile when she opens her mouth and licks her lips and fingers that is shocking, she'd use it often. Look I'll show you.'

I was taken aback as Frid slowly opened her mouth and put a finger to her lips in mock thoughtfulness. Then flicked finger and lip with her tongue. Frid was so attractive and sensual, I felt my manhood stir.

She nodded knowingly. 'Yes, it's a clever trick. I've learnt a lot from her.

'So Welsh boy, do you want me to show you this place? I'm free until an hour before the evening meal. The lady expects me to attend her then.'

She stood and offered me her hand, pulling me up. 'Come on I'll show you wonders,' skipping ahead of me up a steep path. Ten minutes later, breathless we arrived at the top of a cliff. The wind tugged at our clothes and hair as I gazed out at the blue sea and white-fringed waves.

Frid stood closer, took my hand again and shouted out joyously, 'Wonderful isn't it, sea and emptiness, but so lovely. Look, we are at the edge of the world.'

The land was as close to the setting sun as it was possible to go. Some spoke of a country inhabited by gods over the horizon. When I was a boy, druid Laidcenn had told me that any men who sail west never return, that the sun disappears into a chasm, falls away into a void. Even Sylvester agreed; he told us the Romans knew of no land beyond our shores, no people or life.

Frid led me to a grassy hollow well protected from the wind and we sat on short grass, pink cushions of thrift dotted around us. Above seabirds screeched and wheeled, dancing in the wind. On a cliff face pairs of yellow-headed, blue-eyed gannets courted, necks sinuously twining around each other. Frid held a finger to her lips to silence me. A comical little black and white bird with bright orange feet and a striped red bill landed four paces away. In its beak gleamed slim silver fish; it waddled towards us.

'A puffin; watch, its burrow must be close.'

We saw it disappear. Then she lay back in the sunshine smiling up at me and I kissed her. Her lips were soft and responsive, tasting of summer berries. My heart lifted with happiness, what a place. After some minutes she stopped, pushing me away gently.

'What's it like in Tara? Are there palaces? Does everyone eat pork year-round in the High King's home? I'd hoped Diarmuid would marry me but he's in Lady Ria's thrall. I have to escape, not only from Diarmuid, from my father, from my life.'

She looked at me hopefully, as if I was a saviour.

'Tara is not unlike this place I'm afraid, Frid. It's bigger, the huts better kept, wooden, and thatched not stone and turf. No one goes hungry, but servants and slaves still work hard. There are no palaces, none in all of Ireland. Not like Wales, my home, where the Romans left great houses, villas they called them. Inside them the wind can't blow; they are warm and dry whatever the weather.

'You know I'm not a servant, although Lady Ria treats me like one. I'm a chieftain's daughter, his only living child. Fionn took me as a hostage because my father, Diaré, is powerful and his land is on the border of Connacht and Ulster. Fionn wanted to ensure Father's loyalty. If he changed allegiance, Fionn would have been weakened. If it wasn't for that woman, Diarmuid might have married me, truly he might. I wasn't being foolish when I told you of my hopes, all dashed by that bitch. Now I can't have him, I want to go to Wales and live in one of those villas you talked about. They say in Wales men only take one wife. Is that true?'

'Christians are not allowed more than one wife, anywhere, not only in Wales; Rome, Gaul, everywhere.'

'That sounds so nice. I'll be expected to compete with other wives and concubines when I marry. To be the only one someone loves, imagine that. Take me with you when you leave please, please. I'll give you anything you want, anything, but take me away from here.'

'Frid, I can't take you to Wales, how would I explain that to my master? We have come to take Lady Ria to Tara to mourn her brother. She'll likely ask to take a maid. You could offer to accompany her? From Tara, well who knows. Travellers from Wales and far beyond come to Tara.'

Having someone working for Ria might be useful. If Rignach was right Ria might not tell us everything she planned. Ria would be suspicious of a new maid, but not one from her household. I pushed away the sneaking thought that Frid was so very sweet and fresh, and had told me she'd give my anything to leave. It had been clear what she suggested. Dwynwen need never know. If I was not to be a priest then I could be a man.

I turned back to her and tasted her lips again.

That night a homecoming meal was prepared for Diarmuid and his warriors. A grudging invitation was extended to Math and Aed; hospitality had to be offered to strangers, anyway, we came from the High King. Diarmuid looked at Math suspiciously as he explained why we'd come.

'You want to take away my brother's widow?'

At that moment Ria entered the hall and the room fell silent. I guessed she had spent the entire day preparing. Rignach's description was apt. Ria looked as exquisite as Deidre of legend. Her black hair flowed enticingly around her face. An iridescent gown, light as gossamer, clung to her thighs and breast. The pale blue cloth was expensive, imported from lands far to the east of Gaul. On her head a circlet of silver, a bronze torc shimmered at her neck. She was breath-taking, easy to see why men desired her.

Diarmuid watched Aed and Math's reactions. Aed smiled and turned to his neighbour to comment, as Math gazed long at her, tender and proud. He had known his daughter as a child, moved to see her grown to such lovely womanhood. Diarmuid glowered with anger. He could not know why Math looked at Ria so fondly. From his glare, it was obvious that Diarmuid was a jealous man.

'I am commanded to Tara to mourn my brother at the new High King's command. As a widow, with no children I demand the return of my bride price,' said Ria.

Her voice came rich, soft and calm. Behind her back, however, her fingers and thumb brushed against each other quickly in anxiety, as she had always done whenever she was in trouble as a child. At that moment I loved her, she was my baby sister. I would keep Rignach's warning in my mind, but knew I had to help her. Diarmuid's face darkened.

Ria continued, 'Math, my father's champion, I remember you well. I believe you are here to take me home.'

Diarmuid interrupted, 'I will escort my brother's widow, and no one else.'

The two glared at each other. They were perfectly matched in their beauty and their anger. Ria's eyes alighted on Beah then Tas, lying at my feet.

She exclaimed, 'Kira, it is you. My lovely hound come to me,' clicking her fingers.

Of course, Tas, on hearing her mother's name got up and bounded over to her. Sharp as a knife, Ria stared at me and everything fell into place. I could see her calculating how best to use her new knowledge. She nodded slowly, deciding what to say as she fondled Beah's pelt.

'I do have family in this hall. Brother, why do you sit with the servants? Diarmuid, may I introduce my brother Maelon. He is known as the King over the Sea, named that after my father's death. No longer over the ocean, it would appear.'

I grimaced; the servants I had befriended stared at me astonished. Out of the corner of my eye I saw Frid, hand to her mouth, shocked. I blushed hot and rose to my feet as everyone waited to see what I would say.

'Sister, yes, our mother who is now queen in north Wales has received no word of you for months and was worried. She sent me with Math to ensure all was well. When I travelled to Tara I found Conall dying. After his death, Loegaire asked that you come to mourn with the family. We were concerned to hear of your husband's death. When we were not taken to you immediately, I decided to use subterfuge.'

I looked at Diarmuid and said, 'I hope you will forgive me Lord Diarmuid and understand I acted as a concerned brother? Lord Aed, your neighbour, Math and I stand ready to escort my sister as instructed by the High King.

Diarmuid was as taken aback by this turn of events as everyone else. He frowned and stared at Ria.

His words came slowly, 'I cannot deny a brother's or a High King's request, but insist on escorting my sister-in-law. There are bandits on the roads between here and Tara. It is safer to form a larger party.'

'Thank you. Please let's not delay eating any longer. I am sure you are as hungry as I am?' I said, keen to have the room's attention pass on.

Music played as horns of beer were passed around. The party was subdued. Diarmuid shot jealous glances at Math, who continued to gaze adoringly at his daughter.

As we left Ria pushed to my side. 'Walk me to my hut, brother. How could you not make yourself known to me?'

'I tried. You interrupted. Ordered me to fetch you water.'

'Stupid game playing.'

'We were worried. I've heard dark stories.' I turned to face her. 'Are you really, all right? What is happening between you and that man?'

'I don't want to talk about it. Is that Kira, she looks so like her, but I don't think it can be? The moment I saw her, I knew you had to be here.'

'No, Kira is at home in Wales. She is old, my poor brave hound only has three legs now, she couldn't have made the journey. Tas and Beah are her pups. Tas does look like her mother. She must have recognised her name.'

'Finn trained me when you left. He missed you. I did too, Maelon. When you'd gone, I had no one. Rignach's sons were adults and ignored me. Ness's boys were too young to care. I was alone and Tara felt dangerous. Some of the women were cruel. They said horrible things about Mother and me.'

'What things?'

'That Niall was not my father. That Mother had taken a younger, more handsome man as lover; Math. Is that true? Am I Niall's child or not?'

She looked close to crying.

'Yes, it is likely true, although no one can be certain. It's why he is here with me.'

'I'm not the daughter of the High King. Oh Maelon, no one can know.'

'It is not in anyone's interest to admit that. It's why Math was sent away and not publicly punished. You are a princess whatever. Math's father Brion was a king; Niall's brother. Mother is a queen still. Our line through her is better than Father's. We are descended from a Roman emperor.'

Ria groaned. 'Things are so complicated. I am glad you are here, Maelon. It is good to see you, even though you are only a priest. I need time to think, goodnight.'

Stung by her phrase, "only a priest," I nodded and kissed her hand as she went into her hut. I called out, 'Be ready first thing in the morning.'

I turned, then started. Frid stood by the doorway.

'How long have you been there?'

'Well, King over the Sea, maybe asking you to take me to Wales was not so impossible,' she said with a smile, avoiding my question. 'You are not a servant any more than I am, my lord.' She took my hand, whispering again, 'Take me away from this place and I'll give you anything you ask.'

I let her lead me out of the settlement, back up the cliff to that dip in the land with its view over a moonlit dark sea. It was cold as I covered us with my cloak. She took my hand and placed it on her breast and I lost myself in the wonder of her smooth flesh.

CHAPTER

16

In the morning, I woke lying on a rough bed of bracken and mangy skins looking up at the thatch, sticky and guilt-ridden. The taste of Dwynwen's last chaste kiss, mixed uncomfortably with my memories of Frid last night. How she'd enjoyed our caresses; laughing, happy, although it had turned out she was as new to making love as I. The two girls were so different. I thought how long I'd loved Dwynwen, but…I was a man. What happened was only natural when the woman I adored was far away, wasn't it? My soul shouted back, traitor, liar.

Math and Aed called to me. They'd been up for an hour and had groomed all three horses. Eager to depart, they asked me to check if Ria was ready.

She was, her baggage already loaded on a dappled pony. Frid was joining the party as her maid. I was delighted that I would have the chance to re-visit last night's pleasures. Ria stood beside her horse, neatly dressed in a man's green tunic with leggings and soft leather boots, hair held loosely by a red cap adorned with jay wing feathers. The outfit suited her; her legs long and back curved, if anything she looked more attractive than in her gown the night before. I shook my head, astonished at the woman my sister had become.

She grinned up at me and said, 'Race you to the gate Brother. I'm fast. I'll beat you now I'm grown.'

I was tempted, but took the pony's bridle instead. Ria pouted in disappointment. For a moment we were back in Tara again, carefree. Diarmuid appeared at her back and her demeanour changed at a stroke. It was as if she'd shrunk, become more womanly, in need of protection. Diarmuid saw it too.

'Don't attempt your tricks and wiles on me. I know you too well. Call your maid and we'll be off to visit your damned brother.'

She pouted a second time, this time not for play. She'd been thwarted. Diarmuid and she seemed comfortable together. His words were not spoken harshly, he was teasing her. Last night he behaved as if he hated her, today he seemed in control.

Pink cheeked and dainty, Frid, along with three of his warriors joined the party and we set out east, towards Aed's dún. Diarmuid rode beside me, asking questions about my family and childhood. I told him it had been happy, until I was sent away, aged twelve to Wales, describing the freedom I felt before then. How I'd looked up to my brothers. That Conall and Loegaire had been like young fathers; Niall preoccupied. Diarmuid seemed much affected by my tale.

'Our childhoods sound similar. My father died when I was ten, my mother at my birth. Fionn was my elder by seven years, all the father and mother I ever knew. He was wonderful; brave and strong, good-hearted and generous. He taught me to fight, to drink, about women, taught me everything.'

Diarmuid's voice broke and his shoulders shook.

He continued, 'He was not perfect, he had a vile temper and like me, he could be jealous. I loved him and looked up to him always, until… There I have told you enough. You are too good a listener, Maelon mac Neill.'

He galloped off alone, far to the rear of our small column.

As we rounded a bend in the path, I heard a warning shout; warriors were headed towards us. A group of finely dressed men wearing full war gear cantered along the road, raucous laughter and the sounds of drumming hooves preceding them. We halted. Aed, Math and Diarmuid's warriors hurriedly took up their arms. I moved to Ria's side as I unsheathed my sword. I strained around, trying to check on Frid. I needed to be sure she was safe, but couldn't spot her anywhere. The war party outnumbered us, pulling to a halt some thirty yards away, warily taking up their weapons.

I heard Frid call out. I looked around desperately, afraid she had been ambushed.

Then I saw she was off her pony, running as if her life depended on it, towards one of the men.

'Father, Father, it's me. It's Frid! How I have missed you.'

She flung herself at him. Diarmuid's men relaxed as Frid was welcomed with a hug. The warrior swung her up in front of him onto his horse, his companions re-sheathed their swords. Diarmuid had caught up with us, unarmed he rode on towards the group.

Ria riding beside me whispered as loudly as she dared, 'Damn, it's Dairé of Ulster, Frid's father. He hates us because Fionn captured Frid and has held her hostage these last two years.'

Dairé called out, 'Why it's a party from Cruachan, generously returning my little girl to me, now that Fionn is dead. Thank you,

Diarmuid for both your gifts; for slaying your bastard brother and the return of my child.'

Sharp eyes, the same golden brown as his daughter's inspected us. 'In fine company, Diarmuid. You are with the young King over the Sea and his hounds. My band is returning from High King Conall's wake. You were there, Maelon mac Neill. We Connacht chiefs are not lordly enough to do more than bend our knee to such as you and your sister. You will not remember us.'

He was right. I did not recollect him, but felt it wiser not to own that.

'That is not so Dairé of Ulster. My brother Loegaire pointed you out. Said you were fine warriors, ever loyal to the Úi Neill. I noted you well at the funeral games. I admired your fine weapons and strong men.'

His men looked gratified by my flattery. Diarmuid and Dairé grimaced in unison. Dairé had wanted to pick a fight, but presumably not with me.

He studied Ria carefully, then looked directly at Diarmuid and leered.

'Who could that lovely youth be riding with you, young king? So fair, no beard and such curves. Why it must be Fionn's widow. No doubt her family want her back. They'll forge another alliance since her marriage to Fionn proved short and childless. They will look for another a chieftain. Maybe I should ask for her myself? I doubt they'd wish to see her remain with the man who murdered her husband.'

Diarmuid's face blackened, furious; his hand reached for his sword.

'I did not harm my brother. I will kill any man spreading that lie.'

Math put a hand to his sword ready.

I broke in. 'Diaré, be careful what you say of my sister, the Lady Ria. She is the daughter and sister of kings. Do not presume on that loyalty to the Ui Neill's of which I spoke. My brothers and I expect respect from our clients or we will destroy them utterly.'

Diaré was taken aback. Fear flashed across his face; his men recoiled. I realised the power of my threat. In Ireland, my lineage inspired terror.

Frid's warm amber eyes sparkled, she smiled at me and my heart melted. I'd miss her. She was uncomplicated, brave and honest.

'Father, I have come to like this man and he speaks true. They are escorting the Lady Ria to mourn her brother. I would like to go with them. I long to see Tara.'

'Of course, you can't go with them, you foolish girl. Do you think I have found you, to see you a hostage again? You will return to Ulster with me. Diarmuid, good journey. Thank you again for the return of my daughter.'

I felt disappointment mixed with relief. I had longed for the night, to stroke Frid's thighs again, but that temptation had disappeared. Diaré signalled to his companions and wheeled to canter away. Frid turned, her expression imploring me to speak, to command them to stop. My mouth was dry, I could not say a word. I hardly knew her. I liked her, a lot, was attracted to everything about her; her energy, self-belief, her body. But I was in love with Dwynwen. Wasn't I?

Diarmuid spoke, 'Weasel's piss. They know I am away and have my best men with me. They will raid all my settlements along their path back to Ulster.'

Ria spoke, her hand behind her back, twitching and rubbing once again. 'You and the fiann must turn back and overtake them. They will make straight for home.

'What Dairé said is true isn't it? I will be made to re-marry and I'll have no choice in who that man is.'

As she asked, she gazed at Diarmuid, who looked down, staring at his mount's neck. They were at war these two. He hated her for what he had done, or thought of doing, for her; but he loved her.

I said, 'I'm afraid so. Our mother put it well before her marriage to Einion, King of Llyn and Mona. She told me that royal women are like cattle, a commodity to trade, they have no option but do as commanded. If they are clever or lucky, they marry well. Mother and her lover suffered for love. Mother swore she'd never do so again. Love is not for nobles, not for you and probably not for me.'

I looked down, fiddling with my horse's leather bridle. I'd never admitted to myself that I might not be able to marry Dwynwen before. My resolution hardened. I would win Dwynwen despite it all, my pride was at stake.

Ria bit her lip. 'You must turn back, Diarmuid.'

'Come with me. Return of your own free will.'

Ria asked, 'Maelon, what will Loegaire say? Will there be reprisals? Am I bid to Tara to mourn?'

'Honestly, Loegaire will not care, he and Rignach know. He won't mind if I say it was for the best. I can choose. If you return, they will marry you to the most powerful client who asks. I have no doubt there will be plenty they can pick from. As Niall's only daughter you are a prize, they will give you to whoever is most useful to them.'

Diarmuid's hand grasped his sword tightly, but he didn't move.

Math spoke, 'Are you sure you wish to return? Diarmuid seems a man of dangerous passions. Maelon and I promised your mother we would see to your welfare.'

Diarmuid spoke, 'How dare you say that. What is it to you? Why is it up to Maelon? Ria is my brother's widow. I did not kill him. That is the truth, or may the Goddess strike me dead. I am bitter that it happened, and yes, furious with myself because I argued over Ria with him before his death.

I was riding far behind, raging at life when he was attacked. I should have been at his side. I cannot forgive myself for not being there when he needed me.'

Math sighed. 'Peace, you inflame too fast. Impetuosity is unwise in a warrior. Keeping calm will see you safer than the rush of anger and blood lust, in love as well as war.'

'What do you want Ria? To return to Tara with me, or stay?' I interjected.

'I will go back with Diarmuid; provided he marries me and promises to take no other wives, ever. I will not be second. If he looks at another woman, I and my bride price will disappear home to my brothers, so will his children. You see, Maelon, I am with child, Diarmuid's child.'

Her words fell among us like a rock falling from a cliff.

'Are you sure? Can you be certain it is my child and not Fionn's?'

'Fionn was sterile and by the end, impotent. He could never father a child. Yes, I'm sure. Fionn has been dead for months. I have not bled since the night you returned after his death.'

She looked down and Diarmuid face showed desolation.

'That night,' he whispered, 'an ill-fated night. I hope the child will not be cursed. Yes, I promise. You have my heart, there could never be another.'

'Diaré will race for our cattle and may take revenge for Frid being held hostage unless you ride. You must hurry. Maelon will stay and protect me. We will follow on. Go now, go.'

Diarmuid's face reflected uncertainty.

Aed spoke up, 'We are only two hours from my dún, the borders of my land are near, we will soon be safe. You are welcome to stay at my hall, Lady. Let our party continue while Diarmuid sees to his land and cattle. He can send for you once all is settled.'

Math nodded. 'I will accompany Diarmuid. I fancy there is a fight ahead, any extra sword will help. The wolfhounds, Maelon and Aed will see Ria safe.'

Ria watched them spur their mounts and gallop away. 'He is a good man Math; one would be proud to be his kin.'

'He is, I am proud to call him friend.'

'I too,' added Aed.

Two weeks later, I retraced my steps to Tara with Math, matters resolved in Connacht. Ria and Diarmuid had wed. The fiery pair seemingly happy, although I had doubts as to their future. On my return, I was welcomed heartily, although Loegaire immediately insisted he wanted Patricius gone from Tara.

Patricius was impatient too. 'I can't bear to stay any longer. Those who are not warriors have scarcely any comforts. They scratch a living; starvation lurks if their crops fail. Not even worship is granted them, nor the hope of something better in the next life.'

'Patricius, they have the life their parents had. It may seem poor to you, the son of a magistrate from the Roman empire. To them, it is all they have known. Christ, Lugh, Macha, does it matter?'

He looked disconcerted, then replied thoughtfully, 'Before I was enslaved, I might have said the same. My time alone with the sheep and thoughts has changed my view. Yes, it matters. In Jesus, there is consolation, hope in this world and peace in the next.'

'In that case, you should finish your studies, become a priest.'

'I know that. I plan to journey to Gaul, attend school there, then maybe go on to Rome. Will you come with me?'

'I'd love to visit the lands Maximus my ancestor ruled, but I am still unsure of my faith. I'm not cut out to be a priest. There is someone in Wales, a girl. I love her. I want to make my life with her, not preach and build churches. Come home, visit your parents, your father longs to see you, so does Sylvester. Visit Gaul after that. Beni has always said he wants to return to Armorica, maybe he will accompany you.'

'I will, but one day I will return to Ireland as my vision demanded. I dislike Loegaire as much as he does me, but I shan't give up. I'll convert that miserable sod to Christ properly. Make him believe.'

Loegaire found us a ship bound for Wales; to my regret, it held his fiann, off to raid Welsh shores.

Loegaire shrugged and told me, 'You might as well try to stop the wind as stop our ships reaving. You know that. We have poor land, what keeps us alive is our raiding and trade in slaves and silver. We have to eat.'

'One day you may be on the receiving end. It is a terrible thing to see those you love murdered, raped or captured and enslaved.'

'Enough, it is life. The Welsh should fight back, protect their families, I would. Will you remain in Wales or return to Ireland? Mother insists I should be wary of you, but I'm not. I trust you. If I die, I want you to take on the kingship, hold it until one of my sons is old enough and strong enough to take it. Will you give me your promise?'

He made to remove the hound headed arm-ring I had given him long ago.

'Hold, I have Conall's raven arm-rings, and one of your boar headed rings too. I want you to wear that, it is our bond. I will do as you ask if the chieftains agree at the Tara gathering; but would rather you stay alive so I do not need to.

'I will keep your gift of Fiachrae's land in the North and watch Milchu and his cronies carefully. It is close to Wales and my mother's country. I would like them to suffer fewer raids. I may have to steal my bride and will need somewhere to run. My uncle will not grant me his eldest daughter. I will have her though. I won't give her up.'

As I spoke the words out loud, I felt a shiver; Brychan would never agree. I would have to resort to subterfuge. Would Dwynwen come with me? I was not certain she would. How much did she really love me? Did I love her enough to risk her father's wrath? The memory of Frid's warm laugh sounded in my mind, but I pushed it away.

CHAPTER
17

I returned to Lake Syfaddon late in the summer. The road clung to the hillside until at last, nestling on its shores, the church and school were revealed. Pride swelled in me that I had cleared the land, overseen and built those walls and gathered its thatch. Patricius gasped, morning sun glistened on the sparkling lake, the hills and sky were mirrored on its surface. It truly looked as if another world was in that water, one I could inhabit as easily as my own. We heard excited barking, somehow Kira knew I was back. Tas and Beah barked frantically in response. Sylvester, hair thinner and greying emerged from the church doorway.

On seeing us he bowed his head, to say a short prayer of thanks.

He called out, 'Maelon, Wyn, thanks to our Lord Jesus, you have returned. You are a vision of joy to my ageing eyes. Beni, Gastyn, come and see who is arrived!'

Kira used her three legs to leap at me, knocking me half over in excitement and pleasure. She seemed to remember Patricius too, lavishing rough, warm licks over our faces and arms.

Johannes had died while we were away. One cold morning he had been found lying beside Ellyw's grave, its daily flowers clutched in his hand; old age had taken him. The news brought an unexpected tightness to my throat. I had to silence a sob, thinking that he'd never chide or criticise me again. His irritation with me had been real when I was young, but later our railing and disputing became a routine we enjoyed.

We recounted our adventures, to appreciative gasps from our friends and the new pupils. Sylvester was delighted at Patricius's plan to go to Gaul with Benignus. Patricius and Beni spent long hours planning, with Sylvester listening in, commenting and making suggestions.

Finally, he announced, 'I've made up my mind, I am going to go with you Wyn…um, Patricius. I will have two brave men of the church accompany me into the civilised world. I will travel on from Gaul. I want to see Rome again before I die. 'Gastyn, Maelon, you will have to take over. Gastyn, you are full of faith. The people love you; you will take charge of the church and care for the souls of those who come here to pray.

'Maelon, you must teach scriptures and scribing in the school. Don't you shake your head at me. You are clever, I have taught you everything I know. I have cared for you since you were a boy, and never asked for anything in return until this day.'

Speechless, I realised it was true. Sylvester had been constant, there to advise and protect me throughout my life. I could not possibly refuse. But what about my plans to marry Dwynwen and take her to Ireland?

'Sylvester, I cannot say no, but neither can I take my vows. I am still not sure of my faith,' I stammered.

'One day faith will come my son, but until then you can be a deacon to give you authority. Your learning is the only thing you need. The pupils look up to you. I have watched you with them, teaching practical skills, how to build, how to protect themselves with a sword and how to hunt for food. Now you must teach them the words of Christ, how to read and write and proclaim the Lord's message.

'You will have to draw on your stores of patience, I know that, but you can do it. I will return, God willing, after my travels, in a year or maybe two, then you can make choices as to what you want from life. I'm asking you for two years to ensure Cedric's life's work is not wasted.'

Summer was well advanced, the three needed to be well south before the winter. They had to decide whether to take the high mountain route, late in the year or risk a sea passage. Patricius made a brief visit home to his family to say another farewell. We had called there for a week on our journey back from Ireland, his parents had been overwhelmed with joy at the return of their son and begged him to stay. Patricius was firm, his path lay elsewhere. Math's sons would have to take over the mines when they grew up. Patricius had been called to serve God and would not stay in Wales.

Patricius was tall and charismatic and an asset to the clas. For the weeks he was with us the little church grew its congregation, his preaching formidable. I felt pleased if envious, then anxious. What if Dwynwen preferred him to me? Everyone else seemed to.

Sylvester had sent word of his departure to my uncle. We were summoned to Garth Madron for a farewell feast in his honour.

That evening, as we rode to the court my heart ached to see her. All I could look for, all I could think about. My eyes scanned expectantly through a party waiting at the gate. There were my cousins, but no Dwynwen. Marchell was absent too, where was my grandmother? Brychan would not deign to wait on us, but grandmother loved to see me. Cynog came up and hugged me affectionately.

He whispered, 'Grandmother is ill, she won't be able to come to the meal. She asked if you would go to her hut.'

I hurried to her bedside. She lay under a fine woollen blanket, thin and weary, veins protruding bilberry-blue in her neck and hands. Beside her sat Dwynwen; a weighted wooden spindle twisting constantly in her hands, the woollen thread twitched and danced to the floor. Was it my imagination or did her expression look as pleased as my grandmother's?

'Come, sit beside me, Maelon. Tell me how my daughter and her family fare's, and about your sister in Ireland. Dwynwen, move your stool to one side. Maelon, hold my hand. You look so much like my Anlach when I first knew him.'

Instead of waiting to hear about my mother, she began to reminisce.

'Anlach came with his brother to Dinas Powis, the hill fort Glwys retreated to from his villa on the plain. He was young then, tall and slim, black ringlets, with deep brown eyes I could drown in. I don't need to describe him Dwynwen, he looked like Maelon. There were plenty of young men there, many keen to marry me; as Father's only child they knew I would inherit rich lands.'

Her face darkened. 'Glywys was there, lording it over the princes. He assumed I was his for the taking. The moment Anlach smiled at me, my heart was lost. He made me laugh but didn't act the fool, trying to show off like the others. A younger son but from an illustrious line. I know, I know, your grandfather talked of nothing else but his ancestry. I won't repeat it. He was half Irish with a trace of his grandfather's Gallaecian blood obvious in his looks. I fell in love.

'My father was dubious about the match, but my mind was set. I was nineteen, late for marriage so when I insisted, he agreed. Father hated it when I left with Anlach for Ireland. He was a good man, my husband. I miss him and long to join him.'

Dwynwen and I exchanged a sad glance.

'No Grandmother, we need you, the people need you. You are the calm at the heart of the kingdom. They come to you for advice and your wisdom.'

Grandmother shook her head. 'Your father will be relieved to rule without me. He thinks I interfere, even though he and the people know it is my kingdom. Anlach ruled because he married me, with my consent. The kingdom is mine. Your father worries I could disinherit him, in Inne or Maelon or even Rhain's favour. That he'll be passed over. My son is a jealous man. It's not his fault; his being a hostage at a young age made him so.

'Dwynwen, would you fetch me a glass of buttermilk and some sweet bread? I think I can face nibbling on something?'

My cousin looked delighted. Grandmother was obviously not eating much. She looked frail as if any waft of wind could take her from us.

After Dwynwen left, my grandmother turned her head to gaze at me with a loving but concerned expression. 'Maelon, I see how you watch your cousin, that you adore her, but… I worry. I don't want to say this. I know you are in love. It is hard to hear words of warning or believe them.

'It's not only Brychan's objections that concern me. It is Dwynwen herself. Your grandfather would talk of hounds and that you are too close kindred. That's not why I'm uneasy. Dwynwen is so serious and worries so. She has always taken the cares of her sisters on herself. Ellyw's death and the manner of her mother and step-mother's passing has scarred her. I'm not certain marriage is right for her.'

I didn't want to argue with my grandmother. I set my jaw down hard. I couldn't, wouldn't listen. Grandmother could see my distress.

She put her lined hand on mine. 'I'm sorry. I hope I'm mistaken but I have to tell you of my disquiet, in case... well in case what you hope for doesn't happen. My heart tells me it may not be what the fates have in store for you.'

That night at table all I could see was Dwynwen. I kept looking at her, then away but however hard I tried, my gaze was pulled back to her sweet face.

Brychan was his usual terse self. When told I'd be running the school he commented, 'Young for such a learned position surely? Wouldn't you like Drichan to take charge, Sylvester? He is old but he is saintly.'

Sylvester stood his ground. 'Maelon will do very well, he is a natural leader and the pupils look up to him. It would be a favour, however, if you allow young Cynog to teach. Drichan's memory of Christ's life is, perhaps not quite as sure as it once was. I heard him preaching about the miracle of the loaves and cattle last week. The school has copies of the gospels; those Johannes risked his life for. We must spread the same words as every other school in Christendom, not variations.'

Brychan winced, people loved the tale of miracle of the loaves and fishes. Drichan's memory worsened with each year and when he forgot, he made up his own stories.

'Let's have some songs. Harpist play, daughters sing for me,' he called. 'I wish my mother would join us.'

The atmosphere cheered as his seven eldest daughters stood, singing clear and sweet of loves lost and battles won in the flickering tallow light. Brychan demanded songs of the bravery of his ancestors and Sylvester called for hymns praising the Lord. The girls knew them all. No central fire burnt in the hearth today, it was warm enough without. I could gaze at Dwynwen and her sisters without a care, every eye in the room was on them. I thought Dwynwen's smile seemed directed at me, but they were singing for Sylvester and Patricius's departure. Why wouldn't she look in our direction?

We left late for our ride home, drunk on good beer and sweet song. Dwynwen managed to speak to me before we left.

'I am so glad you are home safely. I mean, well, Grandmother was worrying about you. Not that I wasn't.'

She blushed, it was my moment.

'I'm pleased to be home and see you again too. I've thought of you every day since I left, and your farewell kiss. I couldn't believe it when you appeared on our journey to Powys. I'm sorry I....'

Patricius interrupted us, 'Stop whispering to your pretty cousin. We need to get home. It's an early start tomorrow.'

He smiled winningly at Dwynwen and rode off. I'd no choice but to follow him.

It was strange in the clas without Sylvester. I had never realised how hard he worked. Gastyn and I never stopped; there were lessons to be given, food organised, services taken, pilgrims greeted, the harvest gathered, wood collected for the winter. The tasks felt endless. We were delighted when cheerful Cynog joined us, we desperately needed an extra pair of hands.

My cousin was a born organiser. He commanded villagers collect wood and leave it in the doorway on the way to church services. He suggested they could spend time working rather than leave offerings. This pleased people. It had not occurred to us how difficult it was for families to give the church food. They could more easily spare a child to watch our flocks or collect the cows from the hillside than give us grain. Cynog ordered his father's warriors to help harvest our crops; having brewed tubs of raspberry and honey beer in preparation, weeks earlier.

In exchange for his efforts, each evening we'd take it in turns to read from Johannes precious gospels. Cynog's eyes would glow as he listened and the other pupils seemed to enjoy those quiet moments; although some preferred my lessons with the sword, sling and spear.

Winter and spring passed quickly as we worked, studied and played. We'd receive occasional invitations to Garth Madron when I'd try to steal time alone with Dwynwen. With her sisters as chaperones, we'd walk out and our hands would brush. I'd feel tingling reach my heart whenever that happened. The girls would look the other way if we dawdled behind or ran ahead. The world felt heady and I longed to see her face more as each day passed. I felt made of light when she stood near.

She was a will of the wisp, never letting me take her hand or get too close, often acting distant and distracted. If I tried to hold her in my arms she'd freeze and push me away. She was impossible to understand; one moment warm and enticing, the next formal and cold. When we were alone, she seemed as confused as me, unsure what she wanted or expected. I fantasised constantly about making love to her, caressing her body; but at night my dreams were inhabited by Frid, and our passionate encounter.

One summer morning I was woken by a feather-light kiss on my forehead. I shook my head expecting to see Tas or Beah, but it was Dwynwen. I tried to catch her hand but she was already standing back grinning, fondling the dog's ears. They should have warned me, not let someone creep in. My wolfhounds trusted her, had not barked.

'My brother tells me you need a day to rest, Cousin? He says you work too hard. The day is set fair, it will be hot. I will show you somewhere you'll like, my favourite place in all the world.'

Her pony was outside, mine already saddled beside it. The day promised to be beautiful, pale blue sky and wisps of clouds dissolved above us, the sun warm, with a soft breeze at our backs. She cantered off, calling Beah to follow; I struggled to catch up. We crossed the Wysg at a ford beside a huddle of huts, emerging into a flat-bottomed valley, trotting beside a stream, climbing higher. The valley ended at a steep incline and Dwynwen dismounted, indicating to the right.

We led the ponies beside a boulder strewn river-bed, where short falls of water tumbled and sighed into pools. We reached a high cascade of white froth, falling in sheets onto a smooth rock and gurgled on into a basin two spears deep and wide. The polished stones surrounding it warmed by the morning sun.

'Here,' Dwynwen decreed; throwing down two soft sheepskins.

Pulling a bundle from her pony, she handed me a flask and leather satchel. I called to Beah and walked downstream; ordering him to stay a hundred yards distant, beside another rumbling fall of water in the shade an ash tree. I gave him a rabbit caught the day before to eat, then walked back to Dwynwen. An expression of uncertainty shadowed her face for a moment as she sat and patted the fleece beside her.

'Sit here. What do you think? I love this place; it calls to me each summer. I have never brought anyone here before. Father would be furious. It's not our land, we have crossed the Wysg. Glywys rules here,' she shivered. A shadow clouded her eyes.

'It is a marvel, but, but… I was wondering. Glywys is your betrothed, when will you wed?' I never dared ask her directly about it until today.

'Never, I will run away again. Grandmother refused him years ago, said he had dark rages and was known to be cruel. Grandmother and Father have argued bitterly. Father won't admit it, he's not prepared to lose face, but he regrets agreeing. He has let me put my marriage off, but after harvest Glywys will come.'

'We must flee before then. Dwynwen, marry me instead. I have loved you since the day we met and I was so stupid, corrected your Latin. You can't run away alone, it's too dangerous.'

'I will cut my hair, become a man. You don't have to marry me because you are sorry for me.'

'I'm not. Didn't you hear me? I have loved you since I first saw you. You are the meaning of life to me. I can't bear to think of you with that man, his undressing you. I have a kingdom, my brother has given me rich lands in Ulster. You will be my queen.'

She looked at me troubled and unsure. I picked a hare-bell from the bank.

'Look, this is the colour of your eyes, that foxglove pink and freckled like your cheeks. You are lovelier than anything in this wondrous place. I want you for my own.'

'Don't flatter; come on let's bathe.'

I gulped as she removed her tunic and jumped into the pool wearing only a flimsy linen shift. I shrugged off my clothes quickly, I wore no undergarments and jumped into the pool beside her.

Damn it was cold. That mountain stream was freezing despite the heat of the morning. I felt my manhood shrivel to nothing. Dwynwen splashed beside me, laughing at my gasping and spluttering. I ducked her under the water in retribution, revelling in the smoothness of her slim body and auburn hair. I tried to fondle her but she pushed me away and climbed the bank into the sun. I caught too brief a glimpse of small beautiful breasts and long shapely legs and longed for her.

I pulled out of the water to lie beside her on the warm boulder and told her again how lovely she was and how I wanted to marry her. As I talked, I stroked her hair, my caresses getting longer and longer, reaching down her back. I felt her body soften and relax, responding. As I tried to fondle the roundness of her smooth buttocks, she pushed me away in horror.

'No, Maelon, what are you thinking. I must remain pure, unless I am married before the Lord. You, you are a nearly a priest... how could you try to seduce me?'

I was confused and angry.

'You woke me with a kiss and brought me to this hidden spot. You took off your clothing and jumped nearly naked into the pool. I've asked you to elope with me, we would marry. What was I supposed to think? Don't accuse me of seduction, that was your idea, not mine.'

'I brought you here because I wanted you to see how lovely it is, no more.'

I'd had enough. If she'd let me kiss her, she'd change her mind. I forced my lips onto hers, she froze at their pressure. I didn't stop. Holding her tighter, I ignored her struggling beneath me, kept on kissing her, running my hands down her body, over her breasts.

I heard a rustling behind us. Turning in annoyance to tell Beah off, I saw four men standing on the river bank. They were nudging each other in amusement. Dwynwen gave a yelp of horror.

'A pretty pair,' said their grizzled leader, glass hair beads glistening in the dappled sunlight.

'Must be rich looking at the ponies and the arm-rings on that lad. Who can he be?' replied a spotty youngster.

'Not from our lands, that's for sure, we'd know them. I recognise the girl. She looks like that freckled bastard Brychan, her father. What shall we do? Kill him and rape her?'

Dwynwen screamed again.

'No, Glywys will do that when he finds out his betrothed swam naked with this young dog. I doubt she's still a virgin. Best tie them up and take them to him. If I'm right and it is Brychan's daughter we'll be rewarded. If we are wrong, there'll be a fat ransom judging by their clothes and horses.'

I trembled terrified, could scarcely breathe. I had no weapon and no chance. Even if I called Beah, who might take one man down, to fight naked would be hopeless.

'Let us dress in private at least; the lady deserves that.'

The leader acquiesced. 'Very well, don't try anything. If your girl is who I think she is then she's a whore, not a lady. She will get what's coming to her.'

Taking my clothes and I went downstream to the ash tree, leaning over I whispered to Beah, 'Go home.'

I tied a raven arm-ring to his collar, Gastyn would know I would never remove my brother's ring except in the worst emergency.

I pushed him away. 'Go home. Find Tas.'

He was well trained but would he leave? Beah whined, I coughed and spluttered to cover the sound. I walked back as calmly as my shaking legs would allow. I returned wearing my habit, to whistles and hoots of derision.

'Who'd have thought priests keep anything apart from a holy cross beneath their skirts?'

'This one is not so holy.'

'What about all those thou shalt nots?'

I clenched my fists in anger and frustration. They tied our hands in front of us and made us get up onto the ponies. I surreptitiously kicked off a shoe, praying Gastyn and the hounds would find it, along with six sets of hoof prints and guess what had happened.

I glanced at Dwynwen, who rode beside me, mute. The ride along that valley would have been lovely in other circumstances, after an hour we stopped at a settlement below a flat mountain. When we arrived, it was clear that the men were part of a larger hunting party. Horns blew at our approach and more warriors emerged from the gateway, at the fore their leader, a tall, dark-bearded man of middle years, less than thirty.

Dwynwen murmured in dismay, 'Oh no, it's Woolos.'

And so, it proved, Prince Woolos was collecting taxes and hunting boar. His men had been out searching for tracks and found us instead.

After speaking with them Woolos approached, his face stern.

'Dwynwen, you are soon to be my father's wife. I am surprised to see you here and in the company of just one man?' He looked at me enquiringly. 'Who are you, I understand beneath that tunic you wear gold?'

'I am Dwynwen's cousin, from Ireland. Thank you for your hospitality, this has all been a misunderstanding. My cousin was showing me the waterfalls and pools close to her father's borders.'

'In Ireland, men go naked to view the countryside then?'

My heart sank, there was no chance they would believe nothing had happened between us at those falls. I had hoped to make love to her there. Why should anyone believe my denials?

'Woolos, for the sake of our friendship as children please, believe me. I am still pure. You can get one of your women to,' Dwynwen blushed, 'to examine me if you like. I am intact. Nothing happened.'

'I doubt anyone will accept that, even if the women tell them you are a virgin. I have sent to Garth Madron for your father. I had no choice, the men are bound to talk, my father will have to know.'

'No, please don't let them come here. Take us straight home, Woolos please, please for pity and the Lord's sake. My sister Gwladys is in Garth Madron, she'll be pleased to see you and grateful that you helped keep me safe. I don't want to marry your father, any more than you want me as a mother-in-law. Please, please. My father's fury will be enough to bear.

'Think what Glwys will do to Maelon, his tempers are renowned. He will kill him, and it won't be an easy death. Maelon's brother, the High King loves him. Your shores will be harried and ravaged by Irish raiders if Maelon dies by your family's hand. Your father can't live forever; it will be your problem, not his. Please Woolos, I beg you.'

Woolos looked worried. With a sinking heart, I realised Dwynwen was begging for my life. The two obviously knew each other and the likely consequences of the afternoon too well.

Woolos gestured into the settlement. 'Give me time to think. I wish to God you had not crossed our border today. Talk of the charming young King over the Sea has reached me. How fond your grandmother is of him and that Brychan fears him because of that.'

He glanced at me, dismissive of the dark haired young man causing so much trouble.

I was separated from Dwynwen; sent to a hut distant from the gate and guarded by two men, bread thrown in after me. I was in deeper trouble than ever before. My father's voice sounded again in my memory, 'Be sure not to annoy or antagonise Brychan.'

At dusk, I heard a commotion. Woolos stood at the door of my hut, restraining my furious uncle, red and sweating. Rhain stood beside him and couldn't meet my eye.

'Let me at him, I'm going to kill Inne's damn son. My daughter, how dare you put your stinking hands on her.'

Woolos rumbled, 'Peace, friend. For the love your father showed to me as a foster son, listen. They swear nothing happened. Dwynwen has even offered her virginity be examined. She insists she would not lie with a man until after marriage and the Lord's blessing. You have brought your children up to be godly. This is a harmless dalliance, foolishness. We were all young once, even you.'

Brychan stopped struggling. Woolos still held his arms firmly, but he no longer pulled at him. Woolos risked a joke. 'Tales of your youth in Powys and your wooing Ban are well known across Wales.'

'Yes, and she was with child before we wed, what if …

I spoke, 'No, Uncle. Woolos speaks the truth. I have not lain with Dwynwen. If you think I have damaged her reputation I will marry her. I love her, but that love has been chaste.'

I realised my words were unwise. Brychan expression became apoplectic.

'Let you marry my eldest daughter. Do you take me for a fool? You want to steal my kingdom.' He grasped at his sword and I heard Dwynwen scream out, 'No.'

I cowered, waiting for the blow. Woolos still held his arms and strained; younger and stronger he prevailed, as Brychan struggled and cursed at him.

'Stop. This is my land. My Father and I rule here. I command you cease. The boy is your nephew. It would be a sin to kill him if he is innocent'

Brychan lowered the weapon and scoffed. 'You think your father won't demand his death? You are mistaken. My daughter is promised to Glwys, this Irish cur has dishonoured us both.'

'I hope my father is wise enough not to harm the Irish High King's brother. The King that sends men to harry his coastline each summer,' replied Woolos. 'He will have to be cautious and I suggest you should be too.'

I tried reasoning with my uncle again.

'Uncle, I don't want or need your land. I only returned as escort to Patricius and ask for Dwynwen's hand. I will go home to Ireland. Let us marry and leave for Ulster. I have a kingdom waiting for me. I will be your ally and won't send raiders to Wales. I'll make them go north, or to Armorica and Gaul.'

'Father please, let me go. I don't want to marry Glywys. For,' she hesitated, 'Ellyw's sake, please don't make me.'

We watched for Brychan's response. I held my breath. No one mentioned Ellyw's name to Brychan, ever. He crumpled, looking despairing.

Woolos broke in, 'Let us eat. There is fine game in these mountains. We caught a fat hind yesterday; its haunch is roasted and ready. It is good to see you, Brychan, foster brother and friend. Feast with me, then take your family home.

As we made ready to leave Woolos took me to one side.

He whispered, 'Do not trust Brychan, he will not forget this slight. I learnt that as a youngster in his father's court. Escape while you can. If you don't, you will meet with an accident, one that is fatal. He lives by Christ's tenets but if he is pushed too far, he lashes out.

'This insult is too much to expect him to forgive. Forget Dwynwen, as I try to forget of her sister, Gwladys. I dream of Gwladys each night, call her name in my sleep, she haunts my soul. My father refuses to let me ask for her; it would be sinful because he is to marry her sister. Brychan's girls are enchantresses, their charms are merciless. Take care Maelon of Ireland.'

CHAPTER
18

Humiliated and exhausted I was escorted to our little church that night. I heard Brychan's men snicker and joke about my naked capture.

Gastyn gazed at me. 'You fool Maelon, you put the church at risk, not just yourself. When Beah arrived with your arm-ring I had to go to Brychan. What else could I do? This church is on his land. Anlach gave it to us, but Brychan can as easily evict us.'

'Peace Gastyn, you are right; but she fills my thoughts. I think of nothing but her eyes, her smile and imagine her caress. I have to have her.'

I tried not to think about the kisses beside the stream. If those men had not interrupted us what would have happened? Would Dwynwen have softened and kissed me, loved me back? What would I have done if she hadn't? I'd been so furious that she'd rejected me. I wasn't certain whether I'd have stopped. Might I have forced myself on her, surely not? I shuddered thinking that, hated myself.

I replied to Gastyn, 'I can't bear to think of Glywys's age-pocked hands on her. I met him once. Years ago, when I was travelling with Sylvester searching out relics. Cor Tewdws was in the heart of his kingdom; it stretches from here to the coast and beyond to the river of the swans. He is old, sixty years or more, has scarcely any teeth, is lean as a mangy stoat. His breath smelt foul. I pitied his wife, she was cowed and fearful, flinching each time he spoke.

I'm going to Garth Madron and try one more time. I'll ask for Grandmother's support.'

The thought came, she doesn't want you, won't take you. Why are you risking your life? You're a fool. Then in response came sharp. No, I'm Niall's son. Why shouldn't I have the woman I want?

Gastyn tutted; he seemed untroubled by desires, had never shown any interest in girls, or boys. Gastyn was a pure soul, his love as far as I could tell, directed only to our Lord Jesus.

Three days later, Cynog galloped up to the clas, his pony dripped sweat. Gastyn and I watched him dismount.

'Cousin, I have come to warn you, but may be too late. Father is livid. He has told his guards to capture you. Dwynwen is distraught.'

My heart beat faster and my mouth dried. 'Why? I've done nothing these last days, been nowhere? '

'It isn't these last days you need to worry about. Grandmother had a letter from your mother.'

'Well, what of it?'

'Aunt Inne has heard from your sister in Ireland. She wrote asking Grandmother to tell you that you are a father. The letter told that a chieftain's daughter had died giving birth to your daughter. The girl's name was Freid, Frid, something like that. That girl insisted that she had only ever lain with you, the King over the Sea. It sounded as if cousin Ria believed her. There was no suggestion it was not true. *The child's grandfather asks you to go to him and discuss her future.*

'Grandmother showed Father the letter. He gave it to Dwynwen, saying that you were a seducer. That her reputation had been blackened by a philandering scoundrel.

'To make matters worse Father had to ride to make peace with Glywys. He arrived at our border yesterday; enraged that his bride-to-be is despoiled.'

My heart sank. Could it be true? It was not impossible, but surely laying one time with Frid made it unlikely?

Cynog turned the ponies head to canter off, shouting at he left, 'There is a force about to surround you.'

I had no idea what to do, I had to evade them, run away. I called the dogs, grabbed my cloak and looked around for my sword.

There was no time, moments later Brychan's men galloped up. They surrounded us, horses circling, no smiles of greeting. I knew them well so tried a joke.

'Welcome friends; you seem in a rush for a blessing today.'

Ignoring me, they drew out their swords, then gestured for me to lay down my weapon. I was trussed up and thrown face down over a saddle.

Gastyn was terrified, shaking, but insisted on coming with me. 'I must accompany him. He is our church's deacon. I cannot think what Brychan is thinking arresting his nephew and a churchman.'

The journey felt endless as I bumped along, only able to see the muddy path. I thought of Frid, the girl who had longed to see Wales and live in a comfortable villa, married to someone who loved her. A man who would take her for his only wife. Poor Frid,

I'd done her so much harm, made her hope to be taken away from a life she hated, then betrayed her.

My stomach was sore and aching from the saddle and my sadness by the time we reached Garth Madron. I was thrown into an unlit hut. Gastyn insisted on staying with his brother priest, so he was a prisoner too.

Gasty clucked, 'That it should come to this. How to get you out of this mess. I had an idea on the journey. When he returns from pacifying Glywys we will tell Brychan you have died from a fever. I will lay you out.'

'That's a stupid idea. My playing dead is unlikely to fool anyone Gastyn.'

You won't be pretending. It will seem as if you are lifeless to all but the most knowledgable. You will be cold and barely breathe. It is risky. I'll have to use a strong poison. At first, you'll retch. I'll say you were already ill, fevered. With luck, people won't come too close for fear of contagion.'

'What will you give me?'

I have been experimenting for years. A potion made from a mixture of plants. Some you know, such as wolfsbane and poppy, others you won't.'

'But wolfsbane is deadly.'

'Yes, but I will give you a small dose and will have something to counteract the poison ready. Do you have any other suggestions? Or shall we wait for Brychan's return? When no doubt, you will suffer a painful death.'

'Before I take anything, I want to see her. I want to tell her it's not true.'

'Are you sure it's untrue? When you heard about the letter, you acted like it was.'

'It's probably not, but even if it is, it meant nothing. I missed Dwynwen. I wanted it to be her I was loving, not that girl.'

'Maelon, you can't possibly say that. It will make your faithlessness worse. You know how she is. She would be true to you until death.'

'What would you have me do? I have to see her. I love her, I would die, may die for her. Every night when I try to sleep it is her face I see; she is all I dream of. I can't even remember what that girl looked like.'

Frid's pretty smile entered my mind as I said that. Why did I keep lying to myself and others about her? I wondered.

'I don't know,' Gastyn sighed, 'who am I, a celibate to advise? Sometimes I envied you Maelon, that you have felt warm arms around you, known a woman's touch. Today I don't. I fear for you. I will do what I can to find her.'

We had no chance to enact his plan. Brychan returned that night and came to the hut, ordering the guards to leave.

'So, you snivelling rat, I was right, you are a seducer! My sister's letter proved it. Tomorrow you'll die, slowly. Your testicles first, then your arms, your tongue last. I want to hear you scream.'

'No! I love your daughter more than life. That girl meant nothing. You should know that. You cannot tell me you have never known a woman who was not your wife. I was far away in Ireland, and had never dared mention my feelings to Dwynwen.'

He slapped my face hard. I tasted the metal of fresh blood, felt it trickle over my teeth.

'She is my daughter, your cousin and is betrothed. Was betrothed rather, until you went to the waterfalls with her. We trusted you.'

'I love her and want to marry her; she is still pure. She refused me. I won't pretend I didn't want to make love to her, but she wouldn't let me. You have lost one daughter to ambitious betrothals, don't lose second. Don't make her marry someone she doesn't love. Whatever happens to me, don't make her marry an old man or a cruel man. I have reason to believe Glywys is both of those.'

'Marriages are not for love. They are made to tie kingdoms together. To keep land safe. Why do you think I married the daughters of the kings of Powys and Dumnonia, not some pretty creature to keep my bed warm? Do you think I would let you marry my eldest daughter, claim my throne through her? Dwynwen hates you. She says she will give herself to God, never marry.'

'No, I don't believe you. She would not ask that.'

Turning, he left, saying, 'Dwynwen told me you have a treacherous heart. She said she hates you and prays for your death. Only your grandmother begs for your life, no one else.'

My eyes met Gastyn's, my teeth chattered and stomach churned. For the first time in my life, I could not talk my way out of this. I had no brothers to save me, no Math.

Gastyn asked, 'Will you take my potion now? I can't promise it won't kill you. You'll have stomach cramps at the start, maybe puke. I hope you won't die. I have tested it on sheep, they survived. It's too late to suggest you have a fever. I will say you have taken a poison draft rather than face Brychan's torture. He will call you a coward.'

I nodded. I had seen my father torture men, hostages, enemies or traitors. Men could be killed by inches, lashed or broken, but suffer and die anyway, it was a horrible fate.

'Will you pray with me first?'

'I will pray to Jesus, but also the Goddess, Macha.'

Gastyn looked annoyed to hear the old name and crossed himself. He handed me a cup and knelt to pray. Shuddering I drank, its smell and bitterness horribly familiar. The sour taste whirled me back to Knowth and my childhood. In my memory I stood before the Hag, trembling with dread; clinging tight to Conall's hand in that dark tomb as I swallowed her draught. I felt fear rise, the same terror I had felt in that dark chamber so long ago. Would the Goddess let me live and help me? Or had I betrayed her by becoming a novice priest?

My mouth tingled as my tongue went numb. Gastyn set me to pray aloud, but words gradually got harder to speak. I mumbled and slurred then was seized with terrible colic, had to rush to the guards outside, signalling I needed to empty my bowels, at once. Filthy fluid spouted from me, I felt scoured, as if it would never stop, excruciating cramps seized my guts.

Cold overtook me, I was shivering but at peace. I lay gazing at the thatch above me, floating, watching Gastyn pick up my hand, then feel for my heartbeat. The colours in the hut intensified. In dark corners I saw demons waiting to pull me down, their eyes glowing hot like embers. It would be a shameful death. I realised I would not go to the Otherworld. I would never see my father and brother again. I cried silent tears and watched a raven flying toward me, the bird of death. I heard a woman weeping and looked back at my body. Dwynwen; she had come at last. I tried to raise my hand, to tell her not to cry. My arm did not move, it felt as heavy as lead. As she spoke with Gastyn, I watched the raven settle on a pottery jar in the corner. Its beady eyes gleamed as it cocked its head to one side, waiting for me.

'No! Dear Lord, no! Oh Gasty, what have I done? I was so angry when my father showed me Aunt Inne's letter. Maelon has a child, a daughter, with another woman. Her voice dropped low. 'She died in childbirth, exactly what I fear most, happened. I couldn't bear to marry Glywys, encouraging Maelon seemed a way out… even though I wasn't certain I wanted that. I gave in to the sin of jealousy. Maelon kept saying he loved me. I wanted to hurt him for his betrayal.

'I prayed to the Lord. Prayed he'd die, become as a block of ice on the lake, like his frozen heart. Now look, he is cold, dead. He has gone, hasn't he? What will poor Grandmother say? It's my fault. I took him to the waterfalls; it was my idea. I jumped into the pool. I wanted him, but then I didn't. I was afraid; afraid I'd have a child, be torn apart inside like my mother.'

Befuddled as I was, I wanted to agree with her. She had tempted me. I tried to speak, but those demons sent by Macha sat on my mouth stopping it, suffocating me. I had no breath. I felt myself rise and somehow was out beyond it all. I was riding the raven's back above Lake Syfaddon. My father and Anlach appeared below the water in a rainbow of colour, the hall of the afterlife shimmered beneath its surface. All I had to do was dive into the lake, through that wavy line of light. We flew over our church as Beah and Tas barked below us. Out of rushes at the side of the lake flew two swans, each carrying a baby in its beak. What if they dropped them? I knew I had to catch them and save the children. I couldn't get off, then it came to me the raven was Conall, he'd flown from the Otherworld to help. Faster, faster, Brother, I urged.

Voices disturbed me again, it was Brychan.

'The devil, the tempter, I am glad to see him gone. He is a coward. He's taken the weakling's way out.'

'Father no! It would have been a sin for you to kill your nephew in cold blood. You might have gone to purgatory. The Lord would not have forgiven you murder. It is all my fault, I am to blame. I prayed he would be turned to ice. I'm so sorry now. I have been beseeching the Lord all morning, asking for Maelon to return.'

Brychan seemed to feel pity. I felt him taking up my limp hand.

'Dwynwen he does not breathe, the boy is already cold. The Lord cannot answer your supplications. No-one can return from the dead.'

'But we did not lie together. He was innocent.'

Gastyn interjected, his voice stern, 'The time has come for me to take Maelon to his mother for burial. She will never forgive you if she is not allowed one last goodbye. I must make haste before the body begins to rot. Give me a wagon for the journey to the school and onward.

'You have sinned by threatening Maelon and wishing him dead. Without repentance, your souls are at risk.'

I listened, detached; I was dead, only my shade heard them talk. Dwynwen loves me, a wave of pleasure. Then a wave of pain; but she prayed for me to die, she hates me.

I panicked, Gastyn planned to bury me, not burn me. My shade would haunt this damn hut forever if I was not set free.

I tried to shout, 'Don't bury me. I must have a pyre.'

As I tried, the demons returned, this time with blades. They set about pricking my legs and arms with tiny swords, sharp as needles. There were no longer any birds or babies in sight I realised with relief, they'd disappeared. I could rest, plunge into the lake's waters. Float away into sleep, I wanted to sleep.

I felt a tugging at my face, my mouth, as a paste of sour herbs was spread across my tongue and gums by a finger.

Gastyn was muttering disturbing my rest. 'Dear Lord, please don't let me be too late, he hardly breathes.'

He wound me in a cloth that partially covered my face, tight pressure bound my eyelids closed, my nose and mouth left free. I felt consciousness fade. I was riding the raven's back, no, Conall's back; flying to Tara, going home.

<hr />

My body was pulled and prodded, my cheeks were stung by repeated slaps. I tried to stop them, put up an arm to protect myself. I came to. I was in the school; Gastyn peering at me with a worried expression.

'Maelon. Thank God and all the angels. Can you speak?'

I croaked, tried to sit up but failed, then felt a soft tongue lick my hand; Kira was at my side.

'Don't try to move. I must think. If Brychan realises you live he will kill you and flay me beside you.

'What can I do? What is for the best?

'I will take you to the mines and Math. He will escort you to your mother or if not there to Ireland.

'You fool, all for a woman. She is destroyed too, poor girl. No one will take her, she is ruined. We must leave here.'

He rushed around the clas like a demented goose, throwing things into a cloth bundle.

'Who will care for my herb garden while I am away? It's the worst time of year. What a stubborn fool you are.'

Cynog's face appeared around the doorway. Gastyn stopped, his face showed terror.

'He's alive, praise the Lord.'

'No one must know, please don't tell. If your father discovers the truth, he will destroy the church and its school. I will be sent away, if not worse. All of Sylvester's and Cedric's work will come to nothing.'

I felt a sharp pang of guilt; I'd caused this trouble.

Cynog replied, 'I see that, Gastyn. I shan't, don't worry. I am glad my cousin lives though. All this and he didn't even lay with my sister. Would it ever have been worth it? I hate the trouble women cause. Ellyw, Dwynwen and so it goes on.'

'I'll watch over the school while you take him north, and yes, before you ask, I'll protect your plants if it snows. I'll cover them with bracken from the pile. I know what to do.'

As he spoke, he walked, calmly sorting and organising, placing my sword on the bundle with Gastyn's bag of remedies and food. Cynog created order and calm wherever he went.

Gastyn asked, 'The dogs? What of the hounds? They will only obey Maelon. What shall we do with them?'

Hoarse I whispered, 'Kira must stay with Dwynwen, to protect her. Kira loves Dwynwen. I will leave Tas with Math, and Beah... Could we say Beah was given to Mother? I cannot bear to lose all three dogs.'

Finally, our ponies were loaded and I prepared myself for yet another journey. I looked around sadly. I'd built this peaceful community with my own hands, but while Brychan lived I'd be unlikely to return. What did my future hold?

In Bannavem Gastyn told Math the sorry tale, he shook his head.

'You want me to take him to Ireland? Maelon, I am old, this is my last trip for you. My final payment for the debt of honour. That Gastyn said he will take you to your mother, rather than bury you in your church, may strike Brychan as odd in a day or so. It would me. We will not go north, that's exactly where he'll search. We will take the high road over the hills to the coast. Not to Moridunum, further west, past the goldmines at Dolaucothi. There are coves on that coast known only to the fishermen.'

We waited for the tide to turn and a ship to carry me away.

Glancing at me, Math joked, 'What a pair of fools we are, saying we'd die for love. We damn nearly did.'

The Roman Empire had hardly bothered to conquer that wild and lovely coastline of west Wales; the land fit only for sheep. There were few settlements and less boats. No one was willing to sail us to Ireland. Finally we persuaded an old man and his son with an ancient craft to ferry us across the ocean; but only by paying twice what the decrepit craft was worth.

I was still weak from Gastyn's poison when we reached Irish soil. I faced a short journey to Tara. Math had been undecided as to whether to accompany me to Connacht to visit Ria and his grandchild, or return home to Wales. When we arrived, the decision was made for us, the whisper of war on everyone's tongue. As we got closer, we joined columns of families of the plain; carts, ponies and backs laden with belongings. They were making for the safety of Tara's wooden walls. There had been peace in our land since my grandfather Eochaid's rule, but people knew war meant death. Their homes plundered by armies searching for supplies.

At Tara, my brother's court was in chaos. I found Loegaire standing beside the weapon-stone; the ring and hammer of smiths sharpening swords and axes loud around the enclosure. Loegaire looked pensive, standing alone.

'Hail Brother, the dún is busy?'

'Maelon, Math, by all the gods, it's good to see you. I prepare for war… Ulster has refused to acknowledge my right to the high kingship. It has declared for Fiachrae, so has half of Connacht, our uncle, Fergus too. He's resentful to have lost land to our brothers.

'That snake Nathi escaped three months ago. He had help and made for the sea. By the time we realised he was missing it was too late to set the hounds. I have two of his sons held hostage, but he has others. Killing them will achieve little. I will hold them as bargaining chips. Fiachrae will not waver in his throw for the high kingship, he has wanted it for so long.

'Will you support me? Math, will you? Your fame will encourage others to join my war host.'

We looked around. The gathering of warriors was modest, less than we'd expect. Loegaire looked tense and uncertain. I realised to others my brother was untried, one of Niall's many sons, desperate to keep his father's land and title. Many would believe our uncle had as good a claim and was more likely to bring peace to the land. They might join Fiachrae's army. Say that he should be proclaimed at the gathering and Loegaire should cede the kingship, not fight. They didn't know Fiachrae as I did; cruel and devious, his reign would be terrible. Loegaire needed us badly.

'Of course, I will. Our brothers will come and surely Aed and Diarmuid stand firm in Connacht against Fiachrae.'

He shook his head. 'Aed has not declared for me. Remember it was Father who sent him to slavery, admittedly with Fiachrae's help. I doubt he will fight for either side. Diarmuid; well who knows, he might if he thought we were going to win. Our brothers have too much to lose not to come but they are late, curse them. The men are edgy that we are so few.'

Math winced as he studied the force Loegaire had assembled. They were a shadow of the band that he had captained years before. Where were Loegaire's hearth warriors? They should be taking charge. He stepped out and roared, ordering men to get organised, to prepare their packs, find water. They started at his shouts; a whisper that became a shout, then a cheer.

'Math mac Brain, he has returned. We cannot lose.'

Math looked stunned. He stood taller, shoulders back and barrel chest thrust out. The son of a slave, he had never expected to inherit his father's land nor status. The name mac Brain was reserved for sons of acknowledged wives. Math's position was above a servant but below a lord. His strength and skill as a warrior gained him respect, never before had he been called mac Brain.

At my waist hung Fire Fury, Math's father Brion's sword. Now was the moment to return it. I'd offered before, but that it was my father's last gift to me stopped me insisting, but the sword was Math's birth right. Loegaire would find me another.

'Friend and protector, please take Fire Fury for this battle. Use it to slay the bastard who killed your father, enslaved you and took my school and friends from me.'

Math made a motion to refuse, then paused. He nodded and with a smile lifted the heavy weapon and bellowed out to the men. 'For Úi Neill and glory.'

I heard a familiar voice calling my name. It was Finn, he limped as fast as he could towards us.

'Maelon, Thank Lugh you have come. I despaired of ever seeing you again. This young pup,' he glared at Loegaire, 'thinks I am still capable of combat. Says that no one but me can control the hounds. I agreed and thought he might be right, but knew I would not keep up and would get myself, along with my poor dogs killed. There is one other man who can control the Úi Neill Cú Faoil, and he is here. You must command them, make them tear the heart out of that bastard Fiachrae.'

I laughed. 'I'll never manage them as well as you Finn, but you are too old for conflict. Yes, I will run them.'

I longed to take charge of them and looked forward to my first battle.

A second cheer went up as Math called out, 'The King over the Sea has come to his brother's aid. We cannot lose, he has Jesus on his side. He is a holy man, friend to priest Patricius, who cared for you last year.'

Loegaire looked surprised at the cheering, and, for a second, wary.

'You are popular.'

'You would be too if you converted to Christ. You don't even have to believe, but the people need to think you do. Look around, churches have grown like thistles over Ireland. A king must be in step with his people. Father knew that, it's why he was baptised, even your mother agrees.

'Convert, people will flock to your standard. We could add a fish to your red hand emblem, that would show them they were fighting on the side of the Lord. You'll be surprised how many will come. Fiachrae is notorious for his worship of Lugh. Men may desert if they know you are fighting for Christ.'

Conflicting emotions crossed his face; irritation, scepticism and then at last relief.

'Very well I'll do it. Mother has often said the same. As long as you haven't brought that damned Patricius with you. Cocky swine.'

'No, he's in Gaul. There are other priests in Ireland, but they are afraid of you. Worried the Úi Neill's will have them whipped or enslave them. I'll find one to baptise you in front of the Christian warriors. We will ask if any men want to join you in receiving the blessing.'

'Many are sworn to Lugh. Why would they? Are you sure this will not make me appear weak?'

'I'm certain. Ireland is changing and its kings must change with it.'

Word spread and over the following days men appeared at Tara, many but not all, Christian. They wanted to join the fight against Fiachrae, a pagan with a reputation for cruelty against believers. As they arrived Math began their training, formed them into groups to fight together. Calpernius had often talked of Roman battle tactics, training and how Rome defeated Britannia.

A rag-tag rabble became disciplined and obeyed orders, a force to be feared.

Loegaire recovered his confidence. A dozen days later our brothers arrived, we were ready. It was as well, our scouts reported that Fiachrae's men of the swan approached.

Math said, 'They will be tired from their journey and will only have supplies they have carried or stolen. We are rested, well-fed and ready. Let's pick our ground, tempt them to us.

'Maelon, you have the Cú Faoil and command the southern hound masters. How will we know you? You need an emblem and so do your hounds-men.'

'I could use the red hand and fish like my brother?'

'No, we need to be sure who's in charge and whether they are our dogs. You need a badge of your own. Pick, make it simple, easily seen and fast to paint on shields. What will it be?'

My shield was white with a bronze boss, plain workmanlike. How could I stand out? Dogs were too difficult to paint clearly, I need a design drawn large with a couple of strokes and visible from far away. I'd noticed a vat of yellow gorse flowers, used by the women to dye woollen cloth outside a hut. A yellow circle would suffice. I used a hazel branch, its leaves served as brush, but the result looked more like a flower than a circle, like the spring daffodils that grew on the mountains above Syfaddon. No warrior used a flower for an emblem, flowers were for women. I tried on another shield, again outlining a bold golden circle but once more petals appeared. I studied it from a hundred paces. It was clear, in fact, I liked it, anyway, there was no time. It would have to do.

Math laughed, 'Maelon of the daffodils! So be it. Make your men ready, your shields will dry overnight.'

After two short hours of sleep, I was woken by a guard. I blinked, bemused in the darkness. They told me a chieftain from Fiachrae's band had crept to the gates and demanded to speak with me; his name was Diaré of Ulster.

'Bring him to me.'

Diaré was roughly pushed forward and knelt before me.

Taken aback I told him, 'Get up, I do not want your subservience. Tomorrow you will fight the Úi Neill's. Why are you here?'

'I need to talk to you… about your daughter, my grandchild. I am afraid for her future. Every omen predicts Fiachrae's force will fail. We have seen the blackest of portents. Our camp is afraid. I come to beg you to protect my grandchild if I perish.'

'What do you mean?'

'The march south has gone badly. Many suffered a bloody flux in their bowels. The worst affected are fortunate. They have left and returned to their homes. Fiachrae was one, too weak to carry on. He was left behind in secret, with a dozen men to protect him.

Then wo days ago Nathi and his band set out to hunt, tracking a hind. It took cover in a copse and he sent in hounds to flush her out. There was a great growling and howling. When the dogs returned, they didn't have the deer; rather one carried a dead goose, white as snow in its maws. From a distance it looked like a swan. A huntsman claimed he saw a hare bounding away from the wood, but no hind. The worst of omens, our army is cursed.

'Nathi tried to bluster; but we saw the bird, limp, dead in the hounds' jaws. The hare is the omen of ill fate. The war bands are fearful, there is talk of deserting.

'My grandchild, a girl child,' he hesitated, 'my daughter told me she lay only with you. I counted the moons of her return to us; the time was right. Frid believed the child was yours. Will you acknowledge her?'

'Your daughter was beautiful. I am sorry, I should not have behaved dishonourably. She told me she was a chieftain's daughter, not a servant, but Frid was comely. I...I admired her bravery and her boldness.'

'You will acknowledge the child as yours? Swear to care for her if I die, as Brehon law dictates?'

'I swear Diaré. I will protect your line, after all, it is also mine. I will take the child, should you be slain. You could stay? Fight with me and my brother?'

'No, my fiann stands with Nathi. He would punish them if I betrayed him, besides I swore an oath. I am a man of honour. I am relieved you are too. Care for the babe, King over the Sea, treat her considerately. Order your men to let me return to my camp.'

At dawn, I found Loegaire and explained that our enemy was discouraged and afraid. He called druid Laidcenn, asking him to spread the story around the camp and give heart to our men.

I left to check the hounds; over thirty bayed at my approach. I commanded six hounds-men; each carried a shield with a yellow flower strapped on their back; we needed two hands to control the dogs. I'd tucked Anlach's axe into my belt, shuddering in the knowledge that it might soon whirl its death song once more.

Loegaire's war band had increased day by day as Christians came to support their newly converted high king and his brother, the fabled King over the Sea. Men were encouraged that they could now worship freely without fear of persecution.

We marched toward the sacred River Boinne where our foe waited, five hundred strong, although bards would sing of a thousand in years to come. This was Loegaire's land and that of our father and his father before him, he knew every rise and fall; but so did Nathi, our cousin. We achieved the higher ground. I stared across the river plain, in the distance in a bend of the river was Knowth mound, fortified by my grandfather and sacred to the old gods. Spread before us a war host, close in number to our own, as if reflected in a lake. Nathi must have been disappointed, two weeks ago we would not have matched him.

This battle would weigh heavy in lives and blood. I swallowed, felt fear squeeze my guts so hard I groaned. I had never fought nor raided, unlike most of the warriors standing before me. How would I fare? Conall had talked of battle fury, blood lust and the joy of killing. Would I feel that or freeze and die in my first fight? What a waste of the men standing in front of me in the thin morning sunlight, brave and proud. So many would be slaughtered for Nathi and Fiachrae's ambitions.

I scrutinised their pack, how did it compare with mine? Their handlers struggled to manage thirty to forty animals; they were barely under control. Dogs snapped and snarled at each other, others wandered free, leashes trailing as the hounds-men tried to call them to heel. Some fought over haunches of sheep; they'd fed them! What were they thinking? War hounds should be starved before battle. Finn would be disgusted by their lack of discipline. The dogs would kill and main when the time came, but if they couldn't work together, they might attack their own side or each other. My hounds would leap and harry an enemy, dart in, savage a limb, retreat to leap at a face, then disappear back to may side before a sword thrust harmed them.

Finn would tut and criticise. As I thought of Finn, a memory from my boyhood returned.

"Hounds and wolves hate chaos. They look for a leader. You, Maelon, with your head-hound must lead, always in command."

I listened carefully to the hounds-mens' calls, they were no different to the ones I used. Well, why would they be? I called Beah to my side and crept closer, scarcely beyond their arrows reach. I stood. With firm, loud whistles and calls, I demanded Fiachreae's pack come to me. As I did so I walked steadily backward to my own hounds. Beah gave a loud, low growl, then barked repeatedly, deep and aggressive. He paused and repeated his command.

'Obey or face my fury,' is what his bark cried out. He used it often in Wales, keeping his place as top dog.

All hounds and handlers paused, confused. The dogs' acute hearing causing them to quiet. There was no single master on our opponent's side to countermand my instruction. Beah bayed then, he howled, long and clear. I whistled again as if they were my own.

Thirty war hounds turned as one and came to me. Handlers struggled with leashes as their dogs pulled away. A handful remained, straining at their collars, but the majority were untied, so ran directly up the hill. One bitch approached Beah nuzzle to nuzzle, sniffed, then content stood beside him and barked approval to the newcomers. I ordered the dogs to lie, to wait. My pack obeyed in an instant, the others were slower, but then settled, ears pricked and ready for my command.

Men watched with joy or horror. The armies had been closely matched, now every wolfhound was under my control. Nathi's men knew a terrible attack would begin at the trumpet's sound. Savage teeth would render them crippled or worse. No place in the halls of the Otherworld when your throat is ripped apart.

I pitied them; no despaired for them. They should not die for Fiachrae's and Nathi's ambitions.

Holding my shield as protection from a stray arrow, I marched back to the rise, head high, booming out as Abod Cedric had taught me.

'Welcome to Southern Úi Neill, men of the North. Know me, I am Maelon mac Neill, King over the Sea and deacon of the church; a church of peace and forgiveness. I offer you greetings.'

A whisper travelled through the men ranged before me. My name was well known, if not my face. I stood before them, master of a ravening pack of hell hounds. I would bring death; but I had talked of the church, a forgiving church. Nathi tried to rouse his men to jeer, it came out ragged and soft. The armies wanted to hear what this man with a flower on his shield had to say.

I gestured to Loegaire. 'My brother has converted to Christ and welcomes those men who worship with him in Jesus. We hope you have come in peace and will join me in a Christian service on the sacred site of our ancestors at Knowth. It will bind our lands together; as did my grandfather, Lord of Slaves, when our fore-fathers worked to build the fortress on the mound of the ancients.

'It may be you have not come in peace? In which case, l must loose my hounds. I hope for peace in Jesus' name, so offer you a choice. My kindred in the Lord who wish to join me, I invite to move towards the river. Those men such as my cousin Nathi who hoped to steal my brother Loegaire's kingship may remain with their warriors, to face our wrath.'

I waited, scarcely able to breathe. Could I split the host spread before me using words and threats? Would religion work to divide it? If it stopped blood being spilt, it seemed to me Jesus would approve; but how to appease the old gods? They'd want blood. There was a shuffling as men edged away from Nathi and his warriors.

A hundred or so men melted towards the Boinne. There were scuffles as others drew swords. Most knew fights within a fiann were the surest way to die. Nathi tried to drown out my words. His druids shouted incantations, sending wild curses out towards me, spitting and tearing at their clothes.

I called above the melee, 'Fiachrae show yourself. Where are you? Have you abandoned this war so soon? Do you fear we sons of Niall so much?'

My words were lost to all but the closest of our opponents, but news their leader had abandoned them swept through the host. They were left fearful and silenced. I recognised faces in the remaining men and took the opportunity to sow further discord.

'I am glad that Christian men's blood will not stain this plain today. I am also sad, for brave Milchu and Dairé still stand beside my perfidious cousin.

Milchu is a brave warrior and guardian of the old gods. He will have sling-stones from Lugh of the Long Arm's Mountain, some friends from the south will die under their weight today. Numbers weigh heavier than stones, however. Badbh's' red-mouth crows of war will shriek and gorge on the eyes of his fallen. I wish we could feast as friends and reconcile our differences. We respect the old gods, who have sent you dire warnings these days past.'

Patricius would be appalled, there was no question of respecting the old gods in his church. I knew better.

'Diaré too, well met. I undertake to take care of your heir, a granddaughter, my child.' There I'd said it before everyone, acknowledged the baby. 'It is sad you will not live to watch her grow into a comely woman. Reconsider and stand aside. I will not allow your head be placed at my brother's feet, and your body fed on by beasts. I give you my oath your remains will burn with honour, if you choose to fight, however hopeless that choice.'

Diaré and Milchu looked gratified at being singled out but afraid. They stood in a depleted army, facing five hundred warriors on the high ground, ready to stream down and to overwhelm them. Both were relieved for an honourable way out of inevitable defeat.

Milchu spoke first, loud and clear, 'King over the Sea, thank you for the respect you have shown my warriors and the old gods. I will stand aside in this battle.'

Diaré nodded agreement. 'My fiann will not take arms today. We will discuss your daughter tonight.'

This unsettled the remaining men. The omens were black, warriors they thought brothers had defected and two of their number anticipated defeat. Many moved with Diaré and Milchu to stand beside their Christian comrades. Around two hundred men remained in Nathi's host looking anxious and agitated. I doubted they'd fight. Most would turn and run, no augury needed to foretell a rout.

I heard a familiar voice call, 'High King Loegaire, I too am saddened men must die this day for a false claim on the kingship. I am outraged that your cousin has marched on your land when he held a position of trust as your levier of tribute. The gods and honour demand blood should flow this day. I demand that Nathi son of Fiachrae fight me, Math mac Brain, your champion. In years past Fiachrae enslaved me and tried to kill the King over the Sea. We have a blood-feud to settle.

'I ask that Nathi faces me in combat. Our armies can return home with honour, he and I will fight in their stead. The battle is already won by High King of Ireland, Loegaire and his brother, Maelon, Hound of Ireland. Nathi must be punished for his impudence.'

This was clever; Irish warriors loved to fight, had been bred for it, they hated dishonour above all things, even death. The gods of war must be appeased. Warrior princes, Math and Nathi, would fight instead of the armies. Men could thrill to the duel and tell tales, whatever side they were on. Math's new name for me was astute; he'd drawn on the legend of Chulainn, Hound of Ireland, young, invincible and faithful warrior of his king.

The last of Nathi's men moved away. He was alone and trapped. To give my cousin his due he was stoic, gave no sign of the terror he must feel. He gestured acceptance of the challenge. His household warriors trussed him up and pushed him to Loegaire's feet.

Math was more than a decade older than the last time they'd fought, but so was Nathi. Math was sober, no tricks could help Nathi this time, there was no ten-year-old to beg for mercy. It would be a fight to the death.

Loegaire stood, holding aloft the carved stick of the high kingship. 'I grant my champion's demand. Whatever the outcome I declare Nathi and Fiachrae's lands in Ulster forfeit. In future it belongs to my brother and deacon of the church, Maelon of the yellow flowers. Tomorrow, my brother will hold a Christian service on Knowth mound.

Tonight, we will feast and watch my cousins, Math mac Brain and Nathi mac Fiachrae, fight. Everyone will return home without honour lost, nor blood spilt; every man except for one.'

That night the camps combined, shelters were raised, fires lit and food prepared by the servants and slaves. A great tent was thrown up for the chieftains, weapons ostentatiously left in a mound at the entrance. Nathi, loosely bound, was left in a corner huddled and abandoned, everyone avoiding his bitter gaze.

Music and drumming sounded, heather-scented golden mead circulated, men relaxed as the evening darkened. There was laughter and jokes. We loved to battle, but I mused, most preferred survival as long as honour was intact. Fights would be picked later, fists bared, but first, we waited breathless for the contest to begin.

Math sat beside me drinking weak beer and sent some to Nathi, along with bread. He didn't want it said his opponent was weakened by lack of sustenance. Math was calm, collected. He'd often tried and failed to teach me how to prepare my emotions before any contest. I left him and paced outside the tent, afraid for my friend.

I found Finn waiting. 'I worried about my pack and wanted to tend to the wounded animals. There was no need, by magic it has doubled in size. That was some ruse, I am proud of you. I've never heard of anyone trying such a thing. You won that battle using whistles and words.'

He gazed up at me, trepidation on his wrinkled face.

'They whisper that the Hound, Chulainn is reborn. That the victory was yours alone and if you declare at the summer gathering they will support you, not Loegaire. That you will bring peace and prosperity to the land; like the Noígiallach, Lord of the Hostages; they say you are Niall's true heir.'

Was it true that such things were being said of me? I felt a mixture of emotions, pride mixed with apprehension. I changed the subject hurriedly.

'I didn't want to see so many die, Finn. I was afraid when it came to it. I've never raided nor fought; calling to their pack seemed worth a try. What shall we do with all these animals? We can't possibly feed so many through the winter?'

'Reward those who surrendered by returning the hounds to their owners, it will make you appear magnanimous. Fiachrae's are forfeit, they are yours now. We'll keep the best of those, you can gift the rest. I am coming with you to Ulster, I shan't stay at Tara. We will breed a new pack you and I, the finest in Ireland.'

I hugged the old man. 'That is wonderful. We should go back. The contest will start soon.'

Finn replied, 'Nathi will try something. I know it, even as a boy he was dangerous and clever. Math must take care.'

'Nathi is one man, tied up and alone. What can he do? Math will prevail, it will be the end of my cousin. Watch him though. If you notice anything untoward, give a signal.'

Space had been cleared on a rise in the land to allow a view for as many as possible. Nathi's arms and legs were untied, the two opponents stretched, flexed and bent to prepare. I called Beah to me and stood beside my brother. I drew my sword in case Nathi decided to try to take a hostage. His cold, clear eyes smouldered hatred at me and then Math.

Loegaire shouted for silence and held up an arm. I saw my hound headed arm-ring glimmer on his arm, garnet eyes blood red in the flickering torchlight, it felt a warning. Then he signalled for them to begin. Once again, after so many years the two men faced each other.

They circled warily; well matched for height. Nathi was lithe, his body firm and strong, his moustache plaited and neat below his pox-scarred cheeks. Math's long locks and beard were grey now, but he was still massive and muscular, broad of shoulder, his neck as thick as a tree trunk. He was confident, sure of his advantage.

'Prepare to die, dog,' screamed Nathi, as he lunged at Math. There was a metal slam as iron struck iron, followed by a sharp ring as they disengaged. Everyone flinched. Nathi appeared stunned by the weight of Math's blow. The two came back at each other fast and furious, sword on shield, sword on sword, the noise and skill silencing the onlookers. The tips of their blades flickering so fast they were barely visible. Nathi had to parry and dodge desperately, his shield before his face, moving to deflect each raking thrust. He was breathless, rasping wheezes sounded as he gasped for air. There was fear and desperation in his eyes.

The crowd began to shout, men cheered as Math pressed forward. His huge strength forced his opponent back, out of the fire's light and into the darkness. Men scrambled to make way. Nathi appeared to fall but it was a feint. Math lifted his sword for a heavy blow and bellowed in triumph, time slowed. The sickening truth hit me. Math had underestimated his opponent.

Nathi parried then stabbed upwards, reaching under Math's guard. His thrust dug deep into Math's shield arm, the cut gushed blood, staining the ground and Nathi with a shimmering pool of dark red. Math roared with pain, a wounded bull and he sliced across Nathi's chest in return, severing thick leather armour to open a deep gash into muscle. It was over. The sword fell from Nathi's grasp, his right arm hung useless at his side.

Nathi looked at Math and hissed, 'So bastard cousin, you think you have won. You are wrong. We will meet in the Otherworld very soon. I have finally fulfilled my bargain with Niall. End me, it won't help; you are a dead man.'

The gathered crowd fell silent.

I swallowed. What could Nathi mean?

Blood still streamed from Math's arm, he staggered and looked dazed, weary beyond measure.

Loegaire spat, 'Strike the blow Math. His life is forfeit.'

In a stroke it was done, his throat cut, my treacherous cousin was dead. What of his father, Fiachrae though? Where was he?

Finn hurried over and examined Math's wound, then he took up Nathi's weapon by its ornate handle and carefully wiped its blade on a linen cloth. Smelling the fabric, he shook his head in disgust.

'Poisoned,' he said aloud.

Finn ministered to the hounds; but if anyone in Tara was seriously injured, most trusted him rather than the druids.

He spoke directly to Math; slumped against my side, immobile, his brow covered with perspiration.

'Nathi's blade smells of two corruptions, excrement and wolfsbane. If the poison doesn't slay you, the rot from the shit will. Had it not penetrated to the bone; your blood might have washed it away but the wound is deep. There is filth deep inside the muscle'

Math blanched. I sniffed the rag and agreed, the smell of wolfsbane horribly familiar. Math's sons would have no father because I had asked him to come with me to Ireland.

Math looked at Finn steadily. 'There is only one chance then?'

'Yes, we must do it at once. We cannot wait.'

'So be it; use Fire Fury,'

Math was helped into Loegaire's great tent. Finn went to the hearth to place the heavy weapon into its heart.

Loegaire asked, 'Are you sure?'

With a pained smile Math replied, 'I will manage with one arm, I have another. It is my life I cannot do without. Let us do it and quickly.'

Finn was heating the blade, urging a slave to fan the flames faster. Loegaire ordered the tent cleared and made up a bed of skins.

I stood motionless, unable to move, help or think straight. I had seen Kira lose her leg in this way, but Math as well. How could it be happening again?

Math swigged on a pot of mead and unsteadily knelt beside a bench. He laid out his right arm along the wooden surface. Finn removed his leather belt and handed it to Math, who put it between his teeth. Loegaire nodded to two of his men, who held Math's body steady.

Taking the sword from the fire, Loegaire asked, 'Ready Finn, Math?' He swung the red-hot blade high. It slashed down through flesh and bone above the elbow. There was a heavy thud as Fire Fury hit the bench, followed by a second softer thump as the arm landed on the floor. I heard a hiss as Finn used the glowing blade to staunch a stream of blood staining the earth. The smell of roasting flesh and burning stung my senses.

Math made no sound, fainting away. I hurried to the door to retch; my brave friend would not see. When I returned, he lay flat on the skins, out cold.

Finn knelt beside him. 'Sometimes the shock of the pain and blood loss kills a man, however strong he is. The first hours are the most dangerous. We must wait, hope that poison does not spread.'

Loegaire pulled me to one side.

'He will be unconscious for hours. Come outside.'

Pulling on leather jerkins and cloaks, we emerged into fine rain.

Loegaire's voice was cold and distant. 'You won this day. Every man here speaks of you with admiration. You should have let me battle; then no-one could have suggested the throne was not mine. After today the clans will call for you to be the next high king.'

His pupils glistened, tight black gems, without warmth. I was shaken, gripped with apprehension.

'It was a moment's thought. I had no idea whether their dogs would heed my commands. Little would have been lost if they had not, who would have noticed? I was as surprised as everyone else when they did my bidding.'

'You are too honest brother. You should boast of your exploits. Ask the bards to sing songs of this day and your cleverness; which no doubt they will, although not songs of combat. Real men thrill to battle; they long to fight. You, you don't. Your words of peace are for women, not warriors. You are wise brother, but a coward.'

I was stunned by his harsh words. I bit back a retort that without my advice and Math's help he'd have no warriors, and like as not, no kingdom.

I took a breath. 'Loegaire, I make no claim on the Kingship, nor will I while you live. Chulainn, Hound of Ireland was faithful to his king, as I am to you. I will go to Ulster. I don't want to be your levier. Tomorrow you should order a priest to hold a celebration mass at Knowth.'

'Very well, I will hold trust in you. Heed this, you don't have the stomach of a king. Don't betray me.

'You'll command a Christian mass be held? Really?'

'Yes, it will make sense of these men's journey and bind them to Tara, the Úi Neill's, and you. Give back the hounds to those who lost them, then let them return home.'

I grasped him, holding unrelenting shoulders in a hug, but his body gave not an inch. He had begun to fear me as a rival despite his protestations. It had stung when he accused me of cowardice. A small voice in my head called out, if you were High King, Brychan would not dare refuse you Dwynwen. Had I done right by claiming I didn't want the kingship? My father had said when I was grown, I might try for it. Was this my moment? Could I, should I, betray my brother and grasp the throne as so many of my ancestors had before me?

I did not rest that night, my tortured dreams returned. I was a raven once more, chasing the two swans with babies in their beaks. Huge wings beat on and on, whistling through the air as I gave desperate chase, knowing I had to save the infants. I woke bathed in a cold sweat, panting, afraid. What did it mean? Why was I troubled by this dream? Could it be wolfsbane; was it the poison's stench that reminded me of my old nightmare?

I hurried to Math's side the following morning, to my relief he was awake and trying to sit up. Finn was feeding him bread soaked in warm milk and honey.

'Maelon, my friend, I can be your champion and sworn man no longer. My arm is lost and I am growing grey and slow. Will you count my debt paid?'

'Nonsense, we both know you can use your left arm nearly as well. You taught me to use both, in case of injury in battle. Of course, I release you.'

He shook his head sadly. 'True, but to fight well you need balance, mine will never be the same. If I live, I will return to Wales, Metella and our mines. It was my destiny to kill Nathi, but my fighting days are done. I will sit by the fireside, reminisce of times past and watch my children grow.'

As the sun rose, I sent out word for the Christians to gather. The entire encampment came to join the procession; nearly every man from both armies came. Mumbled excuses were made, but at bottom, those following the old gods didn't want to be left out of the excitement.

Loegaire and I stood side by side at Knowth's summit. Loegaire wearing his finest battle gear, I wore a deep red cloak held by two gold ring brooches at each shoulder. A congregation of Christians, men of Lugh and other gods mingled on the slopes below us.

I spoke first, 'Brave men of this land, I thank you for your support yesterday. Christians will rejoice and those who follow the old ways will not begrudge them this service. There must be no division in our Ireland, men free to worship as they choose. My brother, High King Loegaire mac Neill ,is Christian now, but remembers the old gods fondly.'

Loegaire spoke, 'My people, I also thank you. I gift to those who opposed me, their hounds, they leave with honour intact. There will be no tribute gathering in Tara this Samhain, I will wait until next year. My brothers; sons of Niall will levy from you; they will work as equals. This priest Maelon, he of the yellow flowers, will scribe a list. Each chieftain will have a record of what is expected from his land, I expect no disputes. Your priests may to do the same for those who offer tribute to you and keep records in their churches.

'Maelon, gentle priest of the flowers, please commence your Christian ceremony.'

Priest, before all of the kingdom he had called me priest! Not King! And gentle, using the flowers on my shield against me. Despite what I'd told him about not taking the tonsure. He'd bested me. I could not dispute in front of the assembled armies. Loegaire smiled at me sardonically. I was powerless.

I spoke to the crowd, 'Hear me, I will not stay in Tara. My brother has given me Fiachrae's land in Ulster…to rule. I will establish a school; kings and chieftains can send their sons and daughters to me to study, learn to read, build and debate. I have my first pupils, the son and daughter of my dead brother Conall ,along with High King Loegaire's first-born child.'

There, I had not given in without riposte. I'd said I would rule Ulster, priest or no. Loegaire could not deny me Conall's children in so public a place. Surely last night's dream meant I should protect Conall's two children? I'd given my oath after all. I'd take a child of Loegaire's as hostage too. I had learnt that much from my father.

With gritted teeth, I smiled at my brother. He shrugged, similarly irritated. I'd softened the insult by taking a daughter; he had several after all, but only one son. He could spare the oldest girl to my care.

As commanded I gave the mass, reciting the familiar words I'd spoken with Sylvester, Patricius and Cedric so many times before. Many men of the old religion watched silent and intrigued, but more than that, thoughtful. If Ireland was to become Christian like their new King and so many others, perhaps they should convert. It might be the clever thing to do.

I'd have no choice but approach Palladius and be ordained, but in Ireland priests could marry, despite Rome discouraging them taking wives. Our Celtic church believed priests were better married and happy. If Dwynwen could be persuaded to join me, we could be together. Dwynwen, the thought of her made me sigh. I ached to see her. I had no idea how she felt about me after all that had happened. Did she love me, or was it true that she asked her father to let her marry me to avoid Glywys?

Before Loegaire left for Tara we met again and put aside our annoyance.

'I'm relieved you asked for Conall's children. I cannot guarantee their safety. Take Conall's two surviving widows, along with my daughter Silva and her mother. I'm tired of that damn woman.'

Remembering his adoring expression as he'd watched the lovely Frankish woman at my brother's death bed, I was surprised. I wondered why he was putting her aside.

Finn and I stayed at Knowth watching over Math, who improved each day. He showed no sign of poisoning, and after an early red flare around the stump, it settled, his arm was healing. Each evening I held a service in the little church, day by day the congregation grew. Men and women came to ask for my blessing. I was embarrassed that I was not truly a priest, but enjoyed speaking of the peaceful ways of Jesus. I thought less of the Goddess, kept the tattoo on my wrist hidden.

At last, after so long, I was convinced that the Church's message was right. The old gods were too harsh, too hungry for death. The way of Jesus was the better path. Joy filled my soul. I felt at peace with my conscience. Sylvester had promised I would find faith and finally after years of struggle I had.

CHAPTER
21

We saw Math to the coast days later. I bought him passage to Wales, sending two Welsh slaves and a grizzled warrior who had known him in his youth with him. Math insisted he would return safely to Metella and we would meet again in Wales. As he was helped aboard his face was haggard, jaw gripped with his pain. He'd put the severed arm in a linen bag in his baggage.

'I can still feel my left hand, clasp it shut and move my fingers. I try to reach for things, then I look down and remember. My hand and forearm ache horribly all night long. How can that be when they are in this bag? I will keep my limb and it will be buried with me. I'll be whole again in death.'

I nodded mute, unable to reply.

I returned to Tara to collect the children, ready to journey to Ulster, along with our hounds. Some hundred Christians begged to join me.

Rignach and Loegaire introduced me to my niece and nephew. A solemn boy of five with the look of Conall, sturdy and determined not to cry, stood holding his chubby half-sister's hand protectively. I saw the man he might become and felt sorry, his fate likely to be similar to mine. The children's mothers looked cowed and downcast. In Loegaire's court, they were lowly, unwanted widows. Rignach's expression was sad. I saw she longed to reach out to the children, but discretion held her back.

A small girl ran in and up to Loegaire; pretty, dark curls, exactly the same colour as his own. She threw herself at him. As he reached to swing her up onto his lap, he closed his eyes distressed; holding her tight, face buried in her shining hair. Silence fell across the hall when the tall, golden-haired woman followed the child, no one dared breathe. Anguish crossed Loegaire's face.

'Lanthchilde you are decided. You will leave with Silva and go to Ulster with my brother.'

She replied, her voice musical and rich, a trace of Frankish accent on her tongue. 'I will not stay in this place now I am no longer your wife.'

'You are my wife, you know that, but I have converted. Angias has to be my Christian wife. She is Lugaid's mother, my son's mother. We have only Silva.'

'Only, only; I am the daughter of a king. My father, Merovech is king of a land wider and richer than you can imagine, not like this cold, filthy island. My brother, Childeric is a Roman general. Angias is nothing. In my kingdom Christians are killed or enslaved, worthless. We do not tolerate our gods being dishonoured.'

Swivelling on her heel she stormed from the room.

I raised an eyebrow at my brother. He set his daughter down and brushed her tears away.

'Shush Silva, all is well. Look your uncle Maelon is here. I've often told you stories about him. How we played together as children and all his silly jokes. He will care for you, teach you to read and write. I will visit soon I promise. I'll bring you a pony to ride.'

'I don't want a pony or to learn to read. I want to stay with you. Mother can go with him. Send Lugaid instead.'

She looked up at him through dark eyelashes; a girl who expected to get her own way with her father. Loegaire nodded to Rignach, who led the protesting Silva and Conall's family away.

I waited, watching him struggle to recover.

'I am un-manned brother. I give my eldest and best-loved child to your care. Please look after her. I cannot keep her mother in this court, the women are at war. I am re-living my father's troubles with his three wives. Lugaid has to be accepted as my legitimate son by Christians, as well as those of the old gods. Lanthchilde refuses to agree. I knew she would. They call her the Frankish enchantress. She is proud and will not yield her place as my first wife; she never listens to me or Mother. I cannot bear to look at her beautiful face any longer.'

'But you love her?'

'Is it that obvious? Yes, I will love her till I die, but she is impossible. You may regret demanding a child of mine to foster and teach. I know why you did, very clever. Silva is an adorable little tyrant, her mother simply a tyrant. Go, take them, so I can forget. I will see my daughter when I visit you. Keep her safe. I never want to see Lanthchilde again, it is too painful. But remember this Maelon,' he glared at me, 'she remains my wife. I allow no other man her affection.'

I shook my head wondering to see my strong brother so distressed and was intrigued to learn more of the woman who had bewitched him. The words the Hag spoke to my brother those years before at Knowth, came back to me.

'Do not betray Lugh and the old gods, else those prizes you love most are lost to you.'

I had repeatedly advised Loegaire to forswear Lugh and the old ones. To become Christian like his people, if he wished to rule Ireland. His ambition was to blame for his loss, but so was I.

CHAPTER

22

We marched to take over Fiachrae's forfeit lands. There were many along our road who came for blessings, others simply to see the man who had saved the army of Ulster. Finally, we reached Fiachrae's comfortable dún. Sullen and afraid, his wives, sons and grandchildren waited for us. There was no sign of my uncle. The women swore he had not been seen for many weeks.

Cedric's and Sylvester's voices echoed in my mind as I admired the court's location. Emain Macha, sacred to Macha, the mother goddess, was perfect for my purpose of establishing a school. The bards and filídh had been taught there for generations. A mound built by the old ones, very like Knowth, was set nearby. From it an avenue of quicken trees led to a marsh with black pools reflecting the clouds. The people knew it as sacred; where they'd place offerings into the water to ask for divine assistance.

We would build a fine church and school close by. I hoped find peace in the priesthood, but first I had to destroy Fiachrae's rat's nest and in a Christian manner.

I called my uncle's family to me in his vast hall, even larger than Tara's. Fiachrae had four wives and six concubines, some very young. Nathi's three widows were there too. Many begged to stay, insisting they hated Fiachrae, who was cruel: some made eyes at me despite my habit. I wavered, unsure how to progress, how to balance kindness with safety. Lanthchilde stalked in; without asking she sat beside me.

The first woman brought to us was old, regal and proud. The other wives made way for her with awe. They cowered, avoiding her eye. Stiff with age, she leaned on an intricately carved hazel stick, spirals and snakes climbed its shaft… Granite grey hair was coiled into a high knot on her head, her skin transparent with age. I stared at her. Something about her seemed oddly familiar.

A servant came over and whispered to us. Her name was Bodhmall, Fiachrae's queen and Rignach's sister. Lanthchilde and I exchanged glances. We'd need to be careful.

Her gaze raked us. 'So, you have come at last. I've been waiting for you, boy. You took your time. I warned my husband you had the Goddess's favour. He refused to listen and will yet regret not heeding my words.'

'And this,' cold eyes turned to stare at Lanthchilde, 'is one of the women at your turning, but not yet, not for many moons.'

I shivered to my soul. I was seven again and terrified. I recognised her voice. It was the Hag. Older, but surely it was the priestess of Knowth?

Oblivious, Lanthchilde was polite. 'I am…was High King Loegaire's wife, my lady. Have you anywhere to go now? To kindred perhaps?'

Bodhmall sniffed in disdain. 'I will leave tonight. You will not see me again. I am too tired to bother with such foolishness. I will be looked after.'

Blue eyes flicked at mine, still sharper than flint. 'You have betrayed Macha. I see it all in those robes you wear. The question is will she forsake you? If she does beware.

'I, I was unfaithful, lied about what the bones foretold for my sister's sake. And here you are, King in my husband's place, my son is slain. She has punished me sorely for my deception.'

Turning she hobbled away, her stick tapping the floor with each slow step. I could only watch her bent back disappear and tremble.

Lanthchilde shrugged, then interviewed each of Fiachrae's and Nathi's wives in turn, determining their status. Without any qualms she issued instructions.

'You will return to your family home this day. Maelon Dafodrill, the new ruler gifts you any single jewel you own, however precious, as recompense. If you remarry within a year, you will receive an additional three gold coins as bride price. Your baggage and body, all your body, inside and out, will be searched before you leave. If you take anything extra, everything falls forfeit.'

They were sent with two guards to bring their jewels, told to place them at my feet, then decide which gem to claim.

As they left Lanthchilde whispered an aside, 'It will stop them concealing treasures when they leave, or swallowing them. We are fortunate, only Bodhmall is highly born. Fiachrae married for appearance after her, not for connections. Their families will not dare object to their return, especially if they come with gold.'

Children were led in with the concubines following. I had no idea what to do with them.

Lanthchilde sneered. 'They are your enemy, but it will not do to kill Fiachrae's legitimate children and grandchildren... yet. We cannot know if or when they may be needed.

'The concubines and their offspring we will send as slaves to Wales and Armorica. They will fetch a fair price. The rest we keep as hostages, for now.'

I was disconcerted. I had not asked for her help, although I was grateful. She planned to treat this place as her court. How should I best manage my brother's discarded but beloved wife?

'I do not enslave people, Lanthchilde. We can send them away, but surely as servants, not slaves.'

'They will be safer as slaves and we will too. Servants could return to Ireland. Pretty women such as these, alone, risk being mistreated or used as whores. Why do you know so little of kingship and managing people? Loegaire would have commanded this in an instant. He'd have directed the fiann out to raid.'

'I was sent away at twelve to become a priest. I appreciate your help, although I imagine you'd be ordering the settlement even if I did not. I will not enslave my cousins. I will send the boys to Loegaire as hostages.'

She snorted, then said, 'There is much to do, or we will be robbed. If the people believe you weak your livestock and goods will disappear, as quickly as ants move a mound. We must determine how many head of cattle Fiachrae owns. Work out what remains of his treasury, and who we have to feed. You are supporting too many warriors. They will eat the dún out of its stores. Send the fiann to hunt game for winter at the very least.'

'I will allow you to manage the hall and dún, until I take a wife,' I said, trying to emphasise the word allow.

'I will build my school; I'll need men for that task. Those who wish to go reaving and can do so, gather us wealth. Some may prefer to stay and become monks. Help with building…'

I was right, of those accompanying me from Tara less than half chose to join my fiann. I pulled aside their leader; a strong fellow, as broad as he was tall. I told him that if he went anywhere near my mother's land on the Llyn, I would punish him with death or worse. To my surprise, he quaked with fear and agreed with deference.

I marvelled at it to Finn and he grinned. 'You are no longer twelve and the baby of the tribe of sons bred by Niall. Take a look in Lanthchilde's polished bronze mirror. Your father and your grandfather were huge men, with terrible reputations. Why would they not be afraid of you, despite that priest's robe?'

The remainder were happy to work building my church and school, especially when promised them land or a place in the new monastery. Grudgingly Lanthchilde found me slaves, grain and meat. For once I was content. I worked alongside them, enjoyed the planning and physical labour. We made good progress and I slept well; my dreams restful.

To my delight, my old schoolfriend Benignus arrived at Emain Macha, striding into my hall as we settled to eat. Tanned, but otherwise the same enthusiastic young man, excepting that he wore a richly dyed, purple wool cloak. His warm smile cheered me.

'Maelon, dear friend it is good to see you. I have so much to tell.

'Beni, what is that you are wearing? Isn't that colour reserved for bishops?

He blushed. 'Yes, the Holy Father decreed Ireland should have more bishops. Palladius is elderly and was the previous pope's man. I was to hand, Irish and ordained. It was not on merit, just luck, chance. I can't wait to tell you about good Pope Leo.

You have to visit Rome and meet him. He influenced Emperor Valerian to give Rome primacy over all other churches you know?'

His face glowed with happiness. Despite his protestations, it was clear he was proud of his appointment.

'I am being rude. Let me introduce Princess Lanthchilde, wife of my brother Loegaire, the High King. She is sister to Childeric, you may know of him?

Beni looked shocked and an expression of wariness crossed his face.

'Daughter to the King of the Franks?' he stared at Lanthchilde. Remembering his manners, he swept a low bow. 'My Lady, I am honoured.'

'Maelon, offer your friend some refreshments. Sit, I must organise a welcome meal for the Bishop.'

I was dismissed. Lanthchilde was in command of the household.

I waved weakly at Beni. 'Tell me about your travels before I explain why I am here. How are Sylvester and Patricius?'

'I know perfectly well why you're here. I went to our school, expecting to find you. I wanted you to join me in my mission. Gastyn told me the entire, sorry tale.'

'You went home. Did you… did you see Dwynwen?'

'I did, but not there. Let me tell you about the last year, then I have something for you.'

'Is Dwynwen well? Is she wed?'

'Peace, wait until I tell you everything. Sylvester, Patricius and I made a good journey across Britannia, although Saxon hordes threaten everywhere beyond the River Sabrina. The names, Hengist and Horsa the Saxon leaders, are spoken with awe and fear across the land. We Irish are seen as amateurs, pinpricks, as nothing compared with the threat of the men from the eastern sea.

'In Gaul, it is little different. Attila and his Huns from lands far beyond the mountains have rampaged, pillaging and burning. Lanthchilde's father's land was overrun, as was much of the northern lands of the Empire. They devastated the Western Empire, it was already crippled with famine, two harvests had failed. The barbarians came on horseback and wreaked terrible violence across the land. Emperor Valentinian sent envoys to negotiate. Pope Leo persuaded the Huns to stop at the great river, the Po and not continue onward.

'If the Huns had not left, I might not have seen the glories of Rome or the golden churches of Ravenna. Rome, you cannot believe what a wonderful city it is. Houses and temples tower above you, there are markets with hundreds of traders selling everything in your imagining and more; silks, helmets, oils, jewels, furs. It has vast harbours with huge vessels riding beside high quays. If my eyes had not seen the mass of people living there, rich, poor and slaves, I would have thought it the home of the gods, not mortal men.

'Patricius stayed in Tours at a monastic school, his mother has family there, only Sylvester and I travelled on to Rome. Pope Leo was intrigued when we arrived. No men had been seen from our Isles since Maximus, with his legions, left our shores. Learning that the kings in Ireland are pagan again and our connection through you, Leo decided to see Christianity more firmly established than in the previous pope's time. He ordered me to combat the godless tide that sweeps the northern lands, the Saxons, Vandals and yes, the Franks too. Merovech, that woman's father is one of the worst, he tortures and murders every Christian he finds.

'Sylvester taught us well, we have kept outside church politics, isolated in Wales. We are simple men, preaching from gospels faithfully copied by our good Johannes. Pope Leo was amused that I understood so little and cared nothing for the debates that so bitterly divides the church across the Roman Empire. He made me a bishop, despite my youth. Sylvester is happy teaching in Rome, reading in their libraries, talking to everyone. You must go and see Leo, you'd make a wonderful bishop.'

'Hold, I'm not a priest yet only a deacon. If Dwynwen would marry me I would be content to stay here. I'll support you Beni. I'm building a fine church on the lake; you can take it over as Bishop. I will insist my brother calls me king, not priest.'

'Ah, yes, Dwynwen,' he sighed, 'I must tell you more of Wales.'

'I returned through Tours to visit Patricius. He promises that he will join me later when he completes his studies. He says that his time as a slave, made him fond of Ireland. Sylvester insisted that you and Gastyn should learn of our adventures; he too hopes you might visit him in Rome.

'I took a boat from northern Gaul to the white cliffs of Britannia. Times are terrible in those lands beyond the Sabrina River. Everyone lives in fear of invaders, the Saxon, the Angle and the Jute. I reached our lovely church, so calm and peaceful by the lake. It felt a paradise after the terrors I had seen on my travels. Gastyn's garden grows lovelier each year.

'Gastyn told me of your, ahem… troubles and where you'd fled. He has dared not admit to anyone in Brychan's land that you are alive. He worries constantly as to what will happen when word comes from Ireland that you live. Dwynwen believed you dead at first. She asked to become a bride of Christ and establish a sanctuary, a convent. She and Brychan argued bitterly. He still wanted her to marry, but eventually, he gave way and allowed her to leave. Dwynwen went north to your mother.

'I was overcome with sympathy for you both. The sea route from Mona to Ireland is as short as any, so I determined to go to her... I realised you'd be desperate to know how she fares.'

'How was she? Does she still hate me?'

'Wait, let me explain. When I reached your mother, I learnt more. Dwynwen has retreated to an islet off the shores of Mona, it is reached by a causeway at low tide. Einion built her a shelter, a church beside a well. People from across his kingdom and beyond make pilgrimages to see the holy virgin. They ask her to intercede for them in affairs of the heart, then drink from the fresh waters of the sacred well.

'The story told is her suitor was turned to ice, dead, but Dwynwen's prayers revived him. Somehow it is known you lived, although little mention is made of your name.

'Gastyn told me about your deception, how he used poison. Dwynwen doesn't know, she believes it a miracle.'

He glared at me. 'Dwynwen is thin and looked ill. Kira still guards her, limping around the islet's rocky shores on her three legs. When I arrived on the beach across from Dwynwen's church, Kira swam over the waters, scented me, I guess. She licked me clean in her delight, whined and looked hopeful. It was a day and night before she accepted you were not following behind and returned to the island. Our poor friend set her head and tail down in despair.'

Thinking of my Kira nearly broke me. I could not see or think for a time.

After a pause to let me gather myself, Beni continued. 'When Dwynwen heard for certain you were alive, she laughed and wept. Dwynwen gave me something for you. Here,' he took a wax tablet from his bag.

269

'Thank you, Beni, I don't deserve such a good friend.'

I took the tablet and walked to the lake's shore and sat on a boulder.

I read; 'Maelon,

I was glad to see Benignus today. A bishop! He blessed me and my little church, for which I am grateful.

For months I thought you dead and grieved bitterly, as did your mother. I could neither sleep nor eat for melancholy. My heart was broken, shattered that you were dead because of my actions. It was my guilt and anguish that persuaded Father to allow me to retreat here and not to force me to marry. I am a nun and content in my sanctuary on this island.

You betrayed and deceived me, Maelon. I should rejoice that you live, that God's intercession and my prayers that brought you back to life. It was cruel of you not to tell us you survived. Rumours had reached us from Ireland, but from you, not a word, no relief from our tears. Your mother and I had no certainty until Beni came.

Don't try to search me out. I never want to see you again. You are truly dead to me. I will never change my mind. I am at peace in this little church and can do good here.

Try to live a godly life. Bring up your daughter in the knowledge of Christ.

Dwynwen.'

My heart sunk, the worst of it was she was right. I was doubly thoughtless. How could I have not have sent word to her and my mother that I lived? I had fathered a child on another woman and then tried to seduce Dwynwen. I'd lied to her and to myself.

That night in my bed, for the first time since I was a child, I wept; for my Kira, my ever-faithful friend, for my lost hopes and for how I had treated my cousin and mother. Lying there, I realised I'd always known Dwynwen would refuse me; so had everyone else. I felt resignation, then a faint sense of relief that that she didn't want me. Would I have been happy with someone who's true love had always been the church and Jesus? Who enjoyed reading the gospels and praying more than laughing and living?

Memories of Kira as a puppy, my first friend flooded back. I wept again, but for my hound alone in Wales.

CHAPTER
23

A week later the weather turned, a gale blew in from the coast, torrents of rain turned the land to mud. We could only sit and try to stay warm and dry inside Emain Macha; wait for conditions to improve. Late on the second night of the storm, a rider came to the closed gate, soaked and exhausted. The guards called me to the gateway, asking if they should admit him. It was Diarmuid, Ria's husband.

Dripping he walked into the hall and collapsed from weariness. 'Maelon, your sister and I beg for help, as does my neighbour Diaré. Fiachrae came, he took the babies. He has our son and Diaré's grand-daughter... your child. He insists he will speak only to Niall, Brion or the Welsh bastard from over the sea. Tells us a child will die in two days unless one of them comes. He must mean you as the Welsh bastard, he cannot speak to the dead; Niall or Brion. You have to come with me. He is turned mad with rage and grief. We can get no sense from him.'

As Diarmuid spoke a wave of understanding, then horror and guilt overtook me. My dreams; Fiachrae was the swan I chased. The babies they carried away were my daughter and nephew.

I had not wanted to admit I had fathered a child with Frid. I should have spoken with Diaré after the battle, but was reluctant and used Math's injury as an excuse. If Fiachrae had taken her, I might never see her now. She was motherless, with a father too interested in his own affairs to even look on her face.

'We must leave at once,' Diarmuid demanded.

'We can't ride to Connacht in this storm. You are soaked and cold, half dead.'

'It is not to Connacht we ride.' He hung his head. 'Fiachrae called a meeting of the chieftains at Cethlenn's Isle. He planned a second uprising to reclaim his land. There were fewer warriors than we expected, a ramshackle remnant of his army. We were not convinced there was any chance of retaking Emain Macha. Dairé told him the truth; that we'd lose and bring down Úi Neill wrath on us. Fiachrae was enraged. He told Diaré he'd rue his words and left in a fury. We thought no more of it, but two days later his men stole both babies.'

'Even so, we cannot do anything at night, Diarmuid. I will find you dry clothes, warm food and a rested mount. You must sleep, we can leave at dawn. I will tell my men to prepare.'

Rainwater ran from his sodden hair and down his face. 'It's not men we need. He is alone with the children. He is on the cliff of Cuilcagh, in a cave beside a hawthorn tree. He taunts us by climbing into its branches, a child screaming in his arms. He threatens to drop the babe if we approach. We don't know if he feeds them, or which he holds. In this weather neither will survive long, they will die of cold. We must leave now. It cannot wait until morning.'

I felt my gut wrench. He was right, we couldn't delay, it might mean death for a baby.

I turned to see Lanthchilde standing in the corner listening.

'I will prepare all you need. Go, rouse twenty men, get the horses saddled. I'll see to the rest. You,' she gestured to Diarmuid, 'come with me. I'll find you a change of clothing and warm food.'

Mutely Diarmuid obeyed, shoulders drooping with relief at the temporary respite.

In an hour we were ready to face the rain, wearing waterproof beaver skin hooded riding cloaks, leather breeches and long boots. A slim boy I did not recognise joined me as I woke Diarmuid, whose head rested on the table where he had eaten. Looking more closely at the lad, I realised it was Lanthchilde. Opening my mouth to object, I was forestalled.

'Don't argue and waste time. A baby will need a woman to look after it. What do you know of babies? I'm coming with you.'

I didn't bother to disagree; it would make no difference. She did as she pleased, whether with me or with my brother. Her confidence astonished me, but then so did her abilities.

We set off into the face of the gale. Rain pelted down, we could not see, water filled our eyes and those of our mounts, it ran down our faces and into our noses, drenching, cold and penetrating. Winds howled around us; trees moaned in agony at their blast.

We hunched forward, cling to our reins, praying the weather would improve. I set a steady pace; until light came, we would not be able to canter or push the horses. Diarmuid had taken all day to reach us through the storm. I held little hope of making any faster progress.

At dawn the rain eased, with better visibility, we cantered. Our horses would recover, we had to reach Fiachrae and the babies.

During a brief stop to rest our mounts and eat cold mutton washed down with weak beer I asked Lanchilde, 'Are you managing? You could follow on with two of the men?'

'Don't be a fool, we are safest with together. Yes, I ache, am rubbed raw, so are we all. I don't ask for or need special treatment. I have ridden since I could walk. I can outride most men, you and my husband included. I'm lighter than you, we should swap mounts. You may need a horse with more stamina soon. How much further can it be? We've ridden for hours.'

I didn't doubt her claims. I'd seen her riding each day, she was a skilled horsewoman. I had not been out on horseback since we'd arrived at Emain Macha.

Finally, the sheer cliffs of Cuilcagh came into sight through soft mist. Diarmuid led us into an encampment where a dozen people huddled beside a smouldering fire. One ran to greet us; my sister Ria, eyes swollen and red from tears. She hugged me and then her husband.

'I am so glad you are here. Fiachrae comes out of the cave and holds up a baby. He shouts he'll drop it to its death if Niall doesn't come. He's mad! How can Niall come? He's been dead for years.'

Ria started crying, as Diarmuid tried to comfort her.

'Look!' Lanthchilde pointed. 'In the cave mouth; up there, between the hazel and holly trees, high on the cliff face.'

Fiachrae stood there, a shadow of his former sleek self; thin, white moustache and beard unkempt, wild hair tangled and windswept, his tattooed checks were wrinkled and hollowed. I thought back to my boyhood, how he'd come to Tara, proud in his war chariot, untouchable.

He cradled a child in his arms. It was strangely touching as the old man looked into its eyes, cooed and shushed. He looked down at us and roared with rage. He held the babe above his head and its screams pierced the evening air. Echoing off the cliff face came the sound of his curses and the child's cries.

'I must speak to him while the light remains.'

Taking off my sword, I made to start up loose scree to the cliff.

Lanthchilde stopped me. 'Wait, take him food and milk for the babies. I prepared a bundle before we left.'

She ran to the horses, returned with a bag and flung its strap over my neck; the woman had prepared for every eventuality.

The climb was difficult, hand and footholds crumbled as I reached for them, slowly, so slowly, I ascended. Fiachrae watched, eyes weasel bright, they had not changed I realised. Was he really mad or was this another of his schemes?

'Who comes to call? Is it you Niall, or can it be Brion?'

I spoke in gasps, breathless as I climbed. 'No Uncle, it is Maelon. Your brothers are long gone to the halls of the Otherworld.'

'Gone, gone, so many have left. Come no nearer or this child will die. I will throw it down to its death.'

I wedged myself into the roots of a prickly juniper that grew out of a ledge on the cliff to face him. Twenty feet above me he gazed down into the chasm.

'Uncle, I bring food for you and the babies. You must be hungry? Look I have a package, meat, bread and milk.'

'Yes, we hunger. In death, there is no hunger.'

'The babies will stop crying if you feed them. Their howls pierce the night and stop you sleeping,' I wheedled. 'Let me come closer, then we can talk.'

'Very well. Maelon, is it Maelon? Child of the Welsh woman that destroyed my brother's heart. Her daughter did the same to brave Fionn. You are the son of a sorceress. Can you see into the future, Maelon? I can. I will fly from here with Nathi, north for the summer, south for the winter. Our white wings will beat and bear us aloft, onward together, always.'

He made to jump, holding the child.

I shouted, 'No, here take the bread,' and scrambled closer.

We stared at each other. My uncle's eyes changed, they became crazed, distant and confused.

He spoke, his question sent a shiver through to my core.

'Are you the raven? I see no raven in your eyes, only hounds. I expected a raven, where is it? She told me to wait here. Wait and it would come, the bringer of death.'

I could not pretend.

'In my dreams Uncle, I ride the raven's back. My brother Conall is the bird, but I am his messenger, sent by Macha and Morrigna, goddesses of the dead. Conall is departed, Nathi too is slain. Loegaire rules Ireland.'

Fiachrae spat and hissed at my brother's name.

I continued, 'I have taken Conall's children safe into my care. I am oath-bound to protect them, he did not trust their safety to Loegaire and his wives, he feared for them. Conall sent from the Otherworld for me to protect these two little ones. Can we agree to an exchange? I could foster two children of yours or Nathi's. They are my cousins. I would swear to protect them, protect your bloodline.'

Fiachrae looked thoughtful. 'Yes, we knew you too gentle and tolerant for kingship. Niall loved you, said you were his cleverest child, but he understood your weakness. He told me it would get you slain if you remained in Ireland. I recognised your feebleness; you'd hesitate to strike when you should.

'My wife told me your future. That your hand will triumph. You will suffer, but find no glory. The price, ruthlessness, is more than you are prepared to pay.

'This girl child,' he held up the struggling baby. 'Is she yours? What is her name?'

'I don't know the answer to either of those questions, Uncle. The child could be mine, but her mother seduced me. She seemed to enjoy lovemaking. I might… not have been the first. The child is likely mine; her mother swore so on her deathbed. I have not seen the babe until this moment, don't know her name.'

Gazing at the baby held in his arms I felt bitter shame. I was lying. Frid had been as inexperienced as I. He held my daughter. I had failed her again; even now I'd denied the truth.

Fiachrae stared knowingly at me. 'Your father would understand. He was cuckolded. The girl, your sister, she has two fathers. Niall knew she might be his or more probably our nephew's. Truth is neither man knew, nor did your mother. Niall acknowledged her, but it ate away at him that she might not have been his child. No man wants to be laughed at as a milksop, his wife preferring another. He hated that uncertainty. How will you tolerate it? The child's name should be Deirdre, she of the sorrows, fair and born of sadness. I would do you a kindness to throw her down, unnamed and unacknowledged.'

'No, no! You think me weak, but remember I have your sons and grandsons as hostages. Nathi is dead. I have allowed your wives to leave but the children remain. I will slay every one of them if you kill this child. I swear by Lugh and Jesus.'

Staring him down, I wondered if he would believe me, unsure if I could carry through such a threat myself. He was right I was not callous. Was that such a weakness?

He sighed, 'No one to come after, none to offer me respect in this world. I have lost everything. My time is over, my brothers departed and my heir is slain. I am cursed. Cursed from the day

I did your father's bidding and killed our brother Brion and murdered his sons. Niall's granddaughter's death would be a fitting revenge. I did it all at his command.'

He disappeared into the cave, then returned and walked with a child in each arm to the cliff edge. He teetered, balancing on the brink.

'Uncle no! Think of your sons and grandsons. Let me swear to protect them. In all mercy do not jump.'

A sound startled us. From the twisted and bent hawthorn overhanging the void came a harsh caw. It was a raven, hopping from one leg to another, head to one side watching us, waiting. An omen but of what?

Fiachrae looked afraid, his madness returned to him.

'Macha has come for me. It is her, she brings death and darkness.'

He dropped the screaming babies to the ground and scrambled into the tree, trying to reach the bird. Its beadlike eyes stared dismissively at him, and launched itself, heavy from the branch and was up, circling above us. Its rough screech bounced from the cliff face, echoing through the dusk. Fiachrae climbed on, his skin pierced by thorns. Scratched and bleeding he clambered out onto a slender branch. I struggled up the last stretch of cliff and grasped both children tight to my thudding chest.

My uncle was rambling and cursing, calling to Macha, to Niall and Nathi.

He gave a shout, 'I will fly, fly north. Nathi, son, come with me.'

He leapt, his tunic ripped, leaving fluttering red threads on thorny branches as he flung himself out of the tree. His thin arms beat as if wings for the long seconds it took him to fall to the ground. I looked down to the bottom of the cliff where he lay unmoving, head facing the sky with sightless eyes. I could not celebrate, felt no triumph, only pity mixed with scorn. He'd got all he deserved.

I carried the children into the cave and opened Lanthchilde's package. Bread soaked in milk in a pot, meat along with sweet-scented yellow mead. I gave each child the bread to suck, then tore into the meat myself, famished. The babies looked at me, the older struggled trying to stand and gurgled, smiling. I felt a wave of relief and happiness.

I turned at a soft call. Lanthchilde stood in the light, her body outlined at cave's mouth. Boy's cap discarded, her barley yellow hair flowed waterfall soft, she was lovely in those mannish clothes. Fleetingly I understood my brother's passion, she was beautiful.

'Hold that baby more upright, it's not a bag of grain. Your sister is waiting below the cliff desperate to see her son. We can't descend, it's too dark; we will camp here overnight.'

She bustled in taking charge. The spell was broken. Lanthchilde was no sorceress, a scold more like. I grinned, handing my daughter over to her.

'How did you get up to the cave?'

'Scaled the cliff. You did it, so I knew I'd easily manage. I'm light and strong, it was not difficult,' she replied dismissively. 'Go, call down to Diarmuid and Ria that all is well. I'll make a fire and heat milk for the children.'

In the morning I was roused by Diarmuid cooing at his son, rope around his waist and a basket strapped to his back.

'Ria made me climb as soon as dawn broke,' he said apologetically. 'She's desperate to see our son, little Fionn.' He hesitated, 'I named him for my brother; this child is son for us both.'

We were soon safe below the cliff and Diarmuid called to his men to make ready.

'Not so swift,' commanded Lanthchilde. She held up an arm and six of my men unsheathed their swords, with a soft hiss of metal on leather. 'You told us there was an army of traitors met to overthrow Ulster, Diarmuid?'

'Yes…'

'Where are they?'

'Still at Cethlenn's Isle.'

'Diarmuid, if you want to prove to Maelon and his brother the High King that you are no traitor to the Úi Neills, I have a task for you. Go to them, our men will accompany you as escorts. Tell the assembled army Fiachrae is dead, slain by the King over the Sea using magic. Tell them that Maelon is blessed by the Goddess and Christ.

'We expect tribute for not calling on the gods and his brother to avenge their treachery. They must deliver recompense to Emain Macha by Lughnasahd. One ox, one sheep and a drinking horn from each chieftain; our men will note their names.'

She stared hard at Diarmuid. 'As we saved your son, I anticipate a particularly lovely vessel from his brother-in-law. Ria and your son, will accompany Maelon to his new court, until you return. Not as hostages, as welcome guests, for their safety.'

Lanthchilde's tone brooked no refusal. Her smile was chilly and full of threat. Diarmuid had considered joining an army to overthrow my rule. I realised she was right. It would be foolish to allow an attempted revolt pass unpunished. The tribute demanded was modest compared to their crime. Ria and his baby son would be hostage until her husband's good faith was proven.

Lanthchilde's claim that I had the favour of both old and new gods astute.

'We will leave now,' I ordered, attempting to appear as if I were in charge and this was all my plan; rather than that of Loegaire's Frankish consort.

Back in Emain Macha Lanthchilde gave me my daughter. I held her warily. What was I expected to do with this scrap of humanity?

Her eyes focused on mine; toothless she smiled at me. My heart began to swell and tears formed as I cradled her. I wondered at her tiny hands and perfect fingers, so fragile, needing protection. This baby had never been held by a parent; she was mine, despite all my pretence and denial. In that moment, I knew her name, she would be called Frid, in memory of her bold, beautiful mother.

I felt a chill of fear. I had finally turned to Christ, accepted his teaching. I might yet become a priest. Would the Goddess and old ones punish me for renouncing them?

To the reader;

I do hope you enjoyed this novel. If you did and could find time to write a short review on Amazon, I'd be thrilled to see what you though.

If you would like to read more about Maelon's adventures, then check for the sequel. A draft extract is attached below to whet your appetite. There are photos of some of the places and walks with OS grid references from the book on my website.

semorganhistoricalfiction

There is also there is a free short story set in Wales in 1843, which relates to my first novel:

From Waterloo to Water Street
Available at;
Amazon UK   Amazon US

Wales 1843

Carpenter's apprentice, clever but cautious Will, grapples with resentment that he will not inherit the family farm. Will's jealousy increases when his handsome, radical older brother falls in love with his best friend, Ellen.

Around them the countryside is in turmoil; livelihoods destroyed by unfair tithes and taxes. The workhouse provides a starvation diet for the "deserving poor." Daughters of Rebecca are marching, breaking down toll gates that encircle Carmarthen.

Cantankerous veteran, Thomas Lewis, is tormented by nightmares of the wars against the French in Spain and the Low Countries nearly thirty years earlier.

Could telling Will the story of his campaigns and battles with the 44th help Thomas find peace? What will happen to Will and his family?

Reviews

"Excellent, a real page turner."

"Well-written, great characters, and a fascinating period of history. Must read!"

"The social conditions in Carmarthenshire that led to the Rebecca Riots and the harrowing experiences of warfare at this time are vividly described. A captivating read. I look forward to the sequel."

THE FRANKISH QUEEN

Two months passed in a fog; I worked, oversaw the building of the school and church at Emain Macha, but my spirit was flat, there was no colour to the world. I could barely bother to eat, could not sleep. My future felt desolate, only the gurgling of my baby daughter coaxed a smile, but even for her, my heart did not truly join my lips.

One morning my brother, High King Loegaire rode into the dún. Surprised to see him soon after we'd last parted, I raised an eyebrow in query.

'I miss them damn it. My daughter was the lifeblood of Tara. Without her everything seems dull. And her mother... you know how I feel.'

'Her mother, the tyrant you blessed and cursed me with? The woman you never wanted to set eyes on again! How would I manage without her? She terrifies and organises the servants and slaves, Bishop Benignus and me. We quake when she comes near with her lists of tasks. I've taken to hiding by the lake all day.'

'She is all that. Tara runs less smoothly I admit. Although there is peace in the women's huts and that is a blessing. Where is she?'

He started at a tap on his back. Cat-like, Lanthchilde had stalked up and stood beside his horse.

'The lake, so that's where you are all day, brother. I will send my lists there. You need to keep busy, not mope over what cannot be.' She glared at Loegaire. 'And peace, there is time for that when you are dead. I enjoy an argument.'

Loegaire opened his mouth to reply but the words were swept away by the missile that was his daughter, Silva flinging herself at him.

'Father, Father, I knew you'd come. Mother said not. Let me show you this place, it's lovely. I'll show you Uncle Maelon's hounds, he has taught me how to command them.'

She dragged her father away toward the enclosure, leaving Lanthchilde and me following in their wake.

'He'll expect a banquet tonight. I will go and tell the cooks to prepare.'

She stopped, putting her hand on my arm.

'I worry about you. You need a change, your heart is not in this place, you need hope... so do I. Tonight I am going to ask a boon of Loegaire. If he agrees, I beg for your assistance. Will you promise to help, without question? It is a great favour, but it may assist you as much as me. You Irish would call it a geis.'

'What will you ask?'

'You'll find out tonight. I'm not letting you discuss it with Loegaire first. He won't agree if he is forewarned.'

For the first time in weeks, my interest was piqued. What was this forceful woman planning? She was right, my heart was not in Emain Macha,

That night Lanthchilde was all charm and wit, beautiful but untouchable. She had loosened her barley hair; it glowed, shimmering like the sunset on the lake, her skin soft and white, demanded to be caressed. Her necklace of golden bees with red glass wings seemed to hum with energy, and reflected flickering torchlight onto her breasts.

The shadows behind his eyes told me Loegaire was tormented by her, ached for her. I feared she would push him too hard. He might insist she was his wife and had to obey him; take her by force. If my brother tried to harm Lanthchilde, what should I do?

Their daughter fell asleep at the harpist's tunes and was carried away to her bed. Lanthchilde dismissed the servants. I tried to withdraw.

She stopped me, with a soft hand on my arm. 'Maelon please stay. You are a priest and can read. Loegaire we have to talk of our marriage contract.'

She handed me a rolled vellum sheet. Loegaire flinched as she continued, 'You know what it says. Maelon can read it aloud if you wish. The contract stipulated I was to be your only queen. It states that if I am betrayed, my bride price and I should return home. Brehon law is no different, as a union of equals I should be your queen. I was a Frankish princess when we wed.'

She reached out to him, taking his hand and raised her eyes to his.

'Please Loegaire we are destroying each other, let me leave Ireland. Keep the bride price if you will, or else I promise to use it for Silva in years to come. I cannot bear you more children, you know that, we tried. When our daughter was born, my womb leaked poison for months. You need a son and you have one.

I cannot give you another. I understand why you have married Aegis and set me aside, but I will not be a concubine.

'Let me go. My father, Merovech will protect me; he will give me land. Send Maelon as escort to see me safely home. Let me go, please, for the love we shared I beg you. Release me, I cannot bear to stay.'

Loegaire looked stunned, 'What of Silva?'

'She will not be safe, she must come with me. Benignus will care for Conall's children. Ria will look after Maelon's baby daughter; she is too young for such a journey.'

He bowed his head; he saw the sense in her words.

'Would you go with her Maelon? You have land in Ulster now and a daughter.'

'I... I don't know. I would like to travel, visit Rome. I know nothing of Gaul, let alone the Kingdom of the Franks.'

I felt Lanthchilde's eyes heavy on me.

I sighed. 'I owe a debt to your wife... I've made a promise to her, a geis. I cannot refuse her, any more than you can Loegaire, only bend to her will. She's right, for your heir to be legitimate in a Christian land you must honour his mother as your queen. I, well I need to find my path in this world. I will act as her escort.'

Loegaire's eyes were wet. 'The woman I love stands before me and I must lose her, along with the child of my heart.

'Take this,' he removed his boar headed arm-ring and thrust it at Lanthchilde.

Her hands turned it over and she caressed the boars' heads gently. Her lip trembled and I saw her bite it to stop herself crying.

'If you are ever in need send this to me, or to Maelon. He has its pair. We will come to you unless death prevents us.' His eyes plaintive caught Lanthchilde's. 'Will you give me one last night, beat of my breast, love of my life?'

As they walked from my hall, he pulled her to him; she placed her head on his shoulder. A wave of loneliness and desolation swept over me, for them and me. Where could I find peace and happiness?

Epilogue

I have endeavoured to make this novel of the Dark, (and largely undocumented) Ages a broadly plausible concoction. It is loosely based on facts, legends and archaeological evidence. As there is little contemporary written documentation, other than St Patrick's own Confessio, I have lightly drawn on later sources such as c. 828, Historia Brittonum and the slightly later Anglo Saxon Chronicles, an amalgam of sources that was altered constantly until the eleventh century.

This is a work of fiction, however most of my key characters probably lived at around this time. No one knows the precise chronology as to when: Niall and his sons, Brychan and his family or indeed Maewyn Succus /St Patrick lived.

Maelon Dafodrill was the name of Dwynwen's legendary rejected suitor. He may well have existed, but he was not a prince of Ireland, he was more likely a Powys nobleman. Niall and Inne had one son, Fiachu. Maelon's characterisation is fictional, as are Ria's and Math's, drawing on a number of legends including those of Grain and Diarmuid, the Cattle Raid of Cooley and Chulainn.

There is slim evidence of an early monastic school established around 390 AC in Llantwit Major, near Bovuim/ Cowbridge in south Wales. It was reputed to have been destroyed by Irish raiders some 50 to 60 years after its inception. There is no archaeological evidence of its existence. Iolo Morganwg's eighteen-century account of the ancient school may well be fictitious, as with many, (but probably not all) of his other tales and forgeries. Iolo was born nearby and will have known of the early school(s) in both Llantwit and Llancarfan.

Excavations confirm that there was a school established on the site 50 years after my tale, in the early sixth century, by King Tewdric and /or St. Illtyd. The earlier school is presumed buried beneath that site. The nearby Roman villa Caer Mead has been excavated, with high quality mosaic floors much as described. Some graves have been found within the building.

For St Patrick to have been educated in the Llantwit clas, St Illtyd's second school is too late, so I have used the earlier proposed school of Emperor Theodosius 1. This was first suggested in 1829 by S. Lewis in his Topographical Dictionary of Wales. It is not certain that Patrick was ever educated in such a school. There is longstanding speculation as to the location of Bannavem Taberniae, where Patrick tells us in his Confessions he was born, to Calpernius and Concessa. His father, a deacon, farmed there and his grandfather was a priest, he had two sisters. Patrick was enslaved for at least 5 years but I have slightly shortened that period for my fictional account.

Little Banwen in Breconshire claims to be Bannavem, St Patrick's birthplace. It held a festival in his honour for some years; although other towns in Wales, Cumbria and Scotland stake similar claims. There are Roman mines and a small fort close to Banwen, consequently it is possible there could have been a Roman vicus there, as described in Patrick's Confessions.

If the earlier school existed and was destroyed during an Irish raid, a novice could easily have been taken into slavery, as the site is very close to the Welsh coast. That Milchu owned Patrick/ Patricius, along with the story of his captivity in Sliabh/ Slieve Mis is not recorded in Patrick's Confessions, but is detailed in a later account of his life from the Eighth Century. Patrick notes he was taken into slavery with thousands of others; although he seems a man rather prone to exaggeration in his Confessions more generally!

Another legend exists about Patrick falling out with Loegaire, and threatening that his sons would not rule. Lugaid was excepted at his mother, Angias's intercession. Patrick is also said to have converted two of Loegaire's daughters to Christianity.

In terms of Marchell, Anlach and Brychan's life in Garth Madron/Talgarth, the mid-fifth century dates are reasonable. Many of the Romano-British aristocracy claimed descent from Maximus Maximus, so it's no real surprise that Anlach would have such distinguished forbears. The first documentation of Anlach's genealogy is from the Fourteenth Century, (Jesus College MS29). There are consistent stories that the rulers of Powys and Gwent descended from Maximus, Roman general, and for three years, Emperor of half the Western Roman Empire. As Macsen Wledig, he and his romantic dream of his future wife features in the ancient Welsh folk tales, The Mabinogion.

The Roman Senate declared Maximus, Damnatio Memoriae, actively erasing his name from their history. This is such an intriguing story I have put more details on my website. Magnus Maximus was far more than an upstart Roman general, as usually portrayed, and the issues more complex than Gildas's portrayal of him as the "Betrayer of Briton."

At least five of Brychan's daughters are supposed to have been raped and or abducted. Although these were dangerous times it seems likely that the tales of exactly which of his daughters were raped have become confused over the centuries. Dwynwen was already established as a saint and revered by lovers in the 12th century. The number of early churches established across Cornwall, Brittany and Wales by many of Brychan's reputed twenty-four children suggests there was an energetic mission emanating from his kingdom. Doch, Dingad, Bleddyn, Woolos and Cynog are fifth century Celtic saints, St Elen and St Gratianna late fourth century. Founding a church was sufficient for sainthood in the Celtic church at that time, no miracles were required!

The legend of St Dwynwen is well known in Wales, where she is regarded as the patron saint of lovers. Over recent years, "Valentine cards," i. e. St Dwynwen's day cards are sent on the twenty-fifth of January.

The legend tells that Dwynwen fell in love with a prince named Maelon Dafodrill. Maelon returned Dwynwen's feelings but they could not be together, as Dwynwen's father forbade the marriage, having already promised her to someone else. Regrettably in some stories, Maelon then either rapes or attempts to rape her.

Distraught because of her love for Maelon, Dwynwen prays to fall out of love with him. Dwynwen was visited by an angel in her sleep, who gave her a sweet potion designed to erase all memory of Maelon and it turns him into a block of ice. The angel granted three wishes to Dwynwen.

For her first wish, Dwynwen asked that Maelon be thawed, second that God meets the hopes and dreams of true lovers and third that she should never marry. All three wishes were fulfilled. As a mark of her thanks, Dwynwen devoted herself to God's service for the rest of her life on the small island off the Anglesey coast.

This legend pre-dates the stories of Romeo and Juliet and Sleeping Beauty by many centuries. The iconic remains of her small church are still there, see my website for photos.

High King Niall Noígíallach, he of the Nine Hostages, is a well-known figure in Irish history. It was once suggested one-eighth of the Irish population could claim him as an ancestor, this outrageous claim has some basis in truth as the M222 genetic marker on the Y chromosome does seem to be linked to the name O'Niell, and is very common in certain parts of Ireland. The tale as to how Niall, a younger son, inherited the throne rather than any of his four older brothers is famous; he had an evil stepmother who was a witch, another familiar theme. Niall and Fiachrae's tales also include an interlude with a Hag.

I should mention the names Niall and Brion mutate to Neill and Brain, and are sometimes changed in old Irish and sometimes not. Similarly mac in Irish becomes ap in Welsh, identifying a man's or woman's father and O' technically means 'grandson of.'

Lanthchilde was the daughter of Childeric 1, (437-483), rather than his sister. I decided for the purposes of my narrative, that girl was named after her fictional aunt, my Lanthchilde. The symbol of bees is Frankish and Childric's burial cloak was encrusted with 300 solid gold bees with red glass wings.

Ancient Celtic law was in all likelihood similar to early mediaeval Brehon law; men were allowed several wives and there were ten degrees of marriage defined within that system. Ireland

and Wales had closely aligned systems of law. Kings were expected to abide by the laws as much as their people. The geography of the clans was very complex. I elected to use modern geographic terms, such as Ulster rather than confuse readers. Similarly, Wales was not recognised, even as Cymru then, the people were, "Britons", and lived in small kingdoms such as Powys and Brycheiniog. For clarity's sake, I have used the modern name of Wales.

I shamelessly used dramatic license in choosing Knowth as a location. It is a wonderful passage tomb dating from around 3500 Bc. Maelon and his brothers could not possibly have entered deep into the tomb; it had been closed for thousands of years by 450 AC. Knowth's magnificent stones have arguably the best Neolithic carving anywhere in the world. It is uncertain whether the east and west-facing tunnels in Knowth really aligned with the equinox sunrise, due to rock falls and excavations, although its sister monument, Newgrange aligns with the summer solstice. A moon calendar stone sits in Knowth and there is a theory that standing sound waves could have caused specific refraction patterns in smoke or ash. Knowth has a much later Iron Age hill fort with massive ditches built around the time of Niall's father. Early Christians re-used a small portion of the mound for burials.

Bishop Palladius, along with priest Sylvester, was sent by Pope Celestine I to Ireland, to convert the Scoti in the north of Ireland at around 431AC. There is a suggestion that the missions of Pallidus and Patricius were confused by later historians.

Attila and his Huns ravaged Europe in 452 AC, including the lands of the Franks, but he was paid by Rome to leave. Pope Leo acted as one of three emissaries for the Roman Emperor. Historians speculate that plague may have helped Attila's decision to take the gold.

This tale was inspired, in part, by the beautiful church of St Gasty beside lovely Llyn Syfaddon, Llangorse Lake as it is now known. My website **semorganhistoricalfiction** has photographs of many places that are mentioned in the book and the starting points of some of wonderful walks if you would like to retrace Maelon's steps to the waterfalls, walk along Wolf Mountain, explore the macabre ancient yew beside St Ellyw's church or visit the stone houses in the Town of the Giants on the Llyn peninsular.

Finally, to note that two years after this novel ends, in 455 AC, Genseric leads the Vandals to sack Rome. Could Maelon and Lanthchilde's future be tied to those events?

Key References

———— ‹‹◉›› ————

Candle in the darkness, Celtic Spirituality from Wales; Patrick Thomas

Wars of the Irish Kings; David McCullough

Celtic Britain; Charles Thomas

Anglo-Saxon Chronicles; (for date of Vortigern inviting Hengist and Horsa to Briton)

Confessions of St Patrick

The Legend of Finn McCool; Rosemary Sutcliffe

Fiorentino, Wesley; "Magnus Maximus." Ancient History Encyclopedia

Link to encyclopedia

A Topographical Dictionary of Wales. S. Lewis, London 1849

Gildas; The Ruin of Briton Translated by Hugh Alders Williams

The Lantern Bearers; Rosemary Sutcliffe

LIST OF MAIN CHARACTERS

*Fictional character, not drawn from history or legend

Ireland;

Maelon, Prince of Ireland, son of Niall Noígíallach, Niall of the
    Nine Hostages

*Aed, warrior and Connacht chieftain

Conall, half-brother to Maelon, son of Niall and Rignach

*Diaré, chieftain in Ulster, father of Frid

Diarmuid, brother to Fionn

Fiachrae, half-brother to Niall

*Finn, hound master in Tara

Fionn, Ria's husband, brother to Diarmuid

*Frid, daughter of Diaré

Inne, wife to Niall, Maelon's mother, Anlach's daughter

Kira, Maelon's faithful wolfhound

Laidcenn, druid and bard in Tara

*Lanthchilde, wife to Loegaire, daughter of the King of the Franks

Loegaire, half-brother to Maelon, son of Niall and Rignach

*Math, Champion warrior, illegitimate son of Brion, Niall's half-brother

Milchu, chieftain in Dal Riata territory, (Northern Ireland)

Nathi, Fiachrae's son, Maelon's cousin

*Ness, Niall's Christian wife

Niall Noígíallach/of the Nine Hostages, High King of Ireland

Palladius, Bishop, sent by Pope Celestius to Ireland

Ria, Maelon's sister

Rignach, Niall's first wife

Sylvester, priest.

Wales;

Anlach, Maelon's grandfather, Irish prince

Benignus, pupil at Cor Tewdws, later Bishop at Emain Macha

Brychan, son of Anlach, Maelon's uncle, ruler of Brycheiniog

Calpernius, Maewyn's father

*Cedric, Abod of Cor Tewdws, Marchell's cousin

Cynog, Brychan's son, Maelon's cousin

Dwynwen, Brychan's daughter, Maelon's cousin

Einion, King of Mona and the Llyn, north Wales

Ellyw, Brychan's daughter, Maelon's cousin

Gastyn, pupil at Cor Tewdws

Glywys, King of Glywyssig, (Gwent and Glamorgan)

Marchell, Maelon's grandmother

Maewyn Succus/ Patricius, pupil in Cor Twedws,

(later known as St. Patrick of Ireland)

Melissa, sister to Maewyn/Patricius

Metella, sister to Maewyn/Patricius

Rhain, Maelon's cousin, heir to Brycheiniog

Wyn, see Maewyn above.

Woolos, Prince, son of Glywys

Key Locations

Ireland

Cethlenn's Isle	—	Enniskillen
Cruachan/Rath Crogan	—	Tulsk
Emain Macha	—	Armagh
Lartharne	—	Larne

Wales

Bannavem Taberniae	—	Banwen, Powys
Bovium	—	Cowbridge/Boverton
Cor Tewdws	—	Llantwit Major
Cicucium	—	Brecon
Garth Madron	—	Talgarth
Mona	—	Anglesey
Moridnum	—	Carmarthen
Nidum	—	Neath
River Sabrina	—	River Severn
Segontium	—	Caernarvon
Wyddfa	—	Snowdon

Other

Dumnonia	—	Devon and Cornwall
Armorica	—	Brittany

Printed in Great Britain
by Amazon